IMMIGRANTS

IMMIGRANTS

A LIBRARY OF CONGRESS BOOK

By MARTIN W. SANDLER

Introduction by James H. Billington, Librarian of Congress

HarperCollins*Publishers*

For Louis Sage, who lived the immigrant experience and realized the immigrant's dream

The author wishes to thank Robert Dierker, former senior advisor for multimedia activities of the Library of Congress and Dana Prat former director of publishing of the Library of Congress, for their encouragement and cooperation. Appreciation is expressed to Kate Murphy, Carol Weiss, Heather Henson, Liza Baker, Alan Bisbort, the staff of the Prints and Photographs Division of the Library of Congress, Dennis Magnu of the Library's Photoduplication Service and Judith Gray of the American Folklife Center. As with all the books in this series, this volume and its author owe much to the editorial skill and guidance of Kate Morgan Jackson.

◆

Immigrants
A Library of Congress Book

Library of Congress Cataloging-in-Publication Data
Sandler, Martin W.
Immigrants / by Martin W. Sandler ; introduction by James H. Billington.
p.   cm.
"A Library of Congress Book"
ISBN 0-06-024507-7. — ISBN 0-06-024508-5 (lib. bdg.) — ISBN 0-06-446744-9 (pbk.)
1. Immigrants—United States—History—Juvenile literature.   2. United States—Emigration and immigration—History—Juvenile literature.
3. Immigrants—United States—Pictorial works—Juvenile literature.   4. United States—Emigration and immigration—Pictorial works—Juvenile literature.   I. Title.
JV6450.S25   1995   93-441
3.4.8'73—dc20   C
                                                                                                                                                                          A

Design by Tom Starace with Jennifer Goldman
❖
Visit us on the World Wide Web!
http://www.harperchildrens.com

Our type of democracy has depended upon and grown with knowledge gained through books and all the other various records of human memory and imagination. By their very nature, these records foster freedom and dignity. Historically they have been the companions of a responsible, democratic citizenry. They provide keys to the dynamism of our past and perhaps to our national competitiveness in the future. They link the record of yesterday with the possibilities of tomorrow.

One of our main purposes at the Library of Congress is to make the riches of the Library even more available to even wider circles of our multiethnic society. Thus we are proud to lend our name and resources to this series of children's books. We share Martin W. Sandler's goal of enriching our greatest natural resource—the minds and imaginations of our young people.

The scope and variety of Library of Congress print and visual materials contained in these books demonstrate that libraries are the starting places for the adventure of learning that can go on whatever one's vocation and location in life. They demonstrate that reading is an adventure like the one that is discovery itself. Being an American is not a patent of privilege but an invitation to adventure. We must go on discovering America.

James H. Billington
The Librarian of Congress

The American experience is filled with stories of men and women who in every era have faced enormous challenges and overcome them. None of these stories is more inspiring than that of the millions of people who, particularly between 1870 and 1920, crossed a wild and dangerous ocean in search of freedom and opportunity in a new land. It is an extraordinarily important story as well. For so much of who we are, what we are and what we have accomplished as a nation is due in the largest measure to the sacrifices made and the achievements realized by those who bore the name *immigrants*.

MARTIN W. SANDLER

LEAVING FOR A NEW WORLD

I n the last quarter of the 1800's the United States is about to change dramatically. As the Statue of Liberty stands guard on its eastern shore, millions of newcomers pour into America.

These newcomers are called immigrants. Most come from countries throughout Europe. They are willing to risk everything for the chance to build new lives in what they have heard is a golden land.

Their travels have take
them thousands of mil
across a wild and dangero
ocean. The ocean voyage
only the first of many challeng
they will face.

ost will settle in the teeming American cities. Others will begin their new lives in the vast lands of the American West. Those who do not speak English will have to learn a new language. All will have to adapt to new ways of life.

The immigrants' children are at the center of their dreams. They are the hope for the future. Because of them, their parents are willing to face the unknown.

America Builds

The Record of PWA

The sacrifices will be great, but the immigrants will make them. They will have no choice but to work long hours at jobs others are unwilling to undertake. They will see that their children are educated in the ways of a new world. They will transform the nation and help build a new America.

THE LONG JOURNEY

The millions of men, women and children who will pour into America are both pulled and pushed into the New World. They are pulled by false stories of the quick riches and easy life they will find in the United States. They are pushed out of the Old World by harsh conditions that include hunger, poverty and religious and political persecution. Many of the families are so poor they are evicted from their homes.

Immigration to the United States by Country of Origin: 1820–1925   Total: 36,307,892

'**N**o migration . . . has occurred in the world at all similar to that which is now pouring itself upon the shores of the United States," writes the *New York Tribune* in 1873. Between 1820 and 1920, more than million people will exchange their lot in older countries for a ew life in America.

Africa and All Other 1%
Ireland 12%
Other NW Europe 3%
Italy and Southern Europe 15.5%
Germany 16%
Scandinavian Countries 6%
Asia 2.5%
Canada and Other Americas 10%
Russia and Eastern Europe 10%
Great Britain 11%
Poland and Central Europe 13%

The Tide of Immigration to the United States: 1820–1920

Country	1820–1830	1831–1840	1841–1850	1851–1860	1861–1870	1871–1880	1881–1890	1891–1900	1901–1910	1911–1920
Denmark	189	1,063	539	3,749	17,094	31,771	88,132	50,231	65,285	41,983
France	8,868	45,575	77,262	76,358	35,986	72,206	50,464	30,770	73,379	61,897
Germany	7,729	152,454	434,626	951,667	787,468	718,182	1,452,970	505,152	341,498	143,945
United Kingdom	27,489	75,810	267,044	423,974	606,896	548,043	807,357	271,538	525,950	341,408
Greece	20	49	16	31	72	210	2,308	15,979	167,519	184,201
Ireland	54,338	207,381	780,719	914,119	435,778	436,871	655,482	388,416	339,065	146,181
Italy	439	2,253	1,870	9,231	11,725	55,759	307,309	651,893	2,045,877	1,109,524
Norway/Sweden	94	1,201	13,903	20,931	109,298	211,245	568,362	321,281	440,039	161,469
Poland	21	369	105	1,164	2,027	12,970	51,806	96,720	—	4,813
Spain/Portugal	2,796	2,954	2,759	10,353	9,355	19,348	21,397	36,239	97,084	158,343
Russia (U.S.S.R.)	89	277	551	457	2,512	39,284	213,282	505,290	1,597,306	921,201
Other Europe	4,436	6,302	18,107	40,626	47,059	126,373	518,177	685,469	2,443,014	1,101,599
China	3	8	35	41,397	64,301	123,201	61,711	14,799	20,605	21,278
Japan	—	—	—	—	186	149	2,270	25,942	129,797	83,837
Other Asia	12	40	47	58	143	473	4,399	30,495	93,165	87,444
Canada and Newfoundland	2,486	13,624	41,723	59,309	153,878	383,640	393,304	3,311	179,226	742,185
Central and South America	9,465	19,800	20,746	15,411	12,729	20,404	33,663	35,661	182,662	401,486
All Countries	151,824	599,125	1,713,251	2,598,214	2,314,824	2,812,191	5,246,613	3,687,564	8,795,386	5,735,811

By 1890, New York City alone will have twice as many Irish as Dublin, half as many Italians as Naples, as many Germans as Hamburg and two and a half times as many Jewish people as Warsaw. Harsh as conditions at home may be, it is not an easy decision to leave one's homeland and friends and relatives. It is an emotional and difficult experience, but in villages, towns and cities through-out Europe, scenes of sad farewell become commonplace.

Farewell to old Ireland,
*   the land of my childhood,*
Which now and forever I am
*   going to leave. . .*
I'm bound to cross o'er that
*   wide swelling ocean*
In search of fame, fortune and
*   sweet liberty.*
                —From song,
          "The Emigrant's Farewell"

Good-byes also take place in European ports that become dominated by ships and people leaving for America.

I can remember only the hustle and bustle of those last weeks in Pinsk, the farewells from the family, the embraces and the tears. Going to America then was almost like going to the moon.

—Golda Meir,
Russian Jewish immigrant

Many immigrants had brought on board
balls of yarn, leaving one end of the line
with someone on land. As the ship slowly
cleared the dock, the balls unwound amid
the farewell shouts of the women, the flutter-
ing of the handkerchiefs, and the infants
held high. After the yarn ran out, the long
strips remained airborne, sustained by the
wind, long after those on land and those at
sea had lost sight of each other.

—Luciano DeCrescenzo, "The Ball of Yarn"

The trip from their towns and villages to the po[r]t cities is just the first step on the immigrants' lo[ng] journey. Ahead lies the long and often dangero[us] sea voyage to America. The trip can take from fi[ve] weeks to six months. Passengers are packed tightly aboa[rd] the ship, with little room to move about.

Crossing the Atlantic is a miserable experience. The wooden ships pitch and roll in the high seas, and many passengers are seasick throughout the entire voyage. The threat of fire from a lighted candle or an open cooking fire is all too real. Disease spreads through many vessels, and there is the constant danger of the ships' being destroyed in a fierce ocean storm.

h God, I was sick. Everybody was sick. I
n't ever want to remember anything about
at old boat. One night I prayed to God
at it would go down because the waves
ere washing over it. I was that sick, I didn't
re if it went down or not. And everybody
e was the same way.

—Bertha Devlin, Irish immigrant

Because they are poor, most of the immigrants are forced to make the journey in the least expensive section of the ship, below the deck. Originally designed to transport animals and freight, this steerage section, as it is called, is a terribly crowded, filthy place with little air and little room to move about. Most steerage passengers endure almost the entire voyage without ever breathing fresh air or seeing the open sky.

assengers on the vessels are not all poor. Thousands of wealthier men, women and children also seek a new and freer life in America. They can afford the higher fares that allow them to travel above deck, far removed from the steerage section.

As time passes, ocean travel does improve. By the 1870's, many sailing ships are replaced by steam-driven vessels. The journey is still dangerous, and life in the steerage section is still terribly difficult, but the speedier steamships reduce the ocean voyage to about fourteen days.

ARRIVING IN A NEW LAND

The voyage to America claims the lives of thousands of immigrants through disease or shipwreck, but the vast majority complete the difficult trip. More than 70 percent arrive in the great port of New York City. The millions who enter New York Harbor after 1886 are greeted by a sight they will never forget. It is the Statue of Liberty, symbol of the hopes and dreams of all who make the journey.

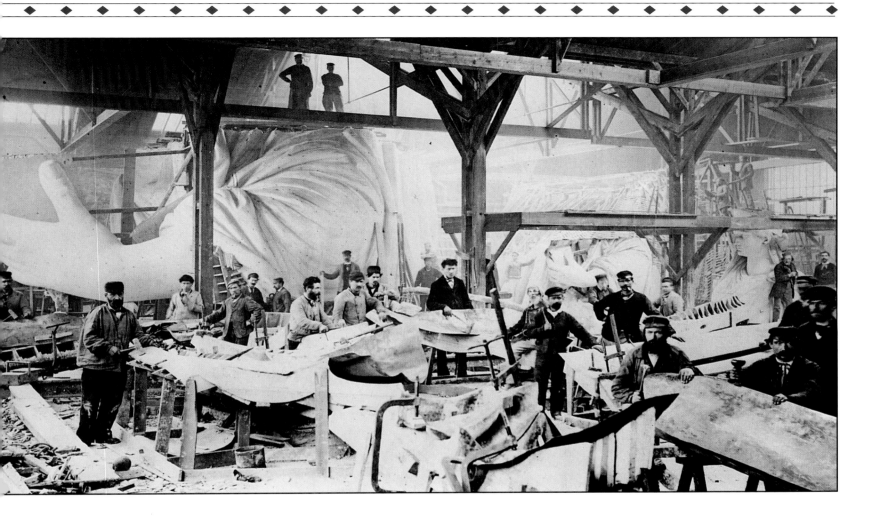

The Statue of Liberty is a gift from the people of France to the people of the United States. It is the creation of Frederic Auguste Bartholdi, whose dream was to build a monument honoring the American spirit of freedom that has inspired the world. In 1874, scores of skilled French laborers begin work on the statue.

The first time I saw the Statue of Liberty all the people were rushing to the side of the boat. "Look at her, look at her," and in all kind of tongues. "There she is, there she is," like it was somebody who was greeting them.

—Elizabeth Phillips, Irish immigrant

The Statue of Liberty is designed to stand 151 feet and one inch high from its base to the torch that Miss Liberty will hold in her hand. It will weigh 225 tons. Long before it is completed, news of the extraordinary gift causes great excitement in America. In 1876, the completed torch is shipped to the United States, where it becomes a major attraction at America's one hundredth birthday celebration in Philadelphia.

On May 21, 1884, more than twelve years of work on the Statue of Liberty are completed. The monument is dismantled and shipped to New York in 214 enormous packing crates. It is then reassembled and re-erected on Bedloe's Island in New York Harbor. On October 28, 1886, President Grover Cleveland leads the festivities as the statue is officially dedicated.

I felt grateful the Statue of Liberty was a woman. I felt she would understand a woman's heart.

—Stella Petrakis,
Greek immigrant

From the moment it is placed in New York Harbor, the Statue of Liberty becomes one of the nation's most important treasures. It will become more than a symbol of freedom. It will also become a symbol of welcome to millions of newcomers who see in America the chance to build better lives for themselves and their families.

The Statue of Liberty is there to greet them, but for the immigrants their ordeal in search of freedom and opportunity is far from over. As soon as their ship docks in the harbor, they line up at the rail, anxious to leave the vessel. There are millions of newcomers pouring in, however. The immigration depot cannot begin to process them all in a single day. After weeks at sea, many of the immigrants are forced to wait on board for as long as four more days.

ELLIS ISLAND

Between 1855 and 1890, the immigration depot where newcomers are processed is Castle Island, a huge round stone structure built in 1808 as a fort. It is here that more than eight million bewildered strangers will be introduced to America.

By 1890, Castle Island cannot handle the ever-increasing flood of arrivals. A new and much larger depot is built on New York Harbor's Ellis Island. Between 1892 and 1920, the busiest years of the facility, more than 23 million newcomers will enter America through Ellis Island. Even more than the Statue of Liberty, it will become the symbol of the immigrant experience.

Ellis Island—you got thousands of people marching in, a little bit excited, a little bit scared. Just imagine you're 14 ½ years old and you're in a strange country and you don't know what's going to happen.

—Albert Mardirossian,
Armenian immigrant

A s the immigrants first set foot on American soil, their faces reveal the sense of anxiety shared by all strangers in a strange new land. Most cannot speak English and most have heard frightening stories of the ordeal that awaits them at Ellis Island.

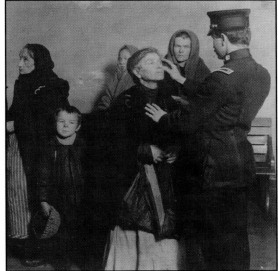

The immigrants' fears are justified. Once inside the Ellis Island facility, the newcomers are forced to wait hours, sometimes days, before undergoing both a physical and a verbal examination. They wait knowing that if they fail either test, they will be sent back across the ocean. The physical examination includes an eye test for trachoma, a disease common in southern and eastern Europe. About 2 percent of all the newcomers fail this or some other test and are forced to return to their homelands.

The verbal examinations are just as difficult, just as terrifying. Uniformed immigration officers, with the aid of interpreters, fire a battery of questions at the newcomers: "Where did you come from? Where are you headed? Can you read and write? Have you served time in prison? Do you have a job waiting for you?" Though most of the immigrants pass the test, it is a bewildering experience.

He asked me a lot of silly questions. You know what I mean? About America, if I knew all about America. Well, I didn't know anything about America.

—Florence Norris, English immi

Why should I fear the fires of hell? I have been through Ellis Island.

—Inscription written on
an Ellis Island wall
by an immigrant

The Ellis Island experience is so bewildering that many immigrants actually lose their names in the process. Often, when the immigrants state their names, the officer writes down what he thinks he hears rather than what is said. When asked their names, many confused newcomers are apt to state the names of their hometowns or their former occupations instead. Some officers, on their own, change European-sounding names like "Valentin" to more American-sounding names like "William." Thousands enter America with their names changed forever.

Finally, for most, the Ellis Island ordeal is over. The immigrants gather on the docks awaiting the ferryboats that will take them across the harbor into New York. Many will journey on to other American cities like Boston, Philadelphia or Baltimore, but hundreds of thousands will make their new home in New York. As they gaze at the skyline of the world's largest city, they can only imagine what lies ahead.

THE TEEMING CITY

The immigrants who pour into American cities in the last decades of the 1800's arrive at a time of great change. The United States, long a country of farms and small towns, is increasingly becoming a nation of city dwellers. The cities offer goods and services that previous generations could never have imagined.

TO THE
VISITING
THOUSANDS

EXTENDS
THE KEY
TO THE
CITY

The cities are exciting, bustling places. They are filled with theaters and museums. They offer the latest in transportation. In every season of the year, they attract tens of thousands of pleasure seekers.

The city dazzled us. We had never seen such buildings, such people, such activity. Maybe the stories were true. Maybe everything was possible in America!

—Slovenian immigrant boy

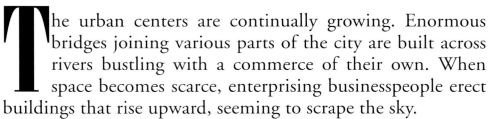

T he urban centers are continually growing. Enormous bridges joining various parts of the city are built across rivers bustling with a commerce of their own. When space becomes scarce, enterprising businesspeople erect buildings that rise upward, seeming to scrape the sky.

The city's department stores and specialty shops are filled with every type of product a person could want. Hundreds of elegant restaurants offer food from around the world. For those who can afford it, the city is truly a magical place.

> *In America there were rooms without sunlight. . . . Where was there a place in America for me to play? . . . "Where is America?" cried my heart.*
>
> —Young immigrant girl

Most of the immigrants, however, are very po... They have arrived in America with alm... nothing. For them, the city is a very differ... kind of place. They cannot afford to shop in ... stores or dine in the restaurants. They cannot ev... afford to live in clean, comfortable homes.

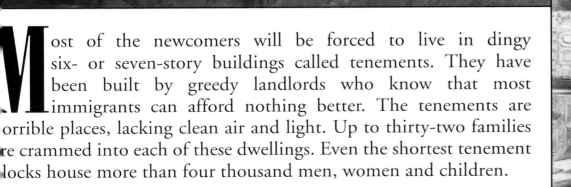

Most of the newcomers will be forced to live in dingy six- or seven-story buildings called tenements. They have been built by greedy landlords who know that most immigrants can afford nothing better. The tenements are horrible places, lacking clean air and light. Up to thirty-two families are crammed into each of these dwellings. Even the shortest tenement blocks house more than four thousand men, women and children.

For many new arrivals the tenement become their work place as well as the place in which they live. Thousands cannot speak English, and until they learn this new language their only way of making money is to take in work at home.

My uncles got jobs in a laundry uptown. My father wasn't so lucky. We took in work at home. But my father never lost hope. "We're in America," he'd say. "We'll work hard and things will get better." And he was right.

—Young Albanian immigrant

hole families work long hours inside the tenements, sewing clothes, making paper flowers and sorting and labeling various types of goods. The pay for this piecework, as it is called, is very low, but the immigrants must do whatever it takes to survive in their new world.

THE CITY STREETS

For most of the immigrant city dwellers, the only escape from the dingy, overcrowded tenements is the street. There is sunlight in the streets, there is fresh air, and there are new arrivals from the Old World to meet and fellow immigrants with whom to share common experiences and news from back home.

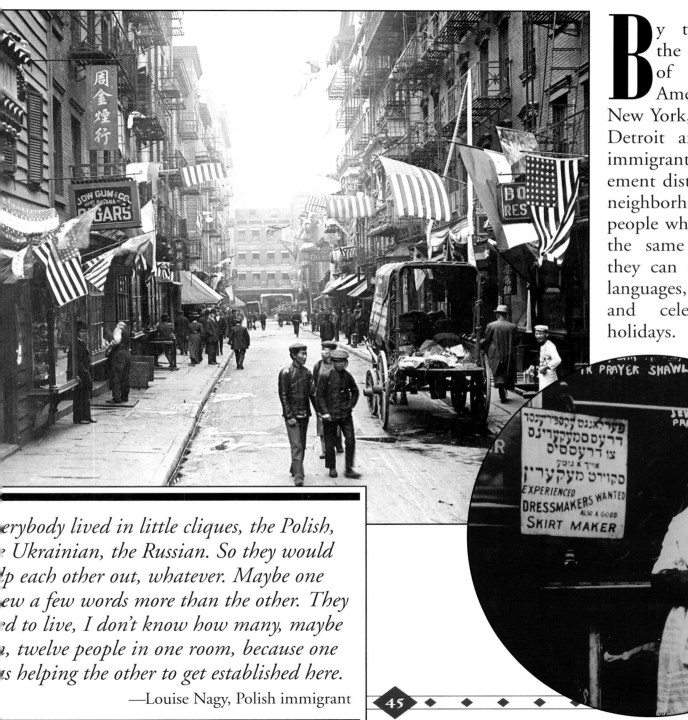

By the beginning of the 1900's, 75 percent of the residents of American cities like New York, Boston, Chicago, Detroit and Cleveland are immigrants. Within the tenement districts they settle in neighborhoods made up of people who have come from the same homeland. Here they can speak their native languages, buy familiar foods and celebrate traditional holidays.

erybody lived in little cliques, the Polish,
Ukrainian, the Russian. So they would
p each other out, whatever. Maybe one
ew a few words more than the other. They
d to live, I don't know how many, maybe
, twelve people in one room, because one
s helping the other to get established here.

—Louise Nagy, Polish immigrant

When I came to this country and I came to a pushcart on First Avenue, and I saw all those fruits and vegetables in February, that gave me such a lift. That I liked.

—Immigrant boy

Increasingly, with every passing year, the streets of many American cities take on the flavor of the Old World. They are filled with pushcarts from which enterprising immigrants, determined to escape tenement work, sell goods of all kinds.

For the immigrants, the streets become the very arteries of life. The newcomers have little money to travel far from their homes, but almost everything they can afford to buy can be found in their neighborhood streets.

etween the streets and the tenement buildings [are] long, dark alleys. Like the tenements, they a[re] unpleasant, dirty places. They are often t[he] meeting spots of neighborhood gangs. Imm[i]grant parents live in fear that their children will [be] influenced by those who have turned to crime out [of] frustration with the challenges of their life in the city.

Most immigrant children, however, avoid the gangs. There are no parks or other open spaces in their neighborhoods, so the streets become their playgrounds. They use their imaginations to create their own games and their own fun.

A GOOD EDUCATION

It is hard to be a stranger in a strange land. It is difficult and often frightening not knowing the language or the nation's ways. There is a way out, though. It is education. In school, the difficult English language can be learned. In school, children can begin to learn what it means to be an American.

Most immigrant parents understand that through schooling their children will have the opportunity to build better lives than they have had. As youngsters' education proceeds, an extraordinary thing takes place. Gradually, many of the children become wiser in the ways of America than their parents. In many immigrant homes, the children make decisions and take on tasks usually reserved for adult members of the family.

I was the one who always went to the gas company to complain about the bill. And I was the one who dealt with the landlords, the real estate agents. I could read the contract or the lease and speak English. I became in a sense a sort of junior father of the family.

—Immigrant boy

For adults as well, education is the avenue to better jobs and a better life. It is also the road to one of their fondest dreams—that of becoming full-fledged American citizens.

My mother began to go to night school, and she immediately began to study for citizenship. She and I studied together ab the Constitution, about the presidents, about the portions of the government, the executive, the judicial, and the congressio She knew all these things and she did pass examination and it was one of the happie days of her life when she became a citizen.

—Morris Moel, Ukraii
Jewish immig

Millions of immigrant men and women attend classes especially created for them. They learn English, they study history and the laws of their new nation. Most attend their classes at night after completing a long day's work. They are determined not only to live in America but to become Americans as well.

HARD WORK

Education is a vital key to building one's future in America, but it does not take the immigrants long to discover that there is another key as well. In America, hard work can lead to success.

From the beginning, Americans have been a most industrious people. Hard work is a national characteristic. Throughout our history, artists, songwriters and journalists have found in the American worker a figure worthy of celebration.

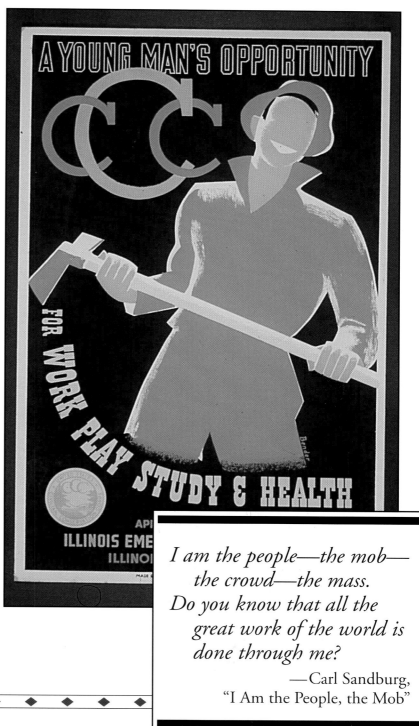

I am the people—the mob—the crowd—the mass. Do you know that all the great work of the world is done through me?

—Carl Sandburg,
"I Am the People, the Mob"

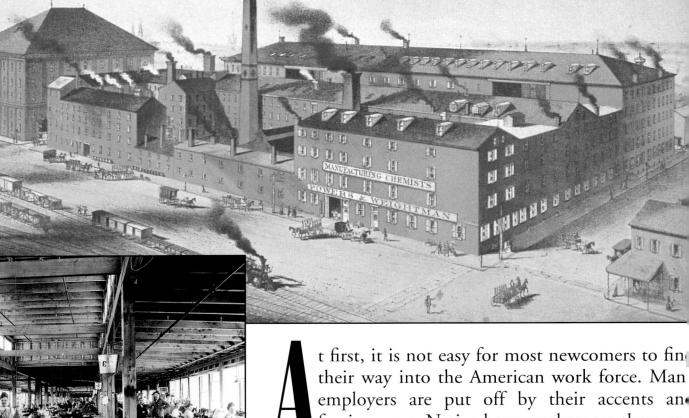

At first, it is not easy for most newcomers to fin their way into the American work force. Man employers are put off by their accents an foreign ways. Native-born workers see them as threat to their own jobs. In a nation caught up i enormous industrial growth, however, labor is greatl needed. Millions of new Americans find work in th nation's ever-increasing factories.

The factories become the workplace not only of the men but of tens of thousands of immigrant women as well. Factory pay is low, and most immigrant families need the wages of both husband and wife.

y mother was a twister in the Lawrence
lls. It was unusual; in Italy there were no
s for women. In fact, people that heard
out it back in the village didn't like the
ea of the women working. But my mother
t she was doing no different from all the
er women, so she decided she was going to
rk. Make some money.

—Josephine Costanzo, Italian immigrant

Those who toil in the factories work long hours under difficult conditions, but soon there are oth[er] avenues of employment for women. As American factories and businesses continue to expand, th[e] need to keep up with orders and other paperwork grows as well. Office workers are needed desperatel[y.] Thousands of immigrant women find work in these offices where they are surrounded by ne[w] inventions such as the typewriter, the dictating machine, the adding machine and the telephone.

The growth of the factories and offices leads to the continued growth of the cities. As more and more people pour in, new buildings, new trolley lines and new bridges must be erected to serve them. Immigrant laborers become an important part of the urban work force.

Building the cities is one thing; keeping them safe and clean is another. More and more police officers are needed to patrol the neighborhoods. Scores of other workers are needed to sweep the streets in summer and to keep them free of ice and snow in winter.

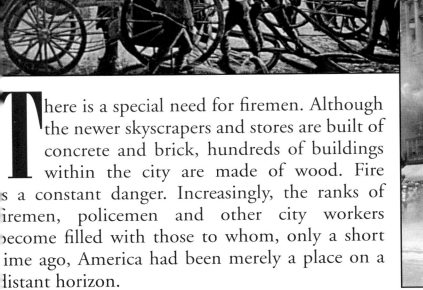

There is a special need for firemen. Although the newer skyscrapers and stores are built of concrete and brick, hundreds of buildings within the city are made of wood. Fire is a constant danger. Increasingly, the ranks of firemen, policemen and other city workers become filled with those to whom, only a short time ago, America had been merely a place on a distant horizon.

WORKING OUTSIDE THE CITY

The immigrants have arrived at a time of great growth outside the cities. The American continent is filled with natural resources. Many lie deep beneath the earth. Mining these resources is a terribly difficult and dangerous job, but thousands of immigrants, anxious to improve their lot, are willing to tackle it. Miles underground, they dig the coal, copper, zinc and other minerals that supply the fuel and raw materials for the ever-demanding American factories.

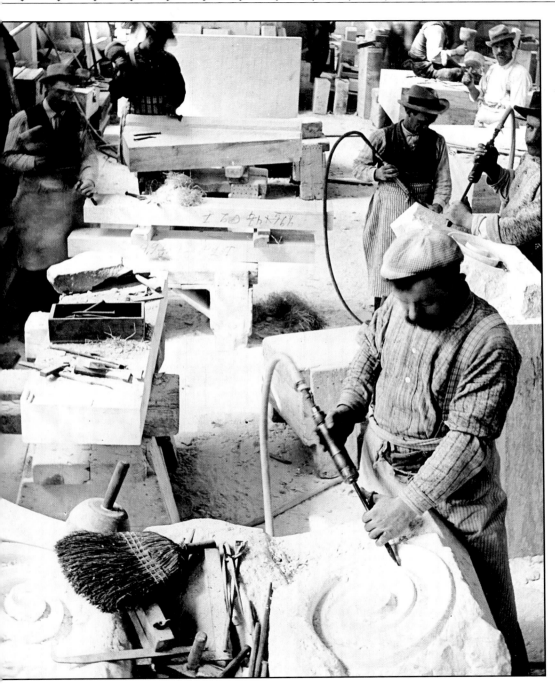

Above the earth, there are great resources as well. The nation's quarries yield enormous amounts of marble and other stone. Many immigrants are employed in mining this resource. Others, trained in Old World countries, use their skills to create magnificent stone carvings that will adorn buildings throughout the nation.

There is another great resource that lies above the ground. America is a land of vast, magnificent forests. Billions of trees yield the lumber from which homes, offices and other buildings are erected. Into the great forests of the midwestern and far northwestern states come lumberjacks, who chop down the trees and haul them off to the sawmills. Many immigrant men find their first jobs in America, surrounded by the tallest living things on earth.

Tens of thousands of other immigrants find work in the nation's steel mills. By 1900, America has become the industrial leader of the world, and by 1910, over half of America's industrial workers are immigrants.

Where would your mines have been dug and worked, where would your great iron industries and constructions . . . have been were it not for the immigrants? . . . It is the immigrant that bears the burden of hard labor . . . and has contributed his full share to the building up of our great country.

—Representative Samuel McMillan of New York, speech to Congress, 1908

The biggest employer of all, by far, is the American railroad system. By the 1870's, great railroad lines run three thousand miles from coast to coast. The earliest of these transcontinental systems have been built largely through the efforts of Chinese and Irish laborers. Millions of other immigrants find work on the railroad. They lay the tracks, keep them open, repair the engines and work in the depots and on the trains.

All those bridges, all those roads, all those railroads—they were built by people who worked hard.

—Joseph Baccardo, Italian immigrant

The railroad becomes the symbol of might and progress, and the immigrants become the symbol of all that can be accomplished in America. Through education and hard work, millions have established themselves in a new world. In the process, they have helped build a nation.

PIONEERS!

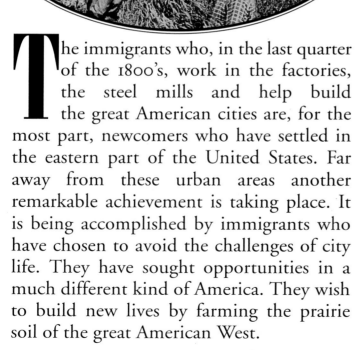

The immigrants who, in the last quarter of the 1800's, work in the factories, the steel mills and help build the great American cities are, for the most part, newcomers who have settled in the eastern part of the United States. Far away from these urban areas another remarkable achievement is taking place. It is being accomplished by immigrants who have chosen to avoid the challenges of city life. They have sought opportunities in a much different kind of America. They wish to build new lives by farming the prairie soil of the great American West.

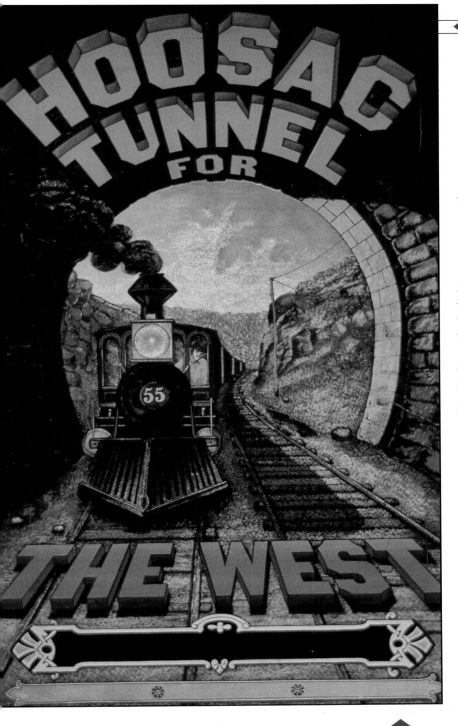

In the last decades of the 1800's, the vast territories of the American West are being settled by millions of courageous men, women and children. The earliest of these pioneers have made the long, dangerous journey across the continent on foot, in covered wagons, and by stagecoach and steamboat. Now the expanding railroad system, which is being built with the aid of immigrant labor, is bringing millions of others to the western lands.

Only an emigrant! son of the soil,
With my hands ready for labor and toil,
Willing for anything honest I be,
Surely there's room on the prairies for me;
—From song, "Only an Emigrant"

For the countless immigrants who want to avoid the crowded cities, the western territories offer the best hope for a new and better life in their new country. Those who can afford it head west by train immediately upon entering America. Others live in the city long enough to earn the train fare and then head west. Increasingly, the connecting western railroad depots take on the look of Ellis Island.

Many of the immigrants come from the Scandinavian countries of Sweden, Denmark, Finland and Norway. Most were farmers in their native lands. No matter how poor they were, they were surrounded by clean air and sunshine. There is plenty of fresh air and sunshine on the western prairies, and there is the opportunity to own their own land. The United States government has provided that 160 acres, or one quarter of a square mile, will be given to any head of a family who will live on the land and farm it for at least five years.

There is opportunity, but there are many hardships as well. Almost no trees grow on the prairie, and the settlers must live in houses made of prairie sod. Often there is too much sunshine. Long periods without rain dry up the land and cause prairie fires and fierce dust storms. In the winter, blizzards cover the prairie with mountains of snow. The greatest hardship of all, though, is loneliness. Unlike the immigrants in the city, who face the challenges of terrible overcrowding, the immigrants who choose to settle in the West must deal with a life in which the nearest neighbor may be thirty or forty miles away.

Using the labor of every member of the family, the immigrant pioneers break the rich prairie soil and plant their crops. They will work every day from sunup to sundown, with little time for rest or recreation. Like the immigrants in the city, those who have chosen to face the challenges of the West are determined to succeed.

Those who survive their earliest hardships are aided greatly by the spirit of inventiveness that sweeps America in the last decades of the 1800's. Every week seems to bring new inventions and new machines. Many of the new machines are designed to make farming more productive. By the late 1870's, farm machinery of every kind dominates the western landscape. More crops than could ever have been imagined can be planted and harvested in less time and with fewer hands than ever before.

By the 1890's, the once empty prairies of the American West are covered with crops. The western immigrants and their fellow pioneers are feeding the nation and much of the rest of the world. Like their fellow immigrants in the East, they too have helped build America.

No wonder that so many Europeans who have never been able to say that such a portion of land was theirs, cross the Atlantic to realize that happiness.

—Alexis de Tocqueville,
early French traveler in America

TODAY'S IMMIGRANTS

The Statue of Liberty still stands guard in the harbor. In every national crisis, she has been our symbol of hope and democracy.

Immigrants from around the world still look to America as the land of freedom and opportunity. Most modern newcomers come from countries different from those of the earlier arrivals. Many come from nations throughout Asia, Africa, the Caribbean, or from various Spanish-speaking countries. Like those who came before them, most will meet the challenges of life in a new land and will realize their dream of becoming citizens of America.

Of course, there's many things I miss about my homeland. It's a beautiful country. But I just couldn't earn a living there. So far it's not been easy here in America either. But my kids are getting a better education. And we have more freedom than we've ever had.

—George Hamayaz, Venezuelan immigrant

Today, four out of every ten Americans are descended from ancestors who passed through Ellis Island. Most are keenly aware of those who were willing to make many sacrifices so that future generations might prosper.

My parents and my grandparents were all born in the old country. They came to America for our sak It was their greatest gift to us.

—Samuel Villani, son
Italian paren

ens of thousands of the most recent immigrants come from African nations. Here, they join tens of millions of African Americans whose ancestors were brought to the United States in chains. Slavery represents this country's most horrible and most inexcusable experience. Yet millions of African Americans have overcome the greatest obstacles of all and have made vital contributions in every area of our society. Like others whose roots lie in countries around the world, they proudly contribute their traditions, beliefs, foods, customs and culture to the mosaic that is America.

he American culture is t[he] culture of many land[s]. What we eat, how we ta[lk], the way we dress and wh[at] we believe are the result of t[he] contributions of people fro[m] every corner of the globe. [We] borrow from every group and a[re] made richer by the borrowing.

On special days I get to dress as my great-grandparents did. It's fun. I'm proud to be an American, but I'm proud of my roots too.

—Girl of Polish ancestry

IMMIGRANTS, ELLIS ISL'D

We are a nation of immigrants. Our forefathers and foremothers have left us their spirit, their cultures and their dreams.

Our cultural diversity is our greatest strength, for we are more than a nation. Thanks to those who dare to be immigrants, we are a nation of nations. It is a heritage of which we should all be proud.

Once I thought to write the story of the immigrants in America. Then I realized that the immigrants were America's story.

—Oscar Handlin, American historian

The Library of Congress

All of the photographs, lithographs, engravings, paintings, line drawings, posters, song lyrics, song-sheet covers, broadsides and other illustrative materials contained in this book have been culled from the collections of the Library of Congress. The Library houses the largest collection of stored knowledge on earth. Within its walls lie treasures that show us how much more than a "library" a great library can be.

The statistics that help define the Library are truly amazing. It has more books from America and England than anywhere else, yet barely one half of its collections are in English. It contains more maps, globes, charts and atlases than any other place on earth. It houses one of the largest collections of photographs in the world, the largest collection of films in America, almost every phonograph record ever made in the United States and the collections of the American Folklife Center. The Library also contains over six million volumes on hard sciences and applied technology.

It is a very modern institution as well. Dr. James Billington, the Librarian of Congress, has defined the Library's future through his vision of a "library without walls." "I see the Library of Congress in the future," he has said, "as an active catalyst for civilization, not just a passive mausoleum of cultural accomplishments of the past."

The Library of Congress was originally established to serve the members of Congress. Over the years it has evolved into a great national library. Unlike almost every other national library in the world, the Library of Congress does not limit the use of its collections to accredited scholars. Ours is a national library made by the people for the people, and is open to all the people. Fondly referred to as "the storehouse of the national memory," it is truly one of our proudest and most important possessions.

Index

Numbers in *italics* indicate photographs, illustrations and charts.

ORTHO'S All About

Annuals

Written by Ann Lovejoy
and Leona Holdsworth Openshaw
Meredith® Books
Des Moines, Iowa

W9-BMH-034

Ortho® Books
An imprint of Meredith® Books

Ortho's All About Annuals
Editor: Michael McKinley
Art Director: Tom Wegner
Copy Chief: Catherine Hamrick
Copy and Production Editor: Terri Fredrickson
Contributing Editor: Ed Malles
Contributing Copy Editor: Martin Miller
Technical Proofreader: Mary Pas
Contributing Proofreader: Kathy Eastman
Contributing Illustrators: Mike Eagleton, Pam Wattenmaker
Contributing Prop/Photo Stylists: Mary E. Klingaman, Diane Munkel, Pamela K. Peirce
Indexer: Donald Glassman
Electronic Production Coordinator: Paula Forest
Editorial and Design Assistants: Kathleen Stevens, Karen Schirm
Production Director: Douglas M. Johnston
Production Manager: Pam Kvitne
Assistant Prepress Manager: Marjorie J. Schenkelberg

Additional Editorial Contributions from Art Rep Services
Director: Chip Nadeau
Designers: Teresa Marone, lk Design

Meredith® Books
Editor in Chief: James D. Blume
Design Director: Matt Strelecki
Managing Editor: Gregory H. Kayko
Executive Ortho Editor: Benjamin W. Allen

Director, Sales & Marketing, Retail: Michael A. Peterson
Director, Sales & Marketing, Special Markets: Rita McMullen
Director, Sales & Marketing, Home & Garden Center Channel: Ray Wolf
Director, Operations: George A. Susral

Vice President, General Manager: Jamie L. Martin

Meredith Publishing Group
President, Publishing Group: Christopher M. Little
Vice President, Consumer Marketing & Development: Hal Oringer

Meredith Corporation
Chairman and Chief Executive Officer: William T. Kerr
Chairman of the Executive Committee: E.T. Meredith III

On the cover: *Rudbeckia* 'Zoto,' *Nemesia* 'Triumph Red,' and pansy 'Padparadja'. Photograph by John Glover

All of us at Ortho® Books are dedicated to providing you with the information and ideas you need to enhance your home and garden. We welcome your comments and suggestions about this book. Write to us at:
Meredith Corporation
Ortho Books
1716 Locust St.
Des Moines, IA 50309–3023

If you would like more information on other Ortho products, call 800-225-2883 or visit us at www.ortho.com

Thanks to
Melissa George, Colleen Johnson, Dave Kvitne, Aimee Reiman, Mary Irene Swartz, Goode Greenhouses of Des Moines, Sloat Garden Center of San Francisco

Photographers
(Photographers credited may retain copyright © to the listed photographs.)
L= Left, R= Right, C= Center, B= Bottom, T= Top, i=inset
William D. Adams: p. 32BR, 60BL, 68BL, 73BRi, 89CRi; **Ball Horticultural Co.:** p. 41TR & CR & BR; **Allen E. Boger:** p. 37BR, 86TL; **Patricia Bruno/Positive Images:** p. 7C; **John E. Bryan:** p. 25B; **David Cavagnaro:** p. 7BC & BRT, 53CRT; **R. Todd Davis:** p. 27T, 31BL, 54CL, 61BR, 63CR, 73TR, 88 Row 1-3, 92TL; **Joseph De Sciose:** p. 66TL; **Alan & Linda Detrick:** p. 8BR, 12, 41BL, 63CRi, 67BCR, 88 Row 2-4, 91 Row 1-3; **Thomas E. Eltzroth:** p. 53BR, 56BL, 57BC, 58TL, 64BLi, 67TR, 74BL, 82BL, 89BR, 90CL; **Derek Fell:** p. 8TL & BL, 15BR, 17BR, 25T, 50CL, 51TR, 55CR, 57TR & CR, 59TR, 60CL, 65CR, 66CL & BR, 68TLi, 70CL, 70BLi, 76TL & CL, 78BLi, 79TR, 81BR, 82TL, 85BCR, 86CL & BL, 87TL & CR, 88 Row 1 1-2, 88 Row 2-1, 89TR, 90TR, 91CRT, 92CL; **Charles Marden Fitch:** p. 8LC, 9BR, 65BR; **George Park Seed Co.:** p. 75TR; **John Glover:** p. 7TRi, 7CR, 8TC, 9CL & CB, 22, 23, 30 all, 31T, 36 all, 37TC, 49BR, 52BL, 53TR & BL & BC, 54BL, 56TL, 58BL, 59BR, 60TL, 61TR, 63TR, 67BL, 68CL, 69CB, 70Ci, 74CL, 76BL, 77BR, 78CR, 80TR & BL & BR, 81CR, 82TR, 83CR, 84BR, 85CRT, 90BR, 91 Row 1-2 & TR & CRB, 92BLi; **David Goldberg:** p. 40 all, 41TL & TC, 43L, 44 all, 45 all; **Jerry Harpur:** p. 4, 7TR, 16T, 26T, 31CR, 62TL & BL; **Marcus Harpur:** p. 67BR, 68TL, 89CR; **Lynne Harrison:** p. 7BR, 24T, 32BRi, 48 all; **Horticultural Photography:** p. 49CL, 50TL, 59TRi, 78TL, 92TR; **Jerry Howard/Positive Images:** p. 37TR, 84CL, 91 Row 1-4; **Bill Johnson:** p. 49TR, 63TL, 67CL, 71CR, 82 Row 1-1 & 1-4; **Dency Kane:** p. 8TRi, 69BR; **Dwight Kuhn:** p. 43R all, 52CL, 67CR, 77TRi; **Janet Loughrey:** p. 32CL, 57BR; **Allan Mandell:** p. 5B; **Charles Mann:** p. 9RCB; **Marilyn McAra:** p. 51BR, 70CR, 72CL; **Stuart McCall:** p. 49CR; **Bryan McCay:** p. 38, 39 all, 42 all; **David McDonald/PhotoGarden:** p. 5T, 83BR; **Michael McKinley:** p. 21TR, 61CR, 72BL, 91BR; **Rick & Donna Morus:** p. 6 Row 5, 6 Row 6; **Clive Nichols:** p. 6TC & BR; 20BL & 26B (The Priory, Kemerton, Worcestershire), 27Li (Graham Strong), 84BL; **Stephen G. Pategas:** p. 6 Row 2, 66BL; **Jerry Pavia:** p. 14B, 15T, 16Li, 21TL & BR, 24B, 28 all, 29 all, 32TL & CR, 52TL, 58CL, 63TRB, 64TL & BL, 69CR, 70BL, 72TL, 73CR, 78CL & BL, 83TR, 85TR, 87TR, 88 Row 2-3, 90TL, 92CLi; **Pamela K. Peirce:** p. 59CR; **Ben Phillips/Positive Images:** p. 69TC; **Proven Winners:** p. 55TR; **Cheryl R. Richter:** p. 6 Row 1, 13T, 82 Row 1-2, 85CR; **Susan A. Roth:** p. 9TR & RCT, 15BC, 16Ri, 33 all, 49TL, 50BL, 51CR, 54TL, 56CL, 63BR & BRi, 67BCL, 69TR, 70TL & TLi, 71BR, 75BR, 79CR & BR, 80BLT, 88BLi, 90BL, 91 Row 1-1, 92BL; **Eric Salmon:** All seedling photos in selection guide, pages 48-92; **Richard Shiell:** p. 7CRB, 53CRB, 55BR, 57CL, 62CL, 64CLi, 66TR, 74TL, 75CR, 77TR & CR, 82 Row 1-5, 84TL, 85CBL, 88BL; **Pam Spaulding/Positive Images:** p. 54CLi; **Albert Squillace/Positive Images:** p. 14T; **Michael S. Thompson:** p. 6 Row 3, 9Ci, 17TL & TC & TR, 20TR, 64CL, 65TR, 67C, 71TR, 80TLL & TLR, 81TR, 82 Row 1-3, 85BR, 87BR, 88 Row 2-2; **judywhite/New Leaf Images:** p. 6 Row 4, 13B, 73BR, 85BCL

Note to the Readers: Due to differing conditions, tools, and individual skills, Meredith Corporation assumes no responsibility for any damages, injuries suffered, or losses incurred as a result of following the information published in this book. Before beginning any project, review the instructions carefully, and if any doubts or questions remain, consult local experts or authorities. Because codes and regulations vary greatly, you always should check with authorities to ensure that your project complies with all applicable local codes and regulations. Always read and observe all of the safety precautions provided by manufacturers of any tools, equipment, or supplies, and follow all accepted safety procedures.

ANNUALS
FOR EVERY SEASON

ALL KIND OF ANNUALS

From geraniums and marigolds to petunias, lobelia and impatiens— even the most common annuals can make your home come alive with exuberant color. They're easy, inexpensive, and practically instant.

Fast growing, free flowering, and festive, annuals live for the moment. They have to— their lifespan is less than a year, and often only a few months. Early annuals leap from the ground and bloom before perennials know it's spring. Some summer annuals party from June until frost. Later bloomers carry on past Labor Day, their flowers fading into winter. Tougher relatives even survive mild winters.

Annuals come in almost every color, size, and shape, and can be quite troublefree. And you can pick annuals to bloom in most seasons. You can mingle pink and blue forget-me-nots among your tulips in the spring and tuck apricot and burgundy winter pansies

beneath your chrysanthemums in the fall. Annuals are ready to jazz up the garden almost any time of the year with instant color.

REFINED OR WILD: Consider California poppy. In the wild, its hot orange blooms come just once, in late spring. But over the years, longer-blooming, many-colored strains have been developed, from Milky White poppies, to the copper and pink Thai Silk that flowers off and on all summer.

TRAILING AND CLIMBING: To gracefully cover almost anything, there is an annual. Climbing annuals will scale a trellis, hide a fence, or clamber through a shrub or vine, adding color for a season. Danglers spill from hanging baskets, tumble off a wall, and pour over large containers.

BEDDING ANNUALS: These plants—compact, and free-flowering—are just waiting to be woven into carpets of color. They're "made" for mass plantings, as well as for infill in parterres and knot gardens. You can use them anywhere, because they're utterly reliable, and sized to fit.

FOLIAGE: Annuals grown for foliage are as useful in beds and borders as they are in window boxes and containers. They bloom, of course, but it's their leaves that earn kudos. Silvery-leaved dusty millers, purple perilla, and cream-streaked snow-on-the-mountain—all provide color, form, and texture.

FRAGRANCE: Potent perfumes distinguish many annuals. Night bloomers like moonflower vine and wild tobacco fill the evening air with mystery, and day bloomers like honey-scented sweet alyssum can be combined to create sunny perfumes for the whole garden.

BIENNIALS: Often used as annuals, these plants have a two-year lifecycle. In their second year, they flower and die. English daisies and forget-me-nots are biennials that are used as annuals.

TENDER PERENNIALS: Recently, many plants that are perennial in warm or tropical settings have been added to the rolls because they're used like annuals. Some are grown from seed, others from rhizomes, and still others from cuttings. Brilliant foliage plants, such as coleus and banana, are examples. You can overwinter them indoors but most are so inexpensive that it's not necessary.

BULBS AND CORMS: Some of the tender perennials you'll encounter will be in the form of small bulbs, or corms, such as elephant's ears and caladiums. They have much in common with the other tender perennials—they can be lifted and stored, but for the most part you don't have to.

HOW TO USE THIS BOOK

The first chapter explores the surprising seasonal effects possible with annuals. The second chapter explains how plant form and structure are the basis for good design. In the third chapter you'll learn some innovative new ways to organize color. The fourth chapter describes annuals for special uses. In the fifth chapter, you'll find instructions for growing annuals either from seeds or as small plants, and tips for care. Finally, there's the Annuals Selection and Growing Guide for over 150 recommended annuals.

Naturalized annuals such as California and shirley poppies, calendula, and lavatera weave a bright tapestry in a meadow garden (right).

Fascinating new foliage annuals such as recent coleus introductions are solid performers for containers (above).

FIRST BLOOMERS

Pansy 'Maxim Rose'

Pansy 'Happy Face White'

Pansy 'Super Swiss Giant'

Pansy, yellow face, blue wings

Pansy 'Joker'

Pansy 'Imperial Antique Shades'

Pansies and forget-me-nots are the classic spring combination with tulips and daffodils. Pansies can be adorably tiny or flagrantly large, and their velvety petals come in almost any color.

Some annuals are almost synonymous with spring. Pansies and forget-me-nots have said "spring's here" for centuries, and modern versions of these old favorites now come in a wide range of tints and tones. And these aren't your only choices—annuals abound that thrive in this cool season.

WITH BULBS: One of the best ways to show off these early birds is to mass them as underplanting for spring bulbs. Blue forget-me-nots foaming through ranks of white tulips make a fetching picture, as do sheets of pink pansies amid yellow daffodils. Livelier pairings can be memorable—pink and purple pansies under rose-toned tulips, or spicy orange tulips rising above blue forget-me-nots.

Other early bloomers can keep spring bulbs company. Wallflowers, cheerful or sizzling hot, have a delicate fragrance: Set a few beneath a window with some narcissus, and the perfume of spring will waft indoors.

SMALL SPACES: Rock walls make lovely homes for the delicate blossoms of baby blue eyes and species tulips. Golden calendulas can soften the edge of a driveway or sidewalk. Plant shady areas (often sunny before the leaves emerge) with a mix of bulbs and wildflowers (grape hyacinth and fried-egg flower, for example). Cheerful, starry English daisies and small violas can nestle naturally beside a mossy rock.

First wave flowers show up early and bow out fast; but before their blooms are fully faded, have replacements ready. But even now it's not too early to look forward to next year.

Leave a few self sowers like forget-me-nots, calendulas, and fried-egg flower, until they set seed. When the seed is ripe, shake them where you want next year's crop to grow or dry them in a paper bag to sow later.

FAVORITE EARLY BLOOMERS

English daisy
  Bellis perennis
Pot marigold
  Calendula
Wallflower
  Chieranthus cheiri and *Erysimum* species
Godetia
  Clarkia
Siberian wallflower
  Erysimum asperum

California poppy
  Eschscholzia californica
Forget-me-not
  Myosotis sylvatica
Baby blue-eyes
  Nemophila menziesii
Pansy
  Viola × wittrockiana
Viola
  Viola species

Wallflower (Cheiranthus) 'My Fair Lady' mix is outstanding for spring bedding in cool areas.

EARLY SUMMER

Beds and borders are filling up fast now. Leaves unfold and buds open. Annuals ease the transition from the tulips to the full magnificence of summer.

BRIDGING THE SEASONS: Use stop-gap annuals to keep your garden full of life while you wait for the glory of summer. Instead of weeding, carpet the ground with blooms while you wait for your ground covers to mature. By high summer, ground covers fill in; cut the annuals away. Also, early summer bloomers, like the spring annuals that preceded them, can hide the browning leaves of bulbs.

They can serve as heralds of plants yet to come. Scented sweet alyssum will foam in pastel clouds where Siberian iris will later show. In dappled shade, welsh poppies grow happily under hostas and rodgersias, whose leaves are slow to wake.

If you want to test new varieties, try sprinkling seed into paving cracks, or along the sidewalk or retaining walls. Sow a pinch of seed in walls, and the clinging plants will hang like living sculpture.

WILDFLOWER MIXTURES: Annual wildflowers are excellent early summer bloomers. California poppies, blue flax, and lupines are splendid self-sowers. Plant mixes that don't contain grasses; they'll likely elbow out your flowers.

In new gardens where grass is not yet planted, wildflower mixes fill summer with delight before you sow or sod. You don't need a meadow for these mixtures; scatter them in sweeps under shrubs and around trees.

Iceland poppies make a colorful transition from spring into summer. Here they have been folded into a bed of bearded iris and foxglove, with white primroses as edging.

Be ready to work annuals among spring bulbs to cover their spent foliage and turn your beds toward summer.

Iceland poppy 'Champagne Bubbles'

Shirley poppy

FAVORITE EARLY SUMMER ANNUALS

Swan River daisy *Brachycome*	Toadflax *Linaria maroccana*
Honeywort *Cerinthe major*	Edging lobelia *Lobelia erinus*
Godetia *Clarkia* hybrids	Sweet alyssum *Lobularia maritima*
Chinese forget-me-not *Cynoglossum*	Stock *Matthiola incana*
China pink *Dianthus chinensis*	Iceland poppy *Papaver nudicaule*
Sweet William *Dianthus barbatus*	Shirley poppy *Papaver rhoeas*

Breadbox or opium poppy

As these petunias take over in summer, they will cover the finished bearded iris plants.

Breadbox poppy 'Danebrog Laced'

HIGH SUMMER

TOP NONSTOP SUMMER ANNUALS

Begonia
  Begonia
Vinca
  Catharanthus roseus
Coleus
  Coleus × hybridus
Cosmos
  Cosmos bipinnatus
Globe amaranth
  Gomphrena globosa
Impatiens
  Impatiens hybrids
Flowering tobacco
  Nicotiana
Geranium
  Pelargonium
Petunia
  Petunia × hybrida
Salvia
  Salvia species
Marigold
  Tagetes hybrids
Narrowleaf zinnia
  Zinnia angustifolia

By midsummer, many annuals are at their peak performance and will continue virtually nonstop until fall.

From sunflowers to daylilies, a symmetrical garden of "hot color" makes a small walled garden come alive, below.

Summer annuals are showboaters; they'll carry your garden through the season with their flurry of flowers and foliage. This is often the most eye-catching season of the year.

CLASSIC COMBINATIONS: Ranks of tall purple cleomes and red amaranths behind swaths of zinnias, 'Orange Zest' salvias, and African marigolds will remind you of an open-air market. White salvias, blue and purple larkspur, and yellow French marigolds or ferny bidens, 'Golden Eye', look nautically crisp. For a more subtle touch, try mingling flowering tobaccos with baby's breath and blue lace flower for a tea-garden display. Cool and pale, Marguerites bloom on lacy foliage all summer. White and pastel cosmos are gentle at the border back, with white cleome and trumpet-flowered woodland tobacco.

BIG AND BOLD: A tiny yard packed full of sunflowers is unforgettable. Top them off with a bang—thread a firecracker vine through the tall stalks. Morning glories are astonishing as they reach for the sky from the sunflowers' golden embrace.

For the tantalizingly tropical, combine big-belled datura 'Evening Fragrance' with bold banana trees and variegated cannas like 'Pretoria'. Tree-like brugmansias reach flowering size in a single season, and may produce flaring flowers by the dozen.

IN SUMMER SHADE: In shady gardens, summer annuals replace spring wildflowers. Some of the best have been improved even

more. New day-neutral coleus come in elegant colors and leaf patterns and stay flowerless as long as they are kept moist. New varieties of impatiens have double or single blooms, with plain or cream-edged leaves. Begonias also have a new look, many with charmingly textured and colored leaves.

'Snowbird' African marigold

'Golden Gate' French marigold

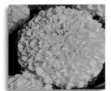

'Mrs. Moonlight' African marigold

Add a splashy fountain of hot summer color with 'Tricolor' Joseph's coat.

COOL SEASON

Where winters are short and mild, cold-tolerant annuals will keep things lively from late fall until spring. Bright calendulas, beloved for their constant bloom, will often carry on all winter. Violet cress, a fragrant, dainty crack filler, will entice you outdoors.

CLASSICS: Pansies are the place to begin. New strains include some baby blues and purples, yellows and rosy pinks, mahoganies, spicy oranges, and copper browns. Winter flowering primroses are equally pleasant, adding height to pansies. Their bright-eyed abundance earns them a place as temporaries anywhere. Mixed with winter bulbs, and evergreen perennials and grasses, these stalwarts bring cheer to window boxes and containers.

GRASSES: Compact ponytail grass adds high drama to winter combinations. Its flossy bloom persists through winter. Or add clumps of bronze and coppery carex, tender grasses

Pansies star among cool-season annuals for adding bright color to borders or backyards. In mild climates, they'll bloom through late winter.

WINTER FAVORITES

Snapdragon
   Antirrhinum majus
	African daisy
	   Dimorphotheca sinuata

Ornamental cabbage and kale
   Brassica oleracea
	Strawflower
	   Helichrysum

Pot marigold
   Calendula officinalis
	Diamond flower
	   Ionopsidium acaule

Annual chrysanthemum
   Chrysanthemum multicaule
	Ponytail grass
	   Stipa tenuissima
	Pansy
	   Viola × wittrockiana

Viola *Viola* species	

Ornamental cabbages and kale blend in a vibrant, well-structured window box planting (above).

Frilly 'Flamingo Plumes' kale

Ornamental cabbage adds bright color (above) or texture (below).

Ornamental kale 'Nagoya Rose' (below) and a calendula (pot marigold) bloom (right) demonstrate their winter hardiness on a frosty morning.

grown as annuals in colder climates. Like ponytail grass, the thready carex brings light-textured movement to stiff winter compositions.

THE CABBAGE FAMILY: Gardeners will have great fun with any of the cabbage family and its dozens of winter-hardy members. To bring out the best of their great, rounded heads, give the cabbages companions with contrasting shapes and complementary colors. Rosettes of 'Red Giant' mustard will set off to perfection frilly 'Peacock' kale. Ruffled 'Northern Lights' kale forms a cabbage-like mound in an array of colors. These plumpers will look dignified with rose- and purple-stemmed kales and darker winter pansies.

BLOOM SEASON CHART

Use this chart to help you plan overlapping seasons of bloom. Annuals are listed in order of bloom, so you can see at a glance which bloom together, which bloom in succession, and which bloom for extra long times. Remember, bloom charts are only rough guides, as bloom seasons differ according to region, weather, microclimates, and cultivars. Blue bars represent bloom seasons. Pink bars represent bloom seasons in mild climates. Broken bars show periods of intermittent bloom.

ANNUALS BLOOM CHART

Plant Name	Spr. E M L	Sum. E M L	Fall E M L	Win. E M L
English daisy (Bellis perennis)				
Ornamental cabbage or kale (foliage) (Brassica oleracea Acephala group)				
Wallflower (Cheiranthus cheirii)				
Forget-me-not (Myosotis sylvatica)				
Pansy or viola (Viola)				
California poppy (Eschscholzia californica)				
Clarkia/Godetia (Clarkia hybrids)				
Flowering flax (Linum grandiflorum)				
Annual chrysanthemum (Chrysanthemum multicaule)				
Canterbury bells (Campanula medium)				
Annual sweet pea (Lathyrus odoratus)				
Annual poppy (Papaver species)				
Pot marigold (Calendula officinalis)				
Begonia (Begonia)				
Blanket flower (Gaillardia pulchella)				
African daisy (Dimorphotheca sinuata)				
Heliotrope (Heliotropium arborescens)				
Sweet alyssum (Lobularia maritima)				
Laurentia (Laurentia axillaris)				
Stock (Matthiola incana)				
Ice plant (Mesembryanthemum)				
Monkey flower (Mimulus × hybridus)				
Nemesia (Nemesia strumosa)				
Baby blue-eyes (Nemophila menziesii)				
Nolana (Nolana paradoxa)				
California bluebell (Phacelia campanularia)				
Annual phlox (Phlox drummondii)				

Plant Name	Spr. E M L	Sum. E M L	Fall E M L	Win. E M L
Snapdragon (Antirrhinum majus)				
Bidens (Bidens)				
Larkspur (Consolida ambigua)				
Dwarf morning glory (Convolvulus tricolor)				
Chinese forget-me-not (Cynoglossum amabile)				
Hare's tail grass (Lagurus ovatus)				
Flossflower (Ageratum houstonianum)				
African daisy (Arctotis stoechadifolia grandis)				
Swan River daisy (Brachycome iberidifolia)				
Browallia (Browallia speciosa)				
Calibrachoa (Calibrachoa hybrid)				
Coleus (foliage) (Coleus × hybridus)				
China pink (Dianthus chinensis)				
Sweet William (Dianthus barbatus)				
Globe candytuft (Iberis umbellata)				
Toadflax (Linaria maroccana)				
Petunia (Petunia × hybrida)				
Butterfly flower (Schizanthus × wisetonensis)				
Vinca (Catharanthus roseus)				
Statice (Limonium sinuatum)				
Lisianthus (Lisianthus)				
Lobelia, all types (Lobelia species)				
Geranium (Pelargonium × hortorum)				
Fan flower (Scaevola)				
Dahlberg daisy (Thymophylla tenuiloba)				
Joseph's coat (foliage) (Amaranthus tricolor)				
Summer forget-me-not (Anchusa capensis)				
Chickabiddy (Asarina)				

Plant Name	Spr. E	M	L	Sum. E	M	L	Fall E	M	L	Win. E	M	L
Caladium (foliage) (*Caladium × hortulanum*)				■	■	■						
Canna (*Canna × generalis*)					■	■						
Bachelor's button (*Centaurea cyanus*)				■	■	■						
Honeywort (*Cerinthe major purpurascens*)	▨	▨		■	■			▨	▨			
Dahlia (*Dahlia*)				■	■							
Snow-on-the-mountain (*Euphorbia marginata*)				■	■							
Gazania (*Gazania rigens*)				■	■	■						
Globe amaranth (*Gomphrena globosa*)				■	■							
Annual baby's breath (*Gypsophila elegans*)				■	■	■						
Ginger lily (*Hedychium*)					■	■						
Strawflower (*Helichrysum bracteatum*)				■	■							
Impatiens (*Impatiens* species)				■	■							
Diamond flower (*Ionopsidium acaule*)				■	■							
Hartweg lupine (*Lupinus hartwegii*)				■	■							
Melampodium (*Melampodium paludosum*)				■	■	■						
Flowering tobacco (*Nicotiana* species)				■	■							
Love-in-a-mist (*Nigella damascena*)				■	■	■						
Basil (*Ocimum*)				■	■							
Penstemon (*Penstemon* hybrids)				■								
Moss rose (*Portulaca grandiflora*)				■	■							
Scarlet runner bean (*Phaseolus coccineus*)				■	■							
Painted tongue (*Salpiglossis sinuata*)				■	■							
Salvia (*Salvia* species)				■	■	■						
Creeping zinnia (*Sanvitalia procumbens*)				■	■							
Dusty miller (*Senecio cineraria*)				■	■							
Catchfly (*Silene*)				■	■							
Ponytail grass (*Stipa tenuissima*)				■	■	■	▨	▨				
Marigold (*Tagetes*)				■	■							

Plant Name	Spr. E	M	L	Sum. E	M	L	Fall E	M	L	Win. E	M	L
Black-eyed Susan vine (*Thunbergia alata*)					■	■						
Canary creeper (*Tropaeolum peregrinum*)					■	■	■					
Garden verbena (*Verbena × hybrida*)					■	■						
Rock bell (*Wahlenbergia*)					■							
Calla lily (*Zantedeschia*)					■	■						
Spider flower (*Cleome hassleriana*)					■	■						
Cosmos (*Cosmos* species)					■	■						
Wishbone flower (*Torenia fournieri*)					■	■						
Zinnia (*Zinnia*)					■	■						
Ornamental pepper (*Capsicum annuum*)					■	■	■					
Celosia (*Celosia* species)					■	■						
Morning glory, moonflower, cypress vine (*Ipomoea* species)					■	■						
Four-o'clock (*Mirabilis jalapa*)					■	■						
Nasturtium (*Tropaeolum majus*)					■	■						
Ornamental gourds (*Cucurbita pepo*)						■						
Hyacinth bean (*Dolichos lablab*)					■	■						
Sunflower (*Helianthus*)					■	■						
Tree mallow (*Lavatera* hybrids)					■							
Annual fountain grass (*Pennisetum setaceum*)					■	■						
Castor bean (*Ricinus communis*)					■	■						
Gloriosa daisy (*Rudbeckia hirta pulcherrima*)					■	■						
China aster (*Callistephus chinensis*)						■						
Datura (*Datura meteloides*)						■	■					
Firecracker vine (*Mina lobata*)						■	■					
Perilla (*Perilla frutescens*)								■				
Mexican sunflower (*Tithonia rotundifolia*)						■	■					

FORM AND FOLIAGE

Though their color may attract you first, annuals are a study in structure. Their shapes and forms can fill almost any niche in your garden. If you make form as much of a factor as color, you'll find you can gain much more impact in your garden.

Smaller annuals, such as begonias or marigolds, can make a large statement, but often they do this in a cumulative way. A broad planting of many of the same annual creates a bold swath of color and form. Or they can repeatedly fill in around taller plants in the front of a border, covering plain stems with small mounds of color. For almost any size "hole" in the garden, there's a small annual to fill it.

Middle-sized annuals can be real show-offs, and many, like snapdragons and coleus, steal the show with bold form and bright color. And they allow for a lot of experimentation: if you're not sure how you want to fill the middle part of a border, you usually have at least a few seasons (while your background perennials and shrubs grow) to play with different color and form combinations of annuals. If you're growing dark green or evergreen shrubs in the back of your border, such annuals will really show up against it.

Back-of-the-border annuals add height and mass while more permanent plants are growing to size. Bold plants like banana or sunflowers will give your border some size and shape quickly. Many a perennial garden looks a little puny the first year or two, and a larger annual can ease this transition time greatly.

Their shapes can do even more. Annual grasses and baby's breath soften the texture of more solid looking companions. Sprawlers can spill over pathways, extending the garden and softening the hard line of brick or stone.

To make the most of annuals, mix them in companionable groupings with all sorts of plants. You can use annuals in old standby rows and ribbons—if you wish. But explore their shapes, too, and create contrasts of form as well as color.

Sprawlers and spreaders

Rounded mound

Open airy

Spiky upright

Fans and blades

Big and bold

Weavers and fillers

Abundant and striking foliage contributes architectural form to this annual border featuring hot color combinations of ageratum, red fountain grass, canna 'Pretoria', and 'Torch' Mexican sunflower, backed up by castor beans.

FRONT LINE ANNUALS

Compact, prostrate, or creeping annuals are perfect on the bottom row. They're often used in beds in solid flows, framed by clipped boxwood or herbs, or around the edge of a border or bed.

EDGING: In most gardens, low-growers act as edgers; they delineate beds, soften the lines of hardscape, or fringe a curving path. Portulaca can fill a driveway; leave two bare strips the width between the tires. Low growers can also emphasize companions that are taller. Plumes of feather grass celosia make a pretty haze in a tangled border, but set several clumps in a foamy pool of 'Ruby Fields' twinspur, and both become distinctive. Such structural grouping makes artwork of our plants.

FORMAL SETTINGS: It's terrific fun to make an instant knot garden with annuals. Choose compact, fine-textured plants for the outer edge—globe basil or cigar plant. Next, crisscross in diamond shapes distinctive foliage plants like dusty miller. Basketweave the lines—alternate the plants in each opposing line. When the framework is established, fill it in with masses of annuals.

GARDEN ORNAMENTS: You can tuck statuary or birdbaths into such schemes. Or be more traditional—center beds with red bananas or clumps of cannas. Less flamboyant is a simple basket stuffed with flowers. In a country garden fill a wooden chair seat with flowers. In the city, paint an old bicycle red or blue; pack its panniers with petunias.

Coleus, cannas, geraniums, ageratums, and impatiens form ribbons of color.

LOW-GROWING ANNUALS

Dwarf snapdragon
Antirrhinum majus
Wax begonia
Begonia × semperflorens-cultorum
Pot marigold
Calendula officinalis
Edging lobelia
Lobelia erinus
Sweet alyssum
Lobularia maritima

Basil
Ocimum basilicum
Moss rose
Portulaca grandiflora
Dusty miller
Senecio cineraria
Signet marigold
Tagetes tenuifolia
Garden verbena
Verbena × hybrida

Dusty miller in the foreground adds distinctive texture to this planting, backed by the easy-to-dry heads of globe amaranth 'Buddy Purple', petunia, shrubby burning bush, and the spiked color of cleome 'Violet Queen'.

Colorful cannas create a background for this multi-layered annual garden with 'Flamingo Feather' wheat celosia forming a strong middle tier, and melampodium as the front line (above).

THE MIDBORDER

In mixed borders and perennial gardens, medium-sized plants make the middle tier, a layer that lifts the eye from the ground to shrubs and trees in the garden backdrop.

In large beds with hedging, the intermediates will shine. Runs of larkspur and marguerites or mixed fancy-leaf geranium and bloodleaf provide powerful impact all summer.

WORKHORSES: Adventurous perennial gardeners will offer flowering tobacco 'Domino' and 'Raspberry Ruffle' sunproof coleus middle billing anytime. Few flowers rival the months of unbroken color these workhorse plants provide.

Continual bloomers like honeywort, 'Red Plume' blanket flower, and 'Aurora Yellow Fire' marigolds keep the border bright among repeat perennials that need to rest between bloom. Golden feverfew and variegated 'Powys Pride' snapdragons are strong bloomers, but their foliage holds interest without their flowers.

LIGHTEN UP: Where heavy-looking plants need airy companions, baby's breath will make a foamy mound. Annual grasses add lightness, too, as well as movement—all will dance in every breeze. Plant feathery squirrel tail grass amid mounds of pink mask flower. Love grass (its fluffy seedheads look like pillow fights), burst out between silver-leaved gazanias and tall African marigolds.

MIDBORDER ANNUALS

Snapdragon	Melampodium
Antirrhinum	*Melampodium*
Bachelor's button	Flowering tobacco
Centaurea cyanus	*Nicotiana*
Coleus	Red fountain grass
Coleus	*Pennisetum*
Cosmos	*setaceum*
Cosmos	'Rubrum'
Dahlia	Salvia
Dahlia	*Salvia* species
Lisianthus	Zinnia
Lisianthus	*Zinnia elegans*

Dusty miller, impatiens, foxglove, and alyssum form a strong vertical planting around a birdbath for an enchanting focal point in this formal garden.

THE BACK BORDER

The back of the border can make or break an effective design. Quiet backgrounds serve to set off midborder stars. But the dramatic forms possible with many larger annuals offer a third layer of excitement that lifts the spirits of any composition.

QUIET BACKGROUNDS

Most large annuals are bred for their flair, so it can sometimes be difficult to use them to build a wall of quiet green. Limit your choices to one or only a few kinds of plants to help simplify and avoid clutter.

Some of the best choices for the quiet treatment are large-leaved plants. Canna and castor bean, for example, provide walls of foliage. For shade, consider flowering tobacco (*Nicotiana sylvestris*) and ginger (*Hedychium*).

Don't forget vines for a rapid rear border. Hyacinth bean (*Dolichos lablab*) makes a wonderful wall of deep burgundy. Canary creeper (*Tropeolum peregrinum*) and cypress vine (*Ipomoea quamoclit*) provide lighter green walls of delicate gauze.

JAZZY SKYLINES

Of course, your background plants can become stars in themselves. Punctuate the skyline of your border with a few standouts. Giant sunflowers (*Helianthus*) and Mexican sunflowers (*Tithonia rotundifolia*) have both the stature and the blazing color to play this role to the hilt, as do the showier vines such as black-eyed Susan vine (*Thunbergia alata*) and morning glory (*Ipomoea tricolor*).

Pennisetum 'Burgundy Giant' and 'Carmineus' castor beans form a tall backdrop and contribute impressive stature to an annual bed.

ANNUALS FOR THE BACK

Joseph's coat
  Amaranthus tricolor
Angel's trumpet
  Brugmansia
Canna
  Canna × generalis
Spider flower
  Cleome hassleriana
Elephant's ear
  Colocasia esculenta
Datura
  Datura meteloides

Sunflower
  Helianthus
Banana
  Musa
Flowering tobacco
  Nicotiana sylvestris
Castor bean
  Ricinus communis
Mexican sunflower
  Tithonia rotundifolia

The substance and drama of castor beans, red fountain grass, and tall Nicotiana sylvestris create a backdrop that anchors and enriches the midsize annuals in front.

'Russian Giant' sunflower (above) gives both height and daring whimsy to any planting.

Tender tropicals catch the eye and make historically accurate plantings for Victorian homes. Above, **Canna 'Mrs. P.S. Dupont'** *and* **Begonia 'Cocktail Brandy'** *contribute coordinating pinks to a dramatic garden. At right, wax begonias, blue salvia, cannas, and elephant's ear make a beautiful wall planting.*

TENDER TROPICALS

A century ago, tender tropicals were all the rage. All across the country, front yards boasted mounded beds, usually set in grass or gravel and packed with striped cannas and eye-catching banana trees. Huge, flaunting dahlias had pride of place in such bedding schemes, as did stiff sprays of gay gladiolas and mounds of brilliantly colored amaranths. That innocent Victorian delight in the gaudy soon gave way to more quietly tasteful border plantings. The brash, oversized plants were banished to parks and public places where they continue to please the eye—if not the arbiters of horticultural taste.

VICTORIAN TASTE: In our own gardens, we can recreate the tropical paradise look by arranging groups of tender tropicals in beds or containers. These days, many gardeners prefer to make more naturalistic arrangements, in which the strong lines and potent forms of the plants are played off to full advantage. However, those with Victorian homes may enjoy recreating the exotic formalism of those heritage bedding schemes.

These were very often based on luxuriant foliage plants such as elephant's ear. For a strong combination, pair it with colorful caladiums—the smaller plants mirror the leaf shapes of the larger plants, and create a repetition of form. A black or green elephant's ear is the perfect background for variegated white, green, or red caladiums underneath it. Ginger lily is another plant, usually thought of mostly for its showy blooms, that has impressive foliage. The long, straplike leaves spill over in profusion, and create a mound of shiny foliage.

JUNGLE PLANTS: In hot climates, many jungle understory plants such as angel's trumpets and silverleaf prefer some shade. A site that offers both reflected heat (as from a nearby street or sidewalk) and plenty of indirect light suits many jungle plants to a nicety. This is especially true in areas with long humid summers. The shelter of a covered but open-sided porch often makes a happy home for showy foliage plants that tend to scorch in hot, open gardens.

It's a jungle out there, with deep-toned 'Antiquorum' elephant's ear and yellow brugmansia striving together for the sun.

Foliage dominates in this planting of 'Maurelii' abyssinian banana with canna 'Tropicanna'.

Luscious beauty, 'Flore Pleno' datura is excellent for container plantings or gardens, flourishing in both sun and shade.

TENDER TROPICALS

Angel's trumpet
  Datura and
  Brugmansia
Caladium
  Caladium
Canna
  Canna
Elephant's ear
  Colocasia esculenta

Ginger lily
  Hedychium
Four-o'clock
  Mirabilis jalapa
Banana
  Musa
Castor bean
  Ricinis
Calla lily
  Zantedeschia

A mix of fancy-leaved caladium adds as much color and interest to a planting as any collection of bloomers.

CLIMBERS AND CONTAINERS: Large containers can hold a collection of big-leaved beauties, along with summer bloomers. One of the best summer bloomers is calla lily. Its tubular, trumpeting flowers come in colors from white to apricot and red, and it fits very nicely in a container.

Another choice for a larger container would be datura. Its dramatic, flaring flowers should be viewed up close, and because it can use some shade, it's the perfect plant for a porch or entryway. It has been hybridized extensively, and there are abundant colors and color combinations available.

Either one of these would be fun to use with black-eyed Susan vine or moonvine, as these abundantly flowering, fast-growing vines are just right for tumbling over the edge of a container. Or they could be potted by themselves and allowed to scramble up a support to create a pillar of blooms.

ANNUALS FROM SMALL TO LARGE

Use this chart to help you combine annuals according to size and form. So that you can quickly find an annual of the correct size you need, at a glance, they are organized in order of their height from short to tall. Each annual listed is accompanied by a sketch of its typical form, approximately to scale. Remember that this chart is a rough guide; the size given and the form shown can vary according to the cultivar selected, as well as region, weather, and horticultural practice.

ANNUALS HEIGHT AND FORM CHART

Diamond flower (Ionopsidium acaule) 2"

Edging lobelia (Lobelia erinus) 4"

Sweet alyssum (Lobularia maritima) 4"

Ice plant (Mesembryanthemum) 4"

Baby blue-eyes (Nemophila menziesii) 4"

Swedish ivy (Plectranthus) 4"

Dahlberg daisy (Thymophylla tenuiloba) 4"

English daisy (Bellis perennis) 6"

Sweet potato vine (Ipomoea batatas) 6"

Monkey flower (Mimulus × hybridus) 6"

Forget-me-not (Myosotis sylvatica) 6"

Moss rose (Portulaca grandiflora) 6"

Creeping zinnia (Sanvitalia procumbens) 6"

Pansy (Viola × wittrockiana) 6"

Viola (Viola) 6"

Flossflower, dwarf (Ageratum houstonianum) 8"

Wax begonia (Begonia × semperflorens-cultorum) 8"

Calibrachoa (Calibrachoa hybrid) 8"

Annual chrysanthemum (Chrysanthemum multicaule) 8"

China pink (Dianthus chinensis) 8"

Laurentia (Laurentia axillaris) 8"

Annual phlox (Phlox drummondii) 8"

Garden verbena (Verbena × hybrida) 8"

Impatiens (Impatiens) 8–12"

Snapdragon, dwarf (Antirrhinum majus) 9"

Swan River daisy (Brachycome iberidifoli) 9"

Nemesia (Nemesia strumosa) 9"

California bluebell (Phacelia campanularia) 9"

Wishbone flower (Torenia fournieri) 9"

Summer forget-me-not (Anchusa capensis) 10"

Browallia (Browallia) 10"

Gazania (Gazania rigens) 10"

Melampodium (Melampodium paludosum) 10"

Chilean bellflower (Nolana paradoxa) 10"

Basil, miniature (Ocimum) 10"

Fan flower (Scaevola) 10"

Dusty miller (Senecio cineraria) 10"

Catchfly (Silene) 10"

Tuberous begonia (Begonia Tuberhybrida) 12"

Ornamental cabbage (Brassica olearacea, Acephala group) 12"

Ornamental kale (Brassica olearacea, Acephala group) 12"

Vinca (Catharanthus roseus) 12"

Plume celosia (Celosia plumosa) 12"

Wallflower (Erysimum linifolium) 12"

African daisy (Dimorphotheca sinuata) 12"

California poppy (Eschscholzia californica) 12"

Globe candytuft (Iberis crenata) 12"

Toadflax (Linaria maroccana) 12"

Petunia (Petunia × hybrida) 12"

Flowering tobacco (Nicotiana hybrid) 12"

Shirley poppy (Papaver rhoeas) 12"

Butterfly flower (Schizanthus × wisetonensis) 12"

French single marigold (Tagetes patula) 12"

Nasturtium (Tropaeolum majus) 12"

Rock bell (Wahlenbergia) 12"

Zinnia angustifolia (Zinnia angustifolia) 12"

Blanket flower (Gaillardia pulchella) 14"

Ornamental pepper (Capsicum annuum) 15"

Cockscomb (Celosia cristata) 15"

Wallflower (Cheiranthus cheirii) 15"

Dwarf morning glory (Convolvulus tricolor) 15"

Dahlia hybrids, low-growing seed-grown type (Dahlia) 15"

Love-in-a-mist (Nigella damascena) 15"

Scarlet sage (Salvia splendens) 15"

Snapdragon, medium (Antirrhinum majus) 18"

Rex begonia (Begonia, Rex cultorum hybrids) 18"

Bidens (Bidens) 18"

China aster (Callistephus chinensis) 18"

Bachelor's button (Centaurea cyanus) 18"

Honeywort (Cerinthe major purpurascens) 18"

Clarkia/Godetia (Clarkia hybrids) 18"

Chinese forget-me-not (Cynoglossum amabile) 18"

Sweet William (Dianthus barbatus) 18"

Globe amaranth (Gomphrena globosa) 18"

Annual baby's breath (Gypsophila elegans) 18"

Hare's tail grass (Lagurus ovatus) 18"

Flowering flax (Linum grandiflorum) 18"

Lisianthus (Lisianthus) 18"

Stock (Matthiola incana) 18"

Geranium (Pelargonium × hortorum) 18"

Hybrid penstemon (Penstemon hybrids) 18"

Blue salvia (Salvia farinacea) 18"

Clary sage (Salvia horminium) 18"

African daisy (Arctotis stoechadifolia var. grandis) 20"

Pot marigold (Calendula officinalis) 20"

Yellow cosmos (Cosmos sulphureus) 20"

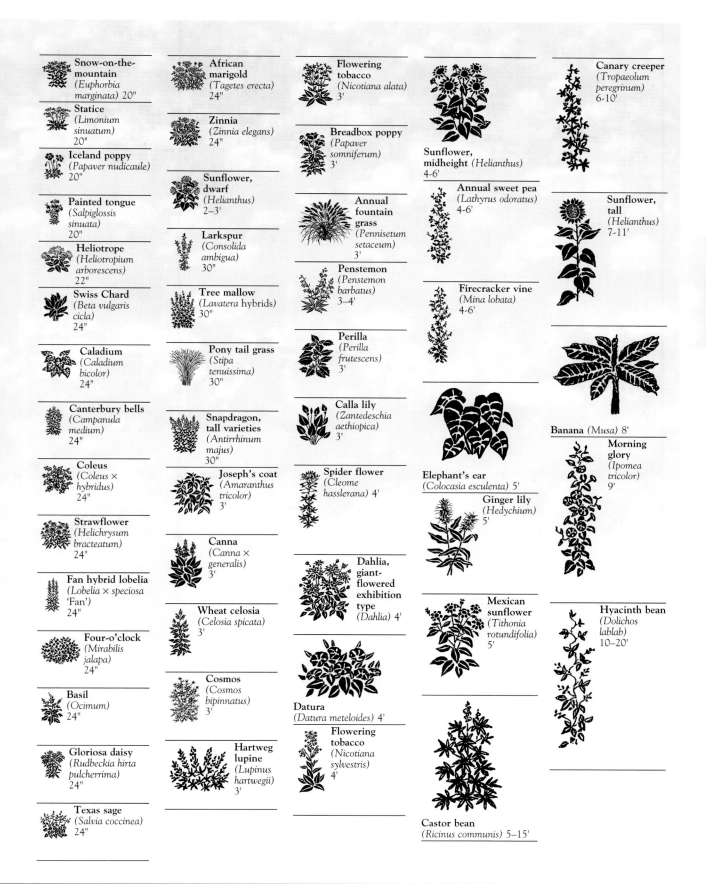

Snow-on-the-mountain
(*Euphorbia marginata*) 20"

Statice
(*Limonium sinuatum*) 20"

Iceland poppy
(*Papaver nudicaule*) 20"

Painted tongue
(*Salpiglossis sinuata*) 20"

Heliotrope
(*Heliotropium arborescens*) 22"

Swiss Chard
(*Beta vulgaris cicla*) 24"

Caladium
(*Caladium bicolor*) 24"

Canterbury bells
(*Campanula medium*) 24"

Coleus
(*Coleus* × *hybridus*) 24"

Strawflower
(*Helichrysum bracteatum*) 24"

Fan hybrid lobelia
(*Lobelia* × *speciosa* 'Fan') 24"

Four-o'clock
(*Mirabilis jalapa*) 24"

Basil
(*Ocimum*) 24"

Gloriosa daisy
(*Rudbeckia hirta pulcherrima*) 24"

Texas sage
(*Salvia coccinea*) 24"

African marigold
(*Tagetes erecta*) 24"

Zinnia
(*Zinnia elegans*) 24"

Sunflower, dwarf
(*Helianthus*) 2–3'

Larkspur
(*Consolida ambigua*) 30"

Tree mallow
(*Lavatera* hybrids) 30"

Pony tail grass
(*Stipa tenuissima*) 30"

Snapdragon, tall varieties
(*Antirrhinum majus*) 30"

Joseph's coat
(*Amaranthus tricolor*) 3'

Canna
(*Canna* × *generalis*) 3'

Wheat celosia
(*Celosia spicata*) 3'

Cosmos
(*Cosmos bipinnatus*) 3'

Hartweg lupine
(*Lupinus hartwegii*) 3'

Flowering tobacco
(*Nicotiana alata*) 3'

Breadbox poppy
(*Papaver somniferum*) 3'

Annual fountain grass
(*Pennisetum setaceum*) 3'

Penstemon
(*Penstemon barbatus*) 3–4'

Perilla
(*Perilla frutescens*) 3'

Calla lily
(*Zantedeschia aethiopica*) 3'

Spider flower
(*Cleome hasslerana*) 4'

Dahlia, giant-flowered exhibition type
(*Dahlia*) 4'

Datura
(*Datura meteloides*) 4'

Flowering tobacco
(*Nicotiana sylvestris*) 4'

Sunflower, midheight (*Helianthus*) 4–6'

Annual sweet pea
(*Lathyrus odoratus*) 4–6'

Firecracker vine
(*Mina lobata*) 4–6'

Elephant's ear
(*Colocasia esculenta*) 5'

Ginger lily
(*Hedychium*) 5'

Mexican sunflower
(*Tithonia rotundifolia*) 5'

Castor bean
(*Ricinus communis*) 5–15'

Canary creeper
(*Tropaeolum peregrinum*) 6-10'

Sunflower, tall
(*Helianthus*) 7–11'

Banana (*Musa*) 8'

Morning glory
(*Ipomea tricolor*) 9'

Hyacinth bean
(*Dolichos lablab*) 10–20'

COLOR PLAY

Annuals are enticing. They offer endless opportunities to play with color. Because they are relatively inexpensive and because they are not hard to move or replace if they don't work out like we want, they should be enjoyed for their experimental nature. We can try combinations of different flowers and forms and colors quickly and easily.

Color work is an art, and there are no rights or wrongs in its application. You can do whatever you want, surround yourself with whatever colors delight your eye. Yet still, it does pay to have some background in color theory, especially if you're considering your first planned border or bed. Use color charts and color wheels if you like, but always let your personal pleasure be your guide.

Harmonious shades interplay and repeat in this late summer garden of annual blooms that includes dusty miller, geraniums, alyssum, petunia, and salvia (above).

A bed of saturated colors dominated by reds provides an intense but integrated planting.

THE VOCABULARY OF COLOR

Artist's terms make useful tools—they help us understand relationships. A *hue* is a pure or fully saturated color, such as spectrum red or blue. The relative brightness or dimness of each color is called its *value* or weight: A pastel pink is light and a murky red is heavy. Highly saturated colors have a high color value: They glow intensely against a green backdrop and carry well across distance. Less saturated colors have lower value and visually recede. A *tone* is either a *shade* (darkened) or a *tint* (lightened) of a hue.

Although there are no strict rules for combining colors, there are a few principles that can help you make attractive and satisfying combinations. For example, hot, highly saturated colors rarely flatter cool, less-saturated colors. But, when the main colors of a combination share the same value or intensity, they will look balanced. If the colors are also close in hue or tint (perhaps a selection of sunset shades), the effect will be harmonious. If you choose partners, on the other hand, with contrasts (as when cool blue and warm orange are mingled), the result will be dynamic.

Always keep in mind, too, that your background or backdrop has a color, and along with that its own value and perhaps shade or tint. Also, remember that oftentimes extremes are not pleasing: A combination that's too harmonious can border on bland, while one that's too dynamic can be jarring.

THE ROLE OF LIGHT

How we see an object changes with the light. Observe your garden through the day. Colors shift from day to night. Morning light is long-angled, pale, and clean. It emphasizes delicate tints and creates long, soft-edged shadows. Noon light overhead bleaches color and casts

Stately white tulips repeat the ivory tones in a bed of pansies, providing rhythmic balance in this planting; the delicate notes of bright lavender contribute a brilliant counterpoint.

Opposite hues of orange wallflowers and blue forget-me-nots provide startling contrast for a heightened sense of drama.

harsh shadows. Evening light is amber, adding warmth and richness. Its shadows make pale colors gleam.

Each light alters the look of foliage and flower color. So does placement; when plants are massed, they reflect light readily. Set them on a porch rail or atop a wall, however, and the backlight will reveal undertones of red, purple, or orange in many leaves. Full sun brings out brilliance in some flowers, yet can overwhelm others (especially foliage plants). Filtered or indirect light (what gardeners call high or dappled shade) may emphasize depths in soft colors that look dull in stronger light.

So when you think about where you will place a plant, try to consider the quality of light it will receive. Will its soft colors be overwhelmed by the noon sun? Does it instead need to be placed where the afternoon sun can bring out its subtleties? Thinking in these terms will help you get the most enjoyment from your annuals.

COLORFUL PARTNERSHIPS

Partnered plants can be supportive or competitive. If you balance their color weight and value, they will appear harmonious. Competitors are higher powered and create tension and drama. Mix grape purple and clarion crimson, for example, and you'll achieve a heavy but harmonious effect. Adding dark orange creates high voltage contrast. For a romantic, misty look, tone down each color to mingled lavenders and pinks. Alone, these harmonize, but stir in some sherbet salmon shades, or orange, and watch the drama increase. To add sparkle, lift the value with white and pale tints of your main colors.

The multicolored leaves of canna and coleus echo and play off one another.

COORDINATING COLORS

When colors of all values are mixed together, the result is often a riot of color. Such a jumble can be very appealing, but it can also be just confusing. If you want to create a more orderly flow of color through the garden, try borrowing a few ideas from textile designers.

COLORWAYS: By looking at how textile designers go about combining colors, you can approach your choices of garden colors systematically. Weavers create colorways, integrated groups of related colors that you can mix and mingle interchangeably.

Picture a handful of fabric patterns in which the same color scheme is repeated. Because they share a common family of color, each individual section harmonizes with the others. The first swatch may be predominately blue, the next one mainly green, another chiefly yellow or orange, but in each case, the secondary colors (which might be bronze, copper, and gold) are drawn from the same pool.

IN THE GARDEN: These ideas apply easily to the plants in your garden, and you can create color themes by using colorways. First, for each bed, select a predominant color—perhaps clear purple in one, sky blue in another, and lemon yellow in a third. Make sure that at least half the plants in each bed have flowers or foliage in this main color. Next, pick a secondary color or colors, that will support your first choice—a hotter purple, perhaps, a darker blue, and an old gold. Choose the remainder of your plants with flowers or foliage in these supportive or secondary colors.

REPETITION: As the colorways move through the various parts of the garden, the main colors take turns at playing the starring role from area to area or season to season while the secondary colors add a unifying theme. The overall effect is constantly changing, yet remains coordinated and

Repeating color themes create a color run throughout this garden. Purples star in alternating beds while softer whites and yellows create patches of muted color. Note that the walkway and pedestal also contribute color, and become part of the overall scheme.

effortlessly attractive. It works because in each bed or section, the main players are ably supported by a united family of secondary colors. The colorway approach greatly simplifies shopping; any plant that does not fit the color guidelines does not go home. It makes plant placement easier as well; since our colors are compatible, we can focus on creating contrasts of form and texture.

COLOR RUNS: Another fun and fascinating way to use color powerfully is to create what weavers refer to as color runs.

Simple color runs take a single color— say, red—and play it for all it's worth, mixing its many tints and shades. You can keep the color run as simple as a single color, or base complex color runs on two or three related colors—blue and purple, or red, orange and yellow (all are neighbors on the color wheel). Simple or complex, be generous with both the lightest tints and the deepest shades. Color runs create a lot of energy in the garden, and can be a lot of fun as well.

BACKGROUND: Color runs and colorways play out against a backdrop of green. Though green is a garden given, like a dressmaker's basic black, it, too, has tints and shades. There are a thousand tones of green which you can loosely cluster as true green, or as blue green, grey green, yellow green; there are greens that are stained with red or purple. Some of the most powerful uses of color in the garden come about because green wasn't taken for granted but instead used to its fullest potential.

Don't overlook the effect that greens can have on other colors. Some gardeners delight in creating complex color runs based on a full palette of greens, including plants that boast green flowers. Or make the backdrop of your garden up with random greens—that is, the background itself can be a color run of greens. On the other hand, by grouping compatible or uniform backdrop greens, you can significantly enhance the effect of colorways and runs.

Various hues of green foliage create a soothing backdrop for this colorful garden. Soft evergreen, vertical deciduous trees, and a carpet of lawn contribute to the canvas for these complex, brighter colors. Although the flower colors are varied, they are all strong and vibrant, creating harmony. The central colors repeat throughout the garden.

French pastels cooled with gray tones make a soft-colored planting that captures and enchants the eye.

Blue is among the coolest of garden colors. For added chill, complement it with pale yellow. Here, this theme is stunningly illustrated by a pairing of 'Victoria' blue salvia and 'Gold Wizard' coleus.

COOL COLOR THEMES

The colors clustered on the blue, green, and yellow side of the spectrum are considered cool; reds, oranges, and purples are hot. Because white is cool and black is warm, a pastel tint (which is whitened) of almost any color works well in combination with other cool colors, but French pastels (which are greyed) look best with warm colors.

Early in the twentieth century, when English gardeners first began making gardens with color themes, nearly all the color combinations were cool, with white flowers and white-streaked foliage. White, as you may have discovered, is very difficult to work with, because few of the endless variations of white match well.

But because white is cool, carefully chosen clear whites can function well in cool themes. When good whites are matched with the cool clear morning sun, the whites in the garden really shine. Or white impatiens can cheer a shady corner. And even though white can be difficult to match perfectly, many gardeners enjoy making white color runs, which are not quite as demanding.

Gardeners who prefer cooler colors will find it much easier (and just as fun) to make a blue garden, using a wide range of blue

White is a difficult color to match in gardens; it often works best blended with grays and silvers in cool, muted plantings.

flowers and foliage, all of which are compatible. Pink and blue pastel gardens are even more popular, particularly when frosted with silvery, grey, or blue-grey foliage. If you prefer a brighter scheme but want a cool look, try blending soft yellows with clean pastel tints—apricot, peach, and salmon—adding lots of chilly grey and muted blue foliage.

A few other general ideas apply to cool color gardens. Remember that less saturated colors recede. So, if you're using pastel shades of these colors, try to place them either close to where you want them to be viewed or in dappled or high shade. If you place them in full, noonday sun they can't help but be washed out.

A cool-color theme garden of massed larkspur and phlox demonstrates how well different shades of blue go together.

This garden of salsa colors pops with bright, hot reds, oranges, and yellows for a warm color theme.

Warm shades of magenta and red darken against dim green foliage; against chartreuse spikes, they will sparkle with electricity.

WARM COLOR THEMES

The warm side of the spectrum—red, orange, and purple—offers irresistible opportunities to indulge in theatrics with pure, fully saturated color.

Heat lovers delight in making salsa gardens filled with the festive, snapping colors of an open-air market. Dramatic sunsets inspire combinations with deeper tones—smoldering purples streaked with flaming reds and brassy oranges, for example.

Orange is generally underused, but your garden can be stunning when you mix it with bronze, copper, brown, and a range of other oranges. You can think of these colors as the colors of fall or halloween, and then give them your own personal spin. In well-matched combinations, these strong colors resonate and will amplify each other—even more so if you mix in slightly lighter shades. It rarely works to blend pastels with fully saturated hues, but step the saturation down a degree or two and you'll make brilliant and successful contrasts.

The deep purple of 'Red Russian' kale is a perfect foil for the warm oranges and golds of these marigold flowers (below).

These distinctively different warm-color blooms coordinate well because their vivid hues are the same color weight.

Background foliage is important too; the darkest shades of reds and purples can vanish into a dim green hedge, but set them in front of gold or chartreuse foliage and the darker, somber colors really sing. If your favorites are the darker colors, remember this factor when you're choosing combinations. Also, if you're wanting to use darker, small bedding plants, try planting gold or chartreuse bedding plants with them—they won't be tall enough to show off against a background, but by placing them this way they will shine.

Alter the look of any color by changing its backdrop: Set a citrus orange marigold against deep purple or mahogany red foliage—the orange will pop out sharply. Back that same marigold with a red or purple of matching weight and the orange will merge instead. Place it in front of murky lavender or smoky blue and orange will now seem cool and dark.

ORGANIZING COLOR: THE WARM RANGE

Penstemon 'Husker Red'

Celosia 'Century Red'

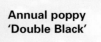

Canna 'Brandywine'

Gazania 'Sunshine'

Salvia 'Carabiniere Blue'

Zinnia 'Border Beauty Rose Shades'

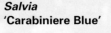

Nemesia 'Carnival'

Celosia 'Apricot Brandy'

Annual poppy 'Double Black'

Nicotiana 'Metro Red'

Mexican sunflower 'Goldfinger'

Marigold 'Orange Jubilee'

Sweet William 'Indian Carpet'

Schizanthus 'Royal Pierrot'

Dahlia 'Smoky Oraule'

Gloriosa daisy

Salpiglossis 'Casino Blackjack'

Cosmos 'Sensation Pink'

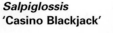

Coleus 'Beauty'

Celosia 'Century Yellow'

Coleus 'Fairway Mosaic'

Coleus 'Black Dragon'

Dahlia 'Rose Branderis'

Zinnia 'Peter Pan Gold'

Coleus 'Black Magic'

African daisy 'Wine'

Wax begonia 'Pink Tausendschon'

Cockscomb celosia 'Jewel Box Yellow'

Red fountain grass

Lavatera 'Mont Rose'

Canterbury bells

Viola 'Lemon Chiffon'

Ponytail grass

Wheat celosia 'Flamingo Feather'

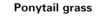

Annual candytuft 'Dwarf Fairy'

Strawflower

Pansy 'Ghost'

Dahlia 'Tanjoh'

Salvia 'Turkestaniana'

Brugmansia

ORGANIZING COLOR: THE COOL RANGE

Dahlia 'Do-De-O'

Blue salvia 'Victoria'

Petunia 'Ultra Blue'

Petunia 'Purple Wave'

Marigold 'Antigua Primrose'

Cerinthe 'Purpurascens'

Heliotrope 'Lemoine Strain'

Dahlia 'Elmira'

Marigold 'Primrose Lady'

Lobelia 'Regatta Marine Blue'

Pansy 'Crystal Bowl True Blue'

Moss rose 'Sundial Fuschia'

Coleus 'Wizard Golden'

California bluebell

Statice

Petunia 'Sugar Daddy'

Nicotiana 'Nicki Lime'

Forget-me-not 'Ultramarine'

Pansy 'Universal True Blue'

Verbena 'Homestead Purple'

Nicotiana 'Lime Green'

Baby blue-eyes

Forget-me-not 'Victoria Pink'

Ageratum 'Hawaii Blue'

Nicotiana 'Starship Lemonlime'

Love-in-a-mist 'Persian Jewels'

Sweet alyssum 'Golf Pastel Lavender'

Nemesia

Dahlia 'All Triumph'

Dusty miller 'Silver Dust'

Viola 'Columbine'

Sweet alyssum 'Wonderland Purple'

Viola 'Gazelle'

Salvia 'Strata'

Annual baby's breath 'Gypsy'

Swan River Daisy

Petunia 'Fantasy Ivory'

Snow-on-the-mountain

Pansy 'Maxim Marina'

Viola 'Penny Lane'

ANNUALS
FOR SPECIAL SPOTS

CONTAINERS

I f your space is limited, or if you want to make a welcome entryway, enliven a poolside, or emphasize a staircase, pack annuals into containers. There are literally hundreds of alternatives—from window boxes and hanging baskets stuffed with trailing vines and cascading petunias to olive cans crammed with red geraniums. Bigger is better; it's easier to keep large pots well watered; small ones dry out quickly.

Dress up permanent evergreen plantings with seasonal annuals, but plan ahead. Sink placeholder pots (bulb pans or 4-inch square pots) around the container edge. Slip in your array of annuals and you won't damage the evergreen roots.

In winter, follow decorative ivies with primroses, cascading double nasturtiums and silvery helichrysums. Use annuals freely in narrow necked pots. For instant elegance, drop hanging baskets of fuchsias or geraniums into tall, narrownecked jars and let the plants tumble down the sides. Remove the hanging

Annuals cascading from containers add color in hard-to-reach spots. Bigger containers are better; small ones dry out too quickly.

Window boxes provide an excellent opportunity to add annual color. Consider the color of the foliage as well as the backdrop for your container when choosing plants and colors.

wires and you have a splendidly mature looking planting in a flash.

Also, keep in mind the foliage of your container annuals. If you like coleus 'Trailing Red', try placing it where it gets afternoon sunlight to show off the leaves to their greatest advantage.

Sweet peas add color and privacy to a wire fence. These climbers block undesirable views and transform unsightly barriers.

Training ornamental gourds onto an arbor creates a charmingly animated garden room.

CLIMBERS

Annual climbers will decorate any surface you like. They can play the role of ground cover, paint a wall in living color, or fill the air with fragrance. Drape them on a slope, or grow them on supports as curtains or as screening for private parts of the yard.

COVER UP: While waiting for foundation shrubs to grow, disguise that new-house siding with annuals. Simply stretch netting across the area to be covered, then plant a few Mexican bell vines at its base. A single cathedral bell vine or goldfish vine will cover half the house by high summer. Canary creeper vine sounds slow, but this determined traveler can cover a garage or a mature fruit tree in one season. Flow rivers of blue morning glories over a homely retaining wall or scale a house with strong netting. Moonflower vine will extend the show, its fragrant white flowers lighting up the night.

SUPPORT: Give spring-flowering shrubs a second season; set lightweight scramblers, such as firecracker vine or sweet peas about their skirts. Heavier vines, such as fernleaf cypress vine need sturdy hosts. Grow the fernleaf in a large tree, not a shrub. Send moonflower vines or morning glories up an old ladder leaning on a tree, or give them runner guides of rubber-coated wire or twine that won't sag under their weight.

'Scarlett O'Hara' morning glory climbs a telephone pole, softening its effect on the surrounding garden.

CLIMBING ANNUALS LIST: (6 FEET AND GREATER)

Chickabiddy
Asarina
Hyacinth bean
Dolichos lablab
Morning glory, moonflower
Ipomoea
Cypress vine
Ipomoea quamoclit
Annual sweet pea
Lathyrus odoratus

Firecracker vine
Mina lobata
Scarlet runner bean
Phaseolus coccineus
Black-eyed Susan vine
Thunbergia alata
Nasturtiums
Tropaeolum majus
Canary creeper
Tropaeolum peregrinum

SHADE

Wax begonias, coleus, and other moisture-loving annuals flourish in damp, shady spots, giving color all season.

Shade offers the opportunity to weave webs of colorful foliage with all its form and texture, and dozens of flowers bloom long and hard in shady settings. But the type of shade will determine what you plant.

DAPPLED: Airy, light shade is ideal; it offers plenty of light and air but blocks the fierceness of the summer sun. Woodland understory annuals like forget-me-nots will thrive in filtered shade, especially with plenty of reflected light from walls or walkways.

DAMP: Wet, moist shade makes streamside annuals—from native monkey flower to tropical begonia and fuchsia—feel at home. Giant Himalayan balsam will rise in thickets in damp locations and scent the air with an orchid like fragrance.

DRY: Shade without much moisture is difficult but a handful of tough annuals will attempt it. Cheerful fried egg flower, baby blue eyes, and foxglove will tolerate dry shade if given periodic boosts with supplemental watering. Hydrophyllic polymers (water-holding gels) will also improve dry soils; with them, a wider range of plants will flourish.

EXTREME: Dense, dank, or bone-dry shades are challenging, but in such situations, raised beds, pots, and containers offer ample alternatives. They can help control the soil and therefore make everything a little easier on plants in these tough spots.

And if your shade gives way to fuller light, there are all kinds of climbing and trailing annuals to expand your palette. A tremendous range of annuals grows beautifully in partial shade, especially where summers are hot, so don't hesitate to experiment with plants you enjoy, even if they are not strictly considered to be shade lovers.

A lush planting of impatiens carpets an area of dappled shade with bloom.

In settings with dense or dry shade, grow annuals in containers; soil can be kept moist.

This pairing of hydrangea and impatiens provides colors as rich as any sun planting.

SHADE ANNUALS

Begonia
  Begonia
Browallia
  Browallia speciosa
Caladium
  Caladium
Coleus
  *Coleus ×
  hybridus*
Elephant's ear
  *Colocasia
  esculenta*

Impatiens
  Impatiens
Diamond flower
  *Ionopsidium
  acaule*
Lobelia
  Lobelia
Monkey flower
  Mimulus
Forget-me-not
  *Myosotis
  sylvatica*

Flowering tobacco
  Nicotiana
Plectranthus
  Plectranthus
Butterfly flower
  Schizanthus
Wishbone flower
  Torenia fournieri
Pansy and viola
  Viola
Calla lily
  Zantedeschia

Shade-loving coleus thrive in pots and soften walls and paved areas of the garden.

HOT SPOTS

If summer heat leaves gardens limp and languid, try an infusion of sun loving annuals to keep them fresh all season. Finding the right plants for the job, however, isn't quite as simple as it sounds because heat lovers don't divide themselves neatly into categories. This is one situation that rewards some experimentation.

ADAPTABLE PLANTS: Some annuals, such as vinca and moss rose, are extremely adaptive, thriving equally in high desert and humid lowland settings. Others, such as African daisy and gazania, thrive in dry heat but fade quickly where summer nights are muggy. Then there are Transvaal daisies; they adore hot days and humid nights. So does the southern classic, cypress vine, but both turn sulky where nights are cool no matter how warm the days may be.

HELP THEM OUT: A lot of annuals can be persuaded to take the heat as long as other needs are met. Generally, humus-rich, well drained soil and plenty of water will do the trick, and sometimes just one supplement is enough. Calendula, baby's breath, geranium, and dusty miller perform brilliantly in hot spots—even if the soil is lean and poor—with ample and regular watering. Prairie plants, such as blanket flower and tickseed, can tolerate an amazing amount of heat and drought when grown in deep, rich soils. Garden verbena and colorful Joseph's coat do best with both great soil and frequent watering.

Moss roses 'Wildfire Mix' (front edge) and 'Sundance Mix' (background) are well suited to the sandy, stony soil of the arid Southwest.

Stone steps create a happy home for this moss rose. Many less hardy blooms, such as the neighboring viola, can handle hot conditions if given a little extra care.

ANNUALS FOR HOT SPOTS

Joseph's coat
  Amaranthus tricolor
Bidens
  Bidens
Ornamental pepper
  Capsicum annuum
Vinca
  Catharanthus roseus
Cockscomb
  Celosia
Spider flower
  Cleome

California poppy
  Eschscholzia californica
Snow-on-the-mountain
  Euphorbia marginata
Blanket flower
  Gaillardia pulchella
Gazania
  Gazania rigens
Globe amaranth
  Gomphrena globosa
Strawflower
  Helichrysum

Statice
  Limonium sinuatum
Sweet alyssum
  Lobularia maritima
Melampodium
  Melampodium
Geranium
  Pelargonium
Petunia
  Petunia
Moss rose
  Portulaca grandiflora

Creeping zinnia
  Sanvitalia procumbens
Dusty miller
  Senecio cineraria
Marigold
  Tagetes
Dahlberg daisy
  Thymophylla tenuiloba
Garden verbena
  Verbena × hybrida
Zinnia
  Zinnia

SPECIAL SPOT, SPECIAL PURPOSE

ANNUALS FOR CUTTING

Floss flower
  Ageratum, 'Blue Horizon', 'Florist's White'
Joseph's coat
  Amaranthus tricolor
Snapdragon
  Antirrhinum
Pot marigold
  Calendula
China aster
  Callistephus
Canterbury bells
  Campanula medium
Cockscomb, celosia
  Celosia

Bachelor's button
  Centaurea cyanus
Spider flower
  Cleome
Cosmos
  Cosmos
Larkspur
  Consolida ambigua
Dahlia
  Dahlia
Snow-on-the-mountain
  Euphorbia marginata
Blanket flower
  Gaillardia
Annual baby's breath
  Gypsophila elegans

Sunflower
  Helianthus
Strawflower
  Helichrysum
Heliotrope
  Heliotropium
Sweet pea
  Lathyrus
Lisianthus
  Lisianthus
Fan hybrid lobelia
  Lobelia × speciosa
Hartweg lupine
  Lupinus hartwegii
Stock
  Matthiola
Flowering tobacco
  Nicotiana

Love-in-a-mist
  Nigella damascena
Annual poppies
  Papaver
Gloriosa daisy
  Rudbeckia hirta
Painted tongue
  Salpiglossis
Salvia
  Salvia
African marigold
  Tagetes erecta
Mexican sunflower
  Tithonia
Calla lily
  Zantedeschia
Zinnia
  Zinnia

ANNUALS FOR DRYING

Celosia, cockscomb
  Celosia
Larkspur
  Consolida
Globe amaranth
  Gomphrena
Annual baby's breath
  Gypsophila elegans

Strawflower
  Helichrysum
Sunflower
  Helianthus
Statice
  Limonium
Hare's tail grass
  Lagurus

Love-in-a-mist
  Nigella
Blue salvia
  Salvia farinacea
Zinnia
  Zinnia elegans

FOLIAGE ANNUALS

Swiss Chard
  Beta vulgaris
Ornamental cabbage and kale
  Brassica
Caladium
  Caladium
Canna
  Canna
Coleus
  Coleus
Elephant's ear
  Colocasia esculenta
Hyacinth bean
  Dolichos lablab
Snow-on-the-mountain
  Euphorbia marginata

Ginger lily
  Hedychium
Licorice plant
  Helichrysum petiolare
New Guinea impatiens
  Impatiens, New Guinea hybrids
Ornamental sweet potato
  Ipomoea batatas
Banana
  Musa
Basil
  Ocimum
Ivy geranium
  Pelargonium peltatum

Annual fountain grass
  Pennisetum setaceum
Perilla
  Perilla
Plectranthus
  Plectranthus
Castor bean
  Ricinus communis
Dusty miller
  Senecio cineraria
Ponytail grass
  Stipa tenuissima
Calla lily
  Zantedeschia

TRAILING ANNUALS

Chickabiddy
Asarina
Tuberous begonia
Begonia Tuberhybrida
Bidens
Bidens
Swan River daisy
Brachycome
Calibrachoa
Calibrachoa
Bush morning glory
Convolvulus tricolor
Ornamental gourd
Cucurbita

Licorice plant
Helichrysum petiolare
Annual candytuft
Iberis
Ornamental sweet potato
Ipomoea batatas
Laurentia
Laurentia
Edging lobelia
Lobelia erinus
Sweet alyssum
Lobularia
Ice plant
Mesembryanthemum

Forget-me-not
Myosotis sylvatica
Baby blue-eyes
Nemophila menziesii
Chilean bellflower
Nolana paradoxa
Ivy geranium
Pelargonium peltatum
Petunia
Petunia
Moss rose
Portulaca
Creeping zinnia
Sanvitalia

Fan flower
Scaevola
Nasturtium
Tropaeolum
Garden verbena
Verbena
Rockbell
Wahlenbergia
Narrowleaf zinnia
Zinnia angustifolia

ANNUALS FOR COOL SUMMER REGIONS

English daisy
Bellis
Swan River daisy
Brachycome
Wallflower
Chieranthus, Erysimum
Godetia
Clarkia
China pink
Dianthus chinensis

African daisy
Dimorphotheca
Annual sweet pea
Lathyrus
Toadflax
Linaria maroccana
Edging lobelia
Lobelia erinus
Stock
Matthiola

Monkeyflower
Mimulus
Forget-me-not
Myosotis
Nemesia
Nemesia strumosa
Baby blue-eyes
Nemophila
California bluebell
Phacelia campanularia

Annual phlox
Phlox drummondii
Painted tongue
Salpiglossis
Butterfly flower
Schizanthus
Nasturtium
Tropaeolum
Pansy and viola
Viola

EDIBLE ANNUALS

(Note: "flowers" refers to flower petals only)

Joseph's coat (leaf and seed)
Amaranthus tricolor
Tuberous begonia (flowers)
Begonia Tuberhybrida
English daisy (flowers)
Bellis perennis
Swiss chard (leaves and stems)
Beta vulgaris
Ornamental cabbage (flowers)
Brassica oleracea

Ornamental kale (leaves and flowers)
Brassica oleracea
Pot marigold (flowers)
Calendula officinalis
Ornamental pepper (fruits of some varieties; most are too hot)
Capsicum annuum
Spider flower (flowers)
Cleome hasslerana
Ornamental gourd (flowers)
Cucurbita
China pink (flowers)
Dianthus chinensis

Hyacinth bean (flower)
Dolichos lablab
Sunflower (unopened young flowers, cooked only; seed)
Helianthus
Ornamental sweet potato (tuber)
Ipomoea batatas
Banana (flowers and fruit)
Musa
Basil (flowers and leaves)
Ocimum
Perilla (leaves, used in sushi)
Perilla

Scarlet runner bean (flowers, young pods under 4 inches long, mature bean seeds)
Phaseolus coccineus
Salvia (flowers and leaves)
Salvia
Signet marigold, 'Lemon Gem', 'Tangerine Gem' (flowers)
Tagetes tenuifolia
Nasturtium (flowers, leaves, young seedheads as caper substitute)
Tropaeolum
Pansy and viola (flowers)
Viola

GROWING ANNUALS

Even beginners can have success growing annuals from seed. Small seeds require fine soil; larger quantities or more demanding plants may require grow lights.

GETTING STARTED

In most parts of the country, garden centers and nurseries provide an exciting range of garden-ready annuals. But even though they offer an increasingly large number of varieties, you can grow annuals from seed in even greater variety and numbers.

FIRST THINGS FIRST

When your only light source is a sunny windowsill, stick with a few pots of quickly sprouting seeds like sunflowers and sweet alyssum. To grow larger quantities or more demanding plants, you'll need to set aside an area for grow lights and flats or seed trays. The serious hobbyist may want to invest in an indoor propagation station. Most have adjustable lights that can be moved as seedlings grow. Most also provide bottom heat from heat cables or pads.

Standard seed trays or flats come in fitted pairs. The rigid outer tray (which should have adequate air and drainage holes) can be filled with lighter-weight inner trays in various sizes. Compartmented flats that keep growing plants separate are most useful for the home grower. One- or two-inch plug trays suit fast growers like marigolds. Larger sixpack pans work well for lobelias and zonal geraniums that need more time indoors. Heavyweight plastic trays last for years and can be cleaned in bleach or disinfectant and water.

WHAT SEEDLINGS NEED

Annuals have the same basic requirement as any other plants, with a few twists. Seedling soil can be purchased or made by adding vermiculite to potting soils. Lumpy mixtures must be pushed through a soil sieve to create a fine textured medium suitable for the smallest seeds. When planting, the rule of thumb is to cover seed to a depth of three times its size (which means the thickness rather than length of seeds like sunflowers).

SEED PACKETS: Read the seed packet for specific tips before planting: some require warmth, others prechilling, and others must be sown directly in the ground where they are to grow, as they will not transplant well. Many seed packets specify the optimal temperature range for germination (usually in the low to 70–75° F. for annuals of tropical origin). They also list average days to germination, which helps you time plantings.

Another handy bit of information on seed packets is the hardiness ranking, usually HA or HHA. Hardy annual (HA) seeds can be

When sowing, scatter seeds thinly to prevent overcrowding.

Cover the seed with soil or compost at a depth equal to three times its size.

Transplant seedlings after true leaves appear to give adequate space and light.

Control water and light, and mark seedlings for easy transfer to the garden.

sown in the fall for spring bloom. Seeds marked HHA or half-hardy annual are frost tender and must be sown in spring to bloom that same season.

WATER AND AIR

Once seeds are sown, the soil must remain evenly moist. Overly wet soil can rot seeds, while dry soil makes for reduced and irregular germination. Many seed trays come with fitted covers of clear plastic which allow

Some annuals are started easily by sowing seeds directly where they are to grow (left). Above, these young nasturtiums have been sown into clay pots in a window box where they can remain all season long.

sprouting to be monitored. The best covers are vented at the sides to let in plenty of air, which helps reduce the possibility of damping off diseases. Removing the cover as soon as growth is noticed will reduce such problems.

So will good air circulation; indeed, air is as vital to healthy seedling growth as water. Adequate air flow promotes husky root systems and can prevent damping off and mildews. A small rotating fan that produces a moderate breeze will also discourage aphids and mites. Moving air will also prepare your seedlings for garden life, where buffeting winds can shock pampered plants.

ANNUAL SEED SOURCES

Abundant Life Seed P.O. Box 772
930 Lawrence Street
Port Townsend, WA 98368-0772
360-385-5660
FAX (360) 385-7455
Catalog $2
Nonprofit Foundation specializing in Northwest natives

W. Atlee Burpee
300 Park Avenue
Warminster, PA 18974
800-888-1447
Catalog free
Very broad selection

Flowery Branch Seed Co.
P.O. Box 1330
Flowery Branch, GA 30542
770-536-8380
Catalog $4
Annuals, fragrant flowers, everlastings

The Fragrant Path P.O. Box 328
Fort Calhoun, NE
Catalog $2
Scented, rare & old fashioned annuals

J.L. Hudson, Seedsman
Star Rt. 2, Box 337
La Honda, CA 94020
Catalog $1
Extraordinary selection

Nichols Garden Nursery
1190 N. Pacific Highway NE
Albany, OR 97321-4580
541-928-9280
FAX: 541-967-8406
Catalog free
Fragrant and cutting annuals

Park Seed
1 Parkton Avenue
Greenwood, SC 29647-0001
800-845-3369
Catalog free
Large selection of annuals

Stokes Seed
P.O. Box 548
Buffalo, NY 14240-0548
716-695-6980
Catalog free
Impressive selection, excellent growing information

Thompson & Morgan
P.O. Box 1308
Jackson, NJ 08527-0308
800-274-7333
Catalog free
Remarkable catalog, huge selection

Serious hobbyists may want to invest in a growing system complete with heat and light control.

GROWING ON

Once annual seedlings germinate, their cultural needs must be met right away. Improper watering, lighting, and temperatures can affect the rapid early growth of most annuals, and quality and performance will suffer permanently.

LIGHT

A commercial or homemade propagation unit will give your annuals the best possible start. It's fine to use ordinary shop-lighting fixtures, as long as they can be adjusted. However, it is vital to use grow lights, which successfully mimic natural sunlight while producing very little heat. Ordinary bulbs can burn young plants without delivering adequate light. Grow lamps are generally set very close to the young plants (an inch or two above their tops), which may necessitate moving the lights daily during active growth.

DAY LENGTH: You also have to consider the length of the 'day' you give your plants, that is, how long to leave the lights on. This must be done manually, but simple to use and inexpensive timing devices (one for each block of lights) can automatically provide the artificial day required. This information may be listed on each seed packet, along with desirable soil temperatures. If not, you can assume that native annuals such as pansies will need about 12 hours of light each day, while annuals of tropical origin, such as tuberous begonias, prefer between 14 and 15 light hours a day.

Don't be tempted to keep them lighted all night as well, for oddly enough, excess light can result in the same kind of leggy or stunted seedlings as inadequate lighting.

MOISTURE

HOW TO WATER: Young annuals also need a regular supply of moisture, both in the air and the soil. Daily misting keeps dry air (common in heated homes) from browning the edges of young foliage. Overhead watering can bruise or break delicate seedlings and often produces irregular soil saturation, leaving some plants sodden and others too dry. Indirect or bottom watering is often recommended for indoor growers, and the easiest way to provide it without danger of drowning vulnerable roots is to line each shelf of the propagation unit with oversized waterproof trays. Water can be added to these each day, and any excess is removed with a turkey baster after about half an hour.

AUTOMATIC SYSTEMS: Some propagation units come with automatic misters and drip line watering systems that can be triggered by timers to deliver measured daily doses of water to each plant or tray. Less complex (and less expensive) systems perform the same services with manual controls.

Where local water is very acid or alkaline, misting and watering with distilled water will avoid pH problems. When growing tropical annuals which prefer constant heat (such as petunias and begonias), have the water at room temperature to avoid stunting plants with cold shock.

TEMPERATURE

COOL OR WARM: Though most seedlings sprout best with bottom heat, the majority of garden plants grow better at slightly cooler temperatures. For hardy annuals, turning off the heat after germination promotes stockier, denser growth. However, many tropical

After seedlings have been transferred to individual cells or pots, they still need good care to keep them healthy until the proper time for outdoor planting.

annuals grow best at higher temperatures and growth will dwindle or halt altogether in cool conditions. Self-regulating heated grow mats will keep a flat of young plants like morning glories or dahlias a comfortable twenty degrees warmer than the surrounding air.

AIR CIRCULATION: Good air circulation remains extremely important as seedlings grow on. Use a small fan to move the air while the grow lights are on (most can be set with the same kind of timer) to keep mildews and molds at bay.

THINNING SEEDLINGS: The gardener's first task after germination is to thin the crop. No matter how carefully you work, it's difficult to sow fine seeds thinly enough to eliminate crowding. Thinning the extras by pulling them out can harm the root systems of the remainder, so it's best to thin unwanted seedlings by cutting off their stems. Nail scissors work beautifully as miniature shears in close quarters, enabling the gardener to be very selective.

POTTING UP

WHEN TO POT: As seedlings mature, they are generally potted up into individual containers. The first "leaves" seedlings produce are called seed leaves or cotyledons. Rounded or elongated, they often bear little resemblance to the plants' true leaves, which begin to appear as the root system develops. When seedlings have two or three true leaves, they are ready to transplant.

HOW TO POT: Seedlings grown in plug trays can be popped into individual four inch pots with no root disturbance. Plants grown in pans or flats may already have interwoven root systems. Pull them gently apart, handling them by their seed leaves in order not to bruise their tender stems, and nestle each into its own new pot, using a light textured potting mixture.

LET THEM ADJUST: Lower light and moist air are essential aids to the root repair the plant must accomplish. Space transplanted annuals further from the lights for a few days, and boost the misting to three or four times daily. To further assist healing, begin feeding weekly with transplant fertilizer (or use ordinary plant feeds, mixing them at half the recommended strength). Once new growth is established, annuals should bulk up rapidly.

PROBLEMS: If instead your seedlings look leggy, pinch back the growing tips (the paired new leaves) to promote more branching. Pinching can be repeated every week to 10 days to encourage compact and bushy plants. If the plants look great already (many annuals are bred for bushy growth), there is no need to pinch them.

HARDENING OFF

As summer draws near, you can begin hardening off your annuals (hardening off is the process of acclimating indoor plants to the outdoors). Cold frames, sheltered but unheated boxes with translucent covers, offer excellent means for this transition. Once your annuals have resumed new growth, they can be set into a shaded cold frame (use an old window screen or cheesecloth to make instant shade). After the first day, the frame's lid can be removed for a few hours each day, gradually exposing the plants to fuller sunlight. Lacking a cold frame, place your plants in a shaded, sheltered part of the garden for a few hours each day, gradually moving them into more sun, but returning them indoors each night. Hardy annuals may be garden ready within a couple of weeks. Tropical plants are more tender and temperamental, and may need three weeks or more of hardening off.

A cold frame (top) is an excellent shelter for transitioning annuals to the outside as the weather warms up. Plants also can be hardened off in a sheltered part of the garden using row covers or some other temporary protection (above).

Greenhouses, nurseries, and garden shops that offer a wide variety of attractive, well-grown plants are the best sources for buying pre-started annuals.

BUYING ANNUALS

When you shop for annuals, be very picky. A perennial that's shopworn may spring back to health, but an annual lives for one season, so buy those that look like they've gotten off to a healthy start.
SHOP AROUND: Visit several nurseries before you buy to get an idea of what's available. Make your purchases at the outlets that have a wide selection of healthy varieties, plants that are attractive, well rooted, and vigorous.

Although it's most rewarding to buy the very best, inexpensive mass-market annuals can be a good value if you shop wisely. If a local store is offering spring bedding annuals at terrific prices, ask the sales clerks when they expect new shipments; then be on hand to pick out the cream of the crop.
AVOID PROBLEMS: Use the photos and information on this page to help you select the best specimens, those that look obviously healthy and boast plentiful new growth. Don't buy annuals with limp or brittle foliage (both are signs of distress). Avoid plants with withered new growth or puckered, discolored

PINCHING POWER

Nursery stock is often smothered with bloom. It may captivate your eye but can overstress the plant's resources when the pampered greenhouse is left behind. To reduce transplant shock, pinch off all mature flowers and buds before planting. (Don't throw them out, float them in a bowl.) You'll be glad you did. The roots will redirect their energy into making bushy plants that will bloom abundantly.

PROPERLY PINCHED

They're hard to part with, but it's always best to pinch off first blooms.

Initially, the young plant looks forlorn, as shown above.

But pinching pays off two months later, with bushy, healthy blooms.

NOT PINCHED

In the second example, the gardener resists advice to pinch back the flower.

During the first week or two after planting, the meager bloom is enjoyed.

But two months later, the unpinched plant bears fewer flowers.

A root-bound plant that is generally healthy can still thrive: simply cut a crisscross in the bottom of the mass.

Then carefully tease roots and soil open before planting. Healthy plants will bounce back within days.

mature leaves—also indicators of stress or disease. Look hard at the leaves of variegated plants, such as coleus; discoloration can be harder to detect.

Healthy plants stand upright; their stems are strong and their roots hold them firmly in their pots. Plants with damaged roots will tilt or flop over, and you may be able to see their anchor roots partially exposed above the soil. Choose compact, sturdy plants over larger but lanky and floppy looking.

LOOK AT THE ROOTS: Check the bottom of each pot: small roots (a few of them) poking from the drainage hole is usually a sign the plant is growing strongly. Make sure;

give the pot a gentle squeeze. If there's some give, the plant is probably a fine choice. If it feels like a rock, however, turn it carefully out of its pot (or ask the nursery staff to do it for you). Ideally, the roots will make a web through which you can still detect the soil. Roots tightly wound in a mass means the plant is root bound and should generally be avoided. If the whole plant looks great, however, it may not be too late. When you plant, simply cut a crisscross in the roots, then tease them open. Healthy plants will respond to this minor surgery, bouncing back in days.

Tip the plant out of its container to check roots; if they're tightly wound, the plant is root-bound and generally should be avoided.

WHAT ARE PLANT PLUGS?

Many nurseries are offering sturdy annual starts grown in plant plugs—wedge-shaped blocks of spongy, semirigid material. Marigolds, dusty miller, and similar seed-grown bedders are often available as inch-long miniplugs. Vegetatively propagated annuals and tropicals, such as coleus, double nasturtiums, and marguerites are grown from cuttings and appear in larger plugs.

Plug starts eliminate or reduce root trauma during transplanting. Popped out of their growth trays and set into 4 inch pots, plants in plugs never stop active growth. Nursery staff will pack them in plastic bags for your trip home (to minimize moisture loss). Transplant them immediately. Pinch off flowers and buds—these little guys need to dedicate their energy to growing up. Losing those first flowers will be hard, but later on, they'll bloom the better for your discipline.

Where they are available, plant plugs are an inexpensive way to purchase annuals in quantity; they should be set out immediately.

INTO THE GARDEN

SOIL PREPARATION

The single most important thing we can do for our plants is to give them nutritious, well-drained soil. Organic farmers say, "feed the soil, not the plants." What they mean is that well-prepared soil offers most plants all they need for sustained growth.

THE BEST SOIL: Good garden soil is a balance of drainage and retention; it allows air and water to pass freely, yet retains enough nutrients to support active plant growth. The easiest way to create a terrific garden is to make raised beds, with a base of top soil or sandy loam topped off with compost or aged manure.

Here's how. Spread a layer of topsoil 8 to 12 inches deep—right on the grass, if it's not extremely weedy. (Put a fabric weed barrier where the path goes, first, as added weed control.) Next, add a thick (6-to 8-inch) layer of compost or aged manure and mound it smoothly. You won't need to till or mix the

beds; you'll mix the layers when you prepare each planting hole. Dairy manure or compost are better choices than peat for topdressing and mulch; peat is extremely difficult to rewet when dry. This thick blanket conserves moisture, helps keep beds weed free, and looks tidy. Over time, earthworms will incorporate the loam with the manure, so add an annual 2- to 3-inch topdressing of manure or compost mulch.

SPACING CORRECTLY

Making great soil is the first step. Next is proper plant placement. Like all plants, annuals grow best when their foliage barely overlaps. The leafy shade conserves soil moisture and encourages the growth of beneficial bacteria that help plants take up nutrients. Overlapping is the key; crowding can encourage fungal growth and mildew.

GIVE THEM ROOM: Unless the annuals you buy or transplant are already fully grown, you'll need to allow room for their natural expansion. The seed packet or plant tag should tell you their mature size (which may

Step 1: Start by laying weed-barrier cloth along the paths. Spread sandy loam 8 to 12 inches deep on top of bed area.

Step 2: Add a 6- to 8-inch layer of compost or aged manure, mounding it smoothly. No need to till.

Step 3: Cover the edges of the weed-barrier cloth with soil, then cover the path with gravel to hold cloth in place.

Build an annual bed in three easy steps. There's no need to mix the beds since earthworms will incorporate the loam and manure over time. Landscape fabric (sometimes called weed-barrier cloth) keeps paths weed free.

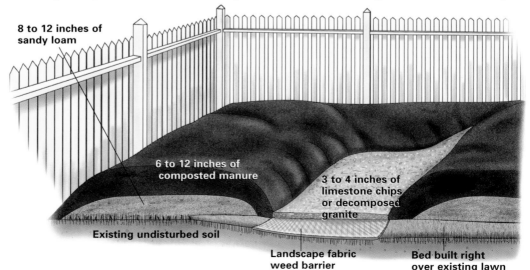

8 to 12 inches of sandy loam

6 to 12 inches of composted manure

3 to 4 inches of limestone chips or decomposed granite

Existing undisturbed soil

Landscape fabric weed barrier

Bed built right over existing lawn

be given as height only) and recommended spacing. For a generous look, space young plants a little more closely than the recommendations, but be cautious. Don't crowd them. Over time, crowded plants tend to be leggy, not bushy. Before you actually start digging, you may find it helpful to mark with stakes the locations of your plants.

INTO THE GROUND

Now all that's left to getting them in the ground is the digging. Annuals benefit from generous ground space, so heed the folk wisdom that says dig a gallon hole for a plant that came in a 4-inch pot.

HOW TO PLANT THEM: If you've constructed a new sandy loam bed, blend the loam and manure you've removed with a potful of compost or good potting soil. (Use the container the pot is in for the right amount.) In an established bed, remove the soil and blend it with an equal amount of compost or aged manure. Fill the planting hole halfway. Gently loosen any tightly wound roots to stimulate new growth. Most annuals have relatively fragile root systems that won't take extensive fussing, so it's best to simply ruffle up the outer roots, leaving the rootball as intact as possible.

Set the plant in place, making sure its crown remains at soil level (just as it was in its pot). Fill in the planting hole with compost and potting soil, firming it in gently as you work. Water well and fluff up or renew the mulch or top dressing around it.

Unfortunately, most planting areas begin with less-than-ideal soil. Even the worst soil can be improved with the proper addition of amendments and compost or aged manure. Once the soil is improved, you're ready to plant. Fill the hole halfway with planting soil, then place the plant, keeping its crown at soil level. Fill with compost and potting soil; water and mulch.

PLANTING IN CONTAINERS

Annuals grown in containers have less water and nutrients available than inground plants: they need more care.

Regular watering is essential, and because of this, drainage holes are vital. Drill the holes, then cover them with a few inches of coarse gravel, or well-rinsed beach stones. Heavy materials will help keep terra-cotta look-alikes from blowing over in the wind. You can set a smaller (minimum size, 5 gallon) pot in a larger ornamental pot; just add drainage layers to adjust the height of the inside pot.

Cover the drainage material with weed barrier; it lets water and air pass but keeps soil out. Sweeten your potting soil with a few cups of activated charcoal. A half cup of water-holding gel to each 5 gallons of soil will keep containers from drying too quickly.

Remember, too, that the frequent watering containers require also washes out nutrients at a rapid rate, so it is vital to fertilize with a regular feeding program. You should, however, keep an eye on your annuals—if you notice a pale crusty

buildup on the soil surface, it could be the insoluble salts of the fertilizer. The remedy? Soak the annual, container and all, in a bucket of water for about 20 minutes and then let it drain thoroughly.

If you have many pots to tend, you may want to invest in a drip system for watering. Run the tubes up the back of a large container or slip them through a drainage hole, taping the line in place before adding soil. The feeder tube can then be split into

several emitters so each annual planted in a large container gets its own water source. Drip lines can be put on timers so water is delivered daily.

CARE AND FEEDING

A long-necked wand attached to your hose makes simple work of watering high hanging baskets.

The old saying, "grow flowers hard and vegetables soft" may apply to perennials but not to all annuals. Many hard blooming tropicals thrive when treated royally. And although some hardy annuals perform well under tough circumstances, most appreciate supplemental water in dry spells and grow best in decent soils.

HOW TO FEED: Tropicals are apt to sulk unless kept in style. Luckily, their needs are modest; adequate warmth, frequent watering and an occasional moderate feeding will help most annuals perform beautifully. As a rule, heavy bloomers grown in sunny settings will appreciate fertilizer more than foliage plants grown in shady spots.

In warm climates, a single spring dose of time release fertilizer gives annuals a good start and will carry them through summer. In cool-spring climates, use liquid feeds (most pelletized time-release fertilizers are not active until soil temperatures reach around 75° F.). If your annual garden is large, you can use liquid root or foliar feeds delivered either by a watering can or hose. What you do is this: blend fertilizer concentrate with water in a pail, add a "Y" connector to your hose with a short siphon hose going into the pail. When you water, diluted fertilizer is delivered to your plants.

TOUGH-TO-REACH PLANTS: You can simplify container watering with a longnecked wand (it will extend your reach—especially for hanging baskets). Or try a turkey baster to get between the leaves and soak the roots directly.

Fertilize hard to reach baskets and containers with fertilizer sticks (make sure you get the sticks for house plants). Push the sticks (which last about 60 days) into the soil beside each annual when you plant it. Each watering washes a small amount of fertilizer into the soil. The sticks are easy to replace.

KEEP THEM BLOOMING: Improved selections have brought us a wide range of long blooming annuals that need relatively little care. Even so, most annuals will perform better if you give them light but frequent grooming. This mainly involves deadheading (removing spent and browning blossoms) and tidying up any yellowed or disfigured foliage.

In many species, seed set is the signal to stop flower production. If allowed to set seed, many species and old fashioned annuals will stop flowering so the seed can ripen.

Deadheading prevents seed from setting. The plant will attempt to set seed with new blossoms and you will have fresh crops of buds all summer. If you pinch back leggy annuals like petunias and African daisies every month or so, they will refurbish themselves and bloom anew for months. Don't decimate the whole plant at once. Just shorten a third of the stems by two thirds of their length each week. By the time you've trimmed the last batch, the first ones will be renewed.

Daily or weekly grooming takes only a few minutes. It also keeps us closely in touch with our plants, making us aware of pest or disease problems almost as soon as they start.

A "Y" connector added to your hose makes it possible to add fertilizer directly to your water source, allowing you to water and feed in one easy step.

Pinch back leggy petunias for blooms all summer. A good rule of thumb: Pinch back a third of the stems by two-thirds of their length about once a month.

Deadheading is a form of grooming. This gardener softly removes spent blossoms of cosmos, preventing seed setting and prolonging the blooming season.

CONTAINER PLANTS: Because of their limited soil, plants in containers need more attention than plants in the ground. In hot months, some containers need daily watering, especially if they receive maximum sun; these repeated waterings leach nutrients from the soil quickly. It's usually better to apply diluted solutions of fertilizers frequently, rather than more concentrated doses once a month. Hanging baskets present specific challenges in container gardening. Wind, sun, and dry air evaporate water from a porous hanging container (clay, wood, wicker) faster than from a container on the ground. In hot, windy climates, plants can sunburn or dry out in a matter of hours. Choose display areas protected from wind or afternoon sun. The best watering method is to take the container down and set it up to its rim in a bucket of water until thoroughly soaked. When using this method, keep plantings lightweight or watering can become a backbreaking task.

STAKING

Where heavy rains are common and in windy, exposed gardens, staking is essential. One approach is to drive a bamboo pole or rebar into the ground. Use a stake a foot longer than the expected stem height; place it 5 or 6 inches out from the plant crown to avoid damaging roots. Sink it a foot into the ground. Secure the stem to the stake with string, fabric or a plant tie, tying every 12 to 18 inches of new growth. In a second method, grow-through supports (far right) are positioned over a plant while it is young; stems and leaves grow through it, hiding the support.

ANNUALS SEED STARTING CHART

All plants are listed alphabetically by botanical name. Consult the maps on page 93 for the dates of first and last frost in your area.

Common name (Scientific name)	When to sow indoors	When to sow outdoors	Ideal temp.	Light or dark	Days to germ.	Notes
Flossflower (Ageratum)	6-8 wks before last frost	After last frost	70-75°	Light	5-14	Best sown indoors
Joseph's coat (Amaranthus)	3-4 wks before last frost	After last frost	70-75°	Either	10-15	Dislikes transplanting
Summer forget-me-not (Anchusa)	6-8 wks before last frost	After last frost	60-65°	Dark	7-21	Tolerates light frost
Snapdragon (Antirrhinum)	8-10 wks before last frost	After soil has warmed	60-65°	Light	10-21	Tolerates some frost
African daisy (Arctotis)	6-8 wks before last frost	Early spring or late frost	60-70°	Either	21-35	
Chickabiddy (Asarina)	8-10 wks before last frost	Best indoors	65-70°	Light	15-30	Sow anytime for indoor use
Begonia (Begonia)	3-4 months before last frost	Not recommended	65-75°	Light	15-30	Difficult to handle, fine seed
English daisy (Bellis)	6-8 wks before setting out	Early spring; late summer in mild areas	65-70°	Light	7-21	Tolerates some frost
Swiss chard (Beta)	4-5 wks before setting out	After soil has warmed	70°	Dark	7	Select best-colored seedlings
Bidens (Bidens)	6-8 wks before last frost	After last frost	55-65°	Dark	10-21	Best sown indoors
Swan River daisy (Brachycome)	6-8 wks before last frost	After last frost	65-70°	Either	7-21	
Ornamental cabbage or kale (Brassica)	6-8 weeks before setting out	Early spring or late fall	65-70°	Light	10-14	Tolerates frost
Browallia (Browallia)	6-8 wks before last frost	Not recommended	65-70°	Light	14-21	Sow anytime for houseplants
Pot marigold (Calendula)	6-8 wks before setting out	Early spring or late fall	65-70°	Dark	10-14	Best sown outdoors
China aster (Callistephus)	6-8 wks before last frost	After last frost	65-70°	Either	7-21	
Canterbury bells (Campanula)	6-8 wks before last frost	Not recommended	55-65°	Light	10-20	Biennial treated as annual
Canna, dwarf (Canna)	6-8 wks before last frost	Not recommended	75-85°	Dark	7-14	Plant seeds vertically
Ornamental pepper (Capsicum)	6-8 wks before last frost	Not recommended	70-75°	Light	20-25	Heat-loving plant
Vinca (Catharanthus)	10-12 wks before last frost	Not recommended	70-75°	Dark	5-15	Perennial in mild climates
Celosia (Celosia)	6-8 wks before last frost	After last frost	70-75°	Either	10-15	Needs warmth for best growth
Bachelor's button (Centaurea)	4-6 wks before last frost	Early spring	60-70°	Dark	10-14	Easily started outdoors
Honeywort (Cerinthe)	2-3 wks before last frost	When soil is warm	70°	Either	5-21	Perennial in mild climates
Wallflower (Cheiranthus)	8-10 wks before setting out	Early to late spring	60-65°	Dark	10-14	Tolerates frost
Annual chrysanthemum (Chrysanthemum)	6-8 wks before last frost	Just before last frost	60-70°	Light	7-14	Tolerates frost
Clarkia/Godetia (Clarkia)	6-8 weeks before last frost	After last frost	60-70°	Light	10-20	Best sown outdoors
Spider flower (Cleome)	6-8 wks before last frost	After last frost	65-75°	Either	10-21	Self-sows
Coleus (Coleus)	8-10 wks before last frost	Only in warm zones, after last frost	70-75°	Light	10-20	Considerable variability in seed-grown types
Larkspur (Consolida)	6-8 wks before setting out	Early spring or late fall	45-50°	Dark	14-30	Best sown outdoors
Dwarf morning glory (Convolvulus)	3-4 wks before last frost, in peat	When soil is warm	70-80°	Either	5-14	Soak seeds 24 hrs before planting
Cosmos (Cosmos)	4-5 wks before last frost	After last frost	70-75°	Either	7-14	Easily sown outdoors
Gourds (Cucurbita)	2-3 wks before setting out	2 wks after last frost	75-80°	Either	7-21	Soak seeds 48 hrs
Chinese forget-me-not (Cynoglossum)	6-8 wks before setting out	Early spring or previous fall	60-65°	Dark	5-10	Tolerates frost; often reseeds itself
Dahlia, dwarf (Dahlia)	8-10 wks before last frost	1-2 wks before last frost	65-70°	Either	10-20	Use tubers for larger types
Datura (Datura)	4-8 wks before setting out	After last frost	65-70°	Either	21-42	Often self-sows
China pink (Dianthus)	8-10 wks before last frost	Early spring or late fall	65-70°	Either	5-20	
Sweet William (Dianthus)	8-10 wks before setting out	Early spring or late fall	60-70°	Either	8-10	Tolerates frost
African daisy (Dimorphotheca)	6--8 wks before setting out	After last frost	60-70°	Either	10-15	Sow fall to winter in mild zones for winter bloom
Hyacinth bean (Dolichos)	6-8 wks before last frost	After last frost	70-75°	Either	10-20	Soak seeds for 24 hrs
California poppy (Eschscholzia)	2-3 wks before last frost	After last frost	60-65°	Either	10-14	Best sown outdoors
Snow-on-the-mountain (Euphorbia)	4-5 wks before last frost, in peat pots	After soil is warm	70-75°	Either	10-15	Self-seeds
Blanket flower (Gaillardia)	4-6 wks before setting out	After soil is warm	70°	Light	15-20	Mild areas: direct-sow in fall
Gazania (Gazania)	6-8 wks before setting out	After last frost	60-70°	Dark	7-14	Easily started
Globe amaranth (Gomphrena)	6-8 wks before last frost	After last frost	70-75°	Dark	15-20	Easily started
Annual baby's breath (Gypsophila)	6-8 wks before last frost	Early spring	70-80	Light	10-20	Sow at intervals to extend bloom
Sunflower (Helianthus)	2-3 wks before planting out	After last frost	68-86°	Either	10-15	Best sown outdoors
Strawflower (Helichrysum)	6-8 wks before setting out	After last frost	70-75°	Light	7-20	Easily started
Heliotrope (Heliotropium)	8-10 wks before setting out	Not recommended	70-75°	Either	21-30	
Globe candytuft (Iberis)	6-8 wks before last frost	After last frost	70-85°	Either	10-20	Repeat sowing extends bloom
Impatiens (Impatiens)	8-10 wks before last frost	Not recommended	70-75°	Light	7-21	Susceptible to damping-off
Morning glory, moonflower, cypress vine (Ipomoea)	3-4 wks before last frost, in peat pots	Best outdoors, 1-2 wks after last frost	70-80°	Either	5-21	Soak seeds for 24 hrs before planting
Diamond flower (Ionopsidium)	Not recommended	Early to late spring, or fall	55-60°	Either	14-21	Self-seeds
Hare's tail grass (Lagurus)	6-8 wks before last frost	Early spring or late fall	55°	Either	15-21	Self-seeds

* See information provided in "Notes" column

Common name (scientific name)	When to sow indoors	When to sow outdoors	Ideal temp.	Light or dark	Days to germ.	Notes
Annual sweet pea (Lathyrus)	6-8 wks before last frost	Early spring	55-65°	Dark	10-14	Soak seeds for 24 hrs
Laurentia (Laurentia)	Mid-winter, Jan-Feb*	Early fall	65-70°	Light	14-21	*Refrigerate after 3 wks
Tree mallow (Lavatera)	6-8 wks before last frost	Early spring	70-75°	Either	14-20	Best sown outdoors
Statice (Limonium)	8-10 wks before last frost	After last frost	65-70°	Either	15-20	Best sown indoors
Toadflax (Linaria)	6-8 wks before planting out	2-3 weeks before last frost	55-65°	Dark	10-15	Repeat sowing extends bloom
Flowering flax (Linum)	2-3 wks before setting out	Late spring	65-70°	Either	15-25	Best sown outdoors
Lisianthus (Lisianthus)	10-12 wks before last frost	Mild zones only, in spring	70-75°	Light	10-20	Difficult to start
Lobelia, all types (Lobelia)	6-8 wks before setting out	Not recommended	65-75°	Light	14-20	Susceptible to damping-off
Sweet alyssum (Lobularia)	6-8 wks before last frost	Early spring, or early fall	60-70°	Light	7-28	Easily started
Hartweg lupine (Lupinus)	6-8 wks before setting out	Early spring or late fall	60-65°	Either	15-25	Soak seeds for 24 hrs
Stock (Matthiola)	6-8 wks before last frost	After last frost*	65-70°	Light	7-14	*Fall sowing for winter bloom in mild areas
Melampodium (Melampodium)	6-8 wks before last frost	Not recommended	70°	Dark	10	Easily started
Ice plant (Mesembryanthemum)	10-12 wks before last frost	After last frost	65-75°	Dark	15-20	Repeat sowing extends bloom
Monkey flower (Mimulus)	10-12 wks before last frost*	Early spring	70-75°	Light	7-14	*Use pre-chilled seeds indoors
Firecracker vine (Mina)	6-8 wks before setting out, in peat pots	2 wks after last frost	70-75°	Either	10-16	Soak seeds overnight
Four-o'clock (Mirabilis)	6-8 wks before last frost	Late spring	70°	Light	7-20	Dislikes transplanting
Forget-me-not (Myosotis)	8-10 wks before setting out	Early spring*	55-65°	Dark	7-14	*Direct seed in fall in mild zones
Nemesia (Nemesia)	8-10 wks before last frost	After last frost, only in cool summer areas	55-70°	Dark	5-21	Susceptible to damping-off
Baby blue-eyes (Nemophila)	6-8 wks before last frost, in peat	Early spring, or late fall in mild zones	55°	Light	10-20	Easily started
Flowering tobacco (Nicotiana)	6-8 wks before last frost	After last frost	70-75°	Light	10-20	Easily started
Love-in-a-mist (Nigella)	6-8 wks before last frost, in peat pots	Early spring to summer, successively	65-70°	Either	8-15	Best sown outdoors
Chilean bellflower (Nolana)	4-6 wks before last frost	After last frost	65-75°	Either	10-20	Difficult to transplant
Basil (Ocimum)	4-6 wks before planting out	Early spring to summer	60-70°	Light	5-15	Easily started
Annual poppy (Papaver)	6-8 wks before last frost	Early spring or fall	70-75°	Dark	20	Best sown outdoors
Geranium (Pelargonium)	10-12 wks before last frost	Not recommended	70-75°	Either	3-25	Seedlings need good light
Annual fountain grass (Pennisetum)	6-8 wks before last frost	Early to mid spring	70°	Either	15-20	Challenging to start
Penstemon (Penstemon)	8-10 wks before last frost	Spring or fall	60-65°	Light	10-30	Some types are perennial
Perilla (Perilla)	6-8 wks before last frost	After last frost	65-75°	Light	15-20	Self-seeds
Petunia (Petunia)	10-12 wks before last frost	After last frost	70-80°	Light	10-20	Best started indoors
California bluebell (Phacelia)	6-8 wks before setting out	Early spring or late fall	55-65°	Dark	12-30	Best sown outdoors
Scarlet runner bean (Phaseolus)	4-6 wks before setting out, in peat pots	2 wks after last frost	60-70°	Either	4-5	Sow with eye facing downward
Annual phlox (Phlox)	6-8 wks before setting out, in peat pots	Early spring; fall in mild areas	55-65°	Dark	10-15	Resents transplanting
Moss rose (Portulaca)	6-8 wks before last frost	After last frost	70-85°	Light	10-20	Easily started outdoors
Castor bean (Ricinus)	6-8 wks before setting out, in peat pots	After last frost	70-75°	Either	15-20	Soak seeds 24 hrs
Gloriosa daisy (Rudbeckia)	6-8 wks before last frost	2 wks before last frost	70-75°	Light	5-10	Self-seeds
Painted tongue (Salpiglossis)	8-10 wks before last frost	After last frost	70-75°	Dark	15-20	Keep dark until germination
Salvia (Salvia)	6-8 wks before last frost*	Not recommended	65-75°	Light	15-20	*Start blue salvia 12 wks before last frost
Creeping zinnia (Sanvitalia)	4-6 wks before last frost	Early spring; fall, in mild areas	70°	Light	7-14	Resents transplanting
Butterfly flower (Schizanthus)	10-12 wks before last frost	Early spring or fall, only in mild zones	60-75°	Dark	7-20	
Dusty miller (Senecio)	8-10 wks before last frost	Early spring, or late fall	65-75°	Light	10-15	Susceptible to damping-off
Catchfly (Silene)	8-10 wks before setting out	Early spring or late fall	60-75°	Either	14-21	Easily started
Pony tail grass (Stipa)	6-8 wks before setting out	Early to mid spring	60-65°	Either	15-30	Easily started
Marigold (Tagetes)	4-6 wks before last frost*	2 wks after last frost	70-75°	Either	5-10	*8-10 wks for African type
Black-eyed Susan vine (Thunbergia)	6-8 wks before last frost, in pea pots	After last frost	65-75°	Either	10-20	Sow outdoors in fall in mild zones
Dahlberg daisy (Thymophylla)	6-8 wks before last frost	After last frost	70°	Light	15-20	Reseeds itself
Mexican sunflower (Tithonia)	6-8 wks before last frost	After last frost	70°	Light	10-14	Easily started
Wishbone flower (Torenia)	10-12 wks before last frost	1 wk after last frost	70-75°	Light	15-20	Best started indoors
Nasturtium (Tropaeolum)	2-4 wks before last frost	1-2 wks after last frost	65°	Dark	7-14	Best sown outdoors
Canary creeper (Tropaeolum)	2-4 wks before last frost	1-2 wks after last frost	65°	Dark	7-14	Best sown outdoors
Garden verbena (Verbena)	10-12 wks before last frost	After last frost	70-75°	Dark	20-30	Keep dark until germination
Pansy or viola (Viola)	8-10 wks before setting out*	Early spring or fall	65-75°	Dark	10-21	*Use pre-chilled seeds
Rock bell (Wahlenbergia)	Mid-winter, Jan-Feb	Not recommended	65-70°	Light	10-28	Grow cool and well-lit
Zinnia (Zinnia)	6-8 wks before last frost	After last frost, when soil has warmed	70-75°	Either	5-10	Outdoor sowing is best for common zinnia

ANNUALS
SELECTION AND GROWING GUIDE

A surprisingly large number of tropicals can be grown as annuals, even in northern gardens. This planting features datura (here displaying seed pods), impatiens, fuschia, petunias and a striped-leaf canna.

characteristics, and a plant portrait. There is also the country of origin, which adds information about the plants adaptations. "Uses" gives suggestions on what roles each plant can best fill in the garden and landscape, and possible companion plants to consider. "Getting Started" gives the basics as to whether and when to start from seed, bulb, or cuttings. "Siting and Care" gives the information needed to successfully grow the plant in the garden, including appropriate time for planting outdoors, soil requirements, recommended distances for spacing, whether it does best in sun or shade, and how to care for it after planting. In "Selecting Varieties" we mention some of the currently available varieties, as well as the qualities for which they have been bred and selected.

A few of these plants are natives, but most have journeyed to America from points of origin around the globe. They have been carried on boats, covered wagons, trucks, and airplanes, spread by hand, wind, insect, trowel, and test tube, some essentially unchanged, others hybridized extensively. We invite you to experience this world of annual beauty.

On the following pages, you will find a gallery of plants that can be grown as annuals. Some may actually grow as perennials in their native environment, and some may occasionally live through winter or reseed themselves and behave like perennials in your garden. But they are all plants that can be brought into bloom, or whatever ornamental quality for which they're selected, within the garden year that they are planted. Some of them will be utterly familiar, others half-forgotten old-fashioned favorites, and yet others recent introductions to the American gardening world. Along with flowers for beds and borders, there are plants to provide foliage effects, blooming vines, ornamental herbs and vegetables, bold tropical beauties, and grasses.

Each listing includes the scientific name, pronunciation, and common name, highlighted

Springtime blooms come in every pastel shade as well as intense colors to delight the winter-weary.

AGERATUM HOUSTONIANUM

*(ah-jur-AY-tum
hoo-stow-nee-AY-num)*

Flossflower

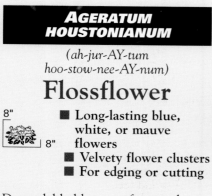

8"
8"

- Long-lasting blue, white, or mauve flowers
- Velvety flower clusters
- For edging or cutting

Dependable bloomers from early summer through fall. Although the dwarf varieties are better known, the tall types are equally garden-worthy. Native to Mexico.
USES: The dwarf varieties make wonderful edgers. Tall varieties are unsurpassed for cutting, and their steel-blue flowers complement hot-colored Mexican sunflower (*Tithonia*) or orange cosmos.

GETTING STARTED: For late-summer bloom, sow seeds outdoors once soil is warm. For earlier bloom, sow inside six to eight weeks before last frost. Plant outside when all frost danger is past. In mild climates, direct sowing in late summer provides winter bloom.
SITING AND CARE: Grows well in sun (or partial shade in hot, dry areas). Space short types 6 to 8 inches apart, tall varieties 12 inches. Rich, well-drained soils are optimum, but tolerates a wide range. Shearing faded flowers promotes nonstop bloom.
SELECTED VARIETIES: 'Blue Danube', 7 inches, rich blue, and 'Hawaii' hybrids 8 inches, in blue, lavender, or white, 'Blue Horizon', 30 inches tall, long-stemmed blue.

Compact 'Hawaii Royal' edges 'Excel Primrose' marigolds (left); tall 'Blue Horizon' is good for cutting (right).

AMARANTHUS TRICOLOR

(ah-muh-RAN-thus TRY-kuh-lur)

Joseph's coat

3'
2'

- Tropical-looking colorful foliage
- Tolerates heat and drought
- Colorful all season

Grown for foliage rather than flowers, the leaves can be red, purple, gold, and green. Native to India and Phillipines.
USES: Excellent for the back of the border, dramatic accent, or even temporary shrubs. Also useful for cutting or as houseplants. Pair them with castor bean (*Ricinus*) or fountain grass (*Pennisetum*).
GETTING STARTED: May be

started indoors in peat pots in midspring, or direct sown outdoors in late spring.
SITING AND CARE: Best grown in warm, sunny, well-drained soils, but tolerates some shade and most soils. Space plants 18 inches apart. Needs only occasional watering and feeding. Staking may be needed.
SELECTED VARIETIES: 'Illumination', 4 to 5 feet tall, blends crimson and gold leaves. 'Aurora Yellow', 3 feet tall, is yellow on top, with lower leaves dark-green. 'Early Splendor' is scarlet above, green below. *A. caudatus*, l (love-lies-bleeding) is 2 to 3 feet tall with long, dark red flower tassels.

Joseph's coat grows 2-9 feet tall, in brilliant hues (left); love-lies-bleeding has long red flower tassels (right).

ANCHUSA CAPENSIS

(an-KOO-suh kuh-PEN-sis)

Summer forget-me-not

10"
12"

- Clouds of tiny blue flowers above mounded foliage
- Grows best in cool regions
- Summer bloom

A South African with one of the most vivid blues in the plant world. Heights range from 8 to 18 inches.
USES: Shorter types work well in the rock garden, where they are perfect mates for California poppy (*Eschscholzia*). Also excellent in pots. Tall varieties are best in the midborder, where other plants hide their leggy habit. They are good for cutting, will naturalize, and go well with daisies, cosmos, and coreopsis.
GETTING STARTED: Direct sow

outdoors after all frost danger, or indoors six to eight weeks before setting out. Plant after last frost.
SITING AND CARE: Space 10 to 12 inches apart in well-drained, infertile soil in sun to light shade. Water well, and feed lightly. Shear after flowering to stimulate bloom. Tall varieties may need staking.
SELECTED VARIETIES: 'Blue Angel' is a trim 9 inches tall with ultramarine flowers. 'Blue Bird' grows 18 inches tall with clouds of tiny indigo-blue flowers.

The intense blue of Anchusa 'Blue Angel' is a wonderful addition to the gardener's palette.

ANTIRRHINUM MAJUS

(an-tih-RYE-num MAH-jus)

Snapdragon

The snapdragon's popularity is justified by its cheerful colors, elegance, and versatility.

18"
10"

- Vertical spikes in bright colors
- Long-blooming
- Wonderful for cutting and bedding

Available in a multitude of jewel-like colors. Perennial in mild areas, native to the Mediterranean.

USES: The range of heights, 6 to 48 inches, supports a variety of uses, from edging to vertical accents.

GETTING STARTED: Start seed indoors six to eight weeks before planting out; may be direct sown outdoors once soil is warm. Don't cover seeds; light is required for germination.

SITING AND CARE: Space 6 to 12 inches apart in rich, well-drained soils, in full sun to partial shade. Tolerates heat well. Pinch young plants and remove spent flowers to provide best vigor and bloom. Fertilize monthly and water moderately. Plant rust-resistant varieties.

SELECTED VARIETIES: Available in dwarf types ('Tahiti', 'Bells', 'Chimes'), intermediate height ('Liberty', 'Black Prince', 'Sonnet'); tall types ('Rocket', 'Madame Butterfly'); cascading habit ('Lampion', 'Cascadia', 'Chinese Lanterns'), and many colors.

ARCTOTIS STOECHADIFOLIA VAR. GRANDIS

(ark-TOH-tis stoh-chad-i-FOH-lee-uh

African daisy

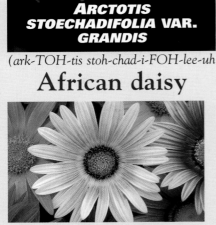

Delectable colors and daisy-shaped flowers make African daisies welcome wherever they are grown.

20"
20"

- Subtle flower colors with contrasting eyes
- Wonderful for cutting
- Drought tolerant

Delicate in appearance, these plants are tough and long-blooming in cool whites, blues, or warm creams, yellows, oranges, and reds. Ranges from 12 to 24 inches tall.

USES: African daisy's moderate height and beautifully-colored blooms are useful throughout the garden. Combine with gazania and gerbera daisy, or weave among perennials. Excellent for massing, cutting, or in containers. It will bloom through winter in mild areas. Flowers close at night.

GETTING STARTED: Can be sown outside in early spring, but best started indoors six to eight weeks before last frost. Use fresh seed, as it deteriorates in storage.

SITING AND CARE: Set plants 12 inches apart in light, sandy soils and full sun. It is best suited to regions with cool summer nights. Removing faded flowers will keep bloom going summer to fall. Water and feed infrequently.

SELECTED VARIETIES: 'T&M Hybrids' is a mix that grows 18 inches tall in a range of colors. *A. hirsuta* is bright orange, 12 inches tall.

ASARINA

(ah-suh-REE-nuh)

Chickabiddy

Also known as twining snapdragon, Asarina grows to 12 feet tall and blooms continually late spring to fall.

10'
1'

- Graceful climber
- Flowers resemble snapdragons
- Rapid grower
- Heart-shaped leaves

This unusual climber has showy 1-inch-long trumpet-shaped flowers in various colors.

USES: Good for training onto trellises, fences, or the stalks of taller annuals or shrub roses. The trailing habit can meander in beds, or be featured in containers.

GETTING STARTED: Sow indoors 10 to 12 weeks before setting out, at surface depth into peat pots. May also be direct sown

outdoors late winter through early spring.

SITING AND CARE: May be planted outdoors in early spring, when temperatures reach 40° F. Space 12 inches apart in full sun, in rich, moist, well-drained soils. Water frequently and feed occasionally.

SELECTED VARIETIES: *A. scandens* is a heavy-bloomer, with snapdragon-like flowers in violet, pink or white; 'Satin Mix' is a color mix, up to 10 feet long. *A. barclaiana* grows to 10 feet, bearing pink flowers that fade to purple. *A. purpusii* 'Victoria Falls' has 2-inch-long, red-purple trumpet flowers and a trailing habit.

BEGONIA REX

(beh-GOH-nee-uh rex)

Rex begonia

18" / 18"

- Large, dramatic foliage
- Beautiful patterns on leaves
- Unusual accent plant

Sometimes called painted leaf begonia, it has traditionally been grown as foliage houseplants.

USES: Rex begonia is useful in gardens and outdoor containers for its elegant foliar patterns and forms. It works well as the centerpiece of container groupings, or in shade gardens, with hostas and ferns.

GETTING STARTED: From seed, grow as for wax begonias. Most commonly available grown in pots. Start by cuttings of leaf vein sections set in a light potting mix, kept evenly moist until rooting occurs.

SITING AND CARE: Rex begonia thrives in light soils, and prefers shade, though sun may be tolerated in cool regions. Keep well-watered and lightly fed. Allow 2 to 3 feet of elbow room for the leaves to show off without crowding.

SELECTED VARIETIES: Seed mixes are available, as well as a large number of named varieties, such as 'Fireworks' (silver with pink zoning and dark green veins) and 'Mardi Gras' (deep pink leaves with purple veining).

Mixed Rex begonias add rich colors and patterns to a shade garden.

BEGONIA X SEMPERFLORENS-CULTORUM

(beh-GOH-nee-uh sem-per-FLOH-renz kul-TOH-rum)

Wax begonia

8" / 9"

- Nonstop bloom all season
- Compact mounds of colorful foliage
- For sun or shade

Extremely popular, wax begonias range in size from 6 to 12 inches, with foliage of green or bronze, and flowers can be white, pink, or red. Native to Brazil.

USES: Color and tidiness make it ideal for edging and massing. It contrasts well with dusty miller (*Senecio*). Good in containers and also as houseplants.

GETTING STARTED: Start indoors; use pelleted seeds. Allow four months from seeding to bloom. Prestarted seedlings may be purchased.

SITING AND CARE: Plant out after last frost, spacing 8 to 10 inches apart. Tolerant of a wide range of conditions, it does best in well-drained soils in the shade. Full sun is also fine in cool-summer regions. Fertilize heavily, and allow soil to dry out between waterings.

Dig and bring indoors in winter.

SELECTED VARIETIES: 'Cocktail' series offers several flower colors on 5- to 6-inch mounds of bronze foliage. The 'Olympia' series is 6 to 8 inches tall with green foliage.

Compact mounds of wax begonia 'Rio Mix' bear glistening foliage and nonstop bloom.

BEGONIA X TUBERHYBRIDA

(beh-GOH-nee-uh too-ber-HY-bri-duh)

Tuberous begonia

12" / 12"

- Brilliant color in shade
- Elegant in hanging baskets and window boxes
- Double or semidouble flowers

Tuberous begonia provides long-blooming flowers in shade. Average height is 1 foot, habit erect or hanging, and colors include white, yellow, orange, red, pink, bicolors, and tricolors.

USES: Cascading varieties in hanging baskets and window boxes, or paired with trailing lobelia. The upright types do well in containers, shady gardens, or under trees.

GETTING STARTED: The seeding process is similar to wax begonia, but takes a bit longer. More often, tubers are started indoors, or planted directly into the garden. Seedlings are also available.

SITING AND CARE: After all danger of frost, plant into rich, well-drained soils, 10 to 18 inches apart, in light shade. Feed and water frequently, taking care of the leaves. Guard against slugs and snails.

Tubers may be overwintered in a dry, cool place.

SELECTED VARIETIES: 'Nonstop' series has 3- to 4-inch double flowers in assorted colors. 'Show Angels' offers bicolors and picotees, and is good for hanging baskets.

The rose-like blossoms of 'Nonstop Rose Pink' are dazzling in shaded settings.

BELLIS PERENNIS

(BEL-liss per-EN-iss)

English daisy

Masses of 'Bright Carpet Mix' English daisies and 'Pink Impression' tulips create a brilliant spring show.

6"

6"

- ■ Dwarf daisies bloom throughout spring
- ■ Wonderful in masses
- ■ Companion for spring bulbs

English daisy, commonly seen throughout its native Europe, is less well-known in the U.S. The 3- to 6-inch plants bear white, pink, or red flowers on single stems.

USES: Pairs beautifully with spring bulbs, forget-me-not (*Myosotis*), and violas. Its diminutive size suits it to rock gardens, edging, and massing.

GETTING STARTED: Indoors, start seeds eight to ten weeks before planting out.

Outdoors, seeds must be started the previous summer for spring bloom; protect over winter in cold winter areas.

SITING AND CARE: Space plants 6 to 8 inches apart in rich, moist, loamy soils, in sun or part shade. Feed early in the season and water frequently. Cut back after flowering. Peak bloom occurs early to late spring. Most successful in cool summer regions.

SELECTED VARIETIES: Choose for dwarfness ('Bright Carpet', 4 to 6 inches), uniformity ('Galaxy', 'Pomponette'), large flowers ('Goliath', 'Habenera'), small flowers ('Buttons'), or individual colors ('Kito', cherry-red).

BETA VULGARIS, CICLA GROUP

(BAY-tuh vul-GAR-iss)

Swiss chard

Stalks of 'Bright Lights' Swiss chard display striped ribbons of color beneath thick-textured leaves.

24"

12"

- ■ Lush, glossy leaves
- ■ Brilliant stalks and midribs
- ■ Vase-shaped growth habit

Striking stalk colors and ruffled, glossy leaves have earned chard a place in ornamental gardens.

USES: A nutritious and long-bearing vegetable, it is now being employed as an accent plant in beds and containers, and being massed to create striped ribbons of color. Try contrasting it with the bengal tiger canna for a wild effect or create a mixed planting with other culinary ornamentals such as opal basil (*Ocimum*).

GETTING STARTED: Direct-sow, 6 seeds per foot, midspring to fall.

SITING AND CARE: Plant in ordinary well-drained soil, in full sun or light shade. Thin to 12 inches apart, selecting seedlings with good colors. Feed lightly and water in dry spells. Harvest outer leaves for eating, if desired; new leaves will grow back. Tolerates some frost, and looks good all winter in mild climates.

SELECTED VARIETIES: 'Bright Lights' has stalks in gold, pink, orange, purple, red, and white, and leaves of green or bronze. 'Ruby Red', or rhubarb chard, has dark red stalks and ruffly, dark green leaves.

BIDENS

(BYE-denz)

Bidens

Bidens' sunny daisy flowers bloom prolifically for the entire growing season, unfazed by weather.

18"

18"

- ■ Masses of small, golden daisies
- ■ Lovely ferny foliage
- ■ Tough and easy to grow

A newcomer to American gardeners, bidens has 2-inch golden-yellow flowers on 2-foot, relaxed, wiry stems of feathery foliage. It blooms spring through fall.

USES: Bidens shines in containers and hanging baskets, happily intermingling with verbena 'Imagination', scaevola, and other cascaders. It's also lovely massed in sunny beds and borders, or cascading over walls. Good for cutting.

GETTING STARTED: Start indoors six to eight weeks before last frost, covering seed to its own depth.

SITING AND CARE: Plant outside after last frost, spacing 12 inches apart in good garden soil, in full sun. Bidens tolerates both cool, wet summers and heat, and is not bothered by pests or disease.

SELECTED VARIETIES: 'Golden Eye' is a 10- to 12-inch prostrate variety, ideal for containers; 'Golden Goddess' is 28 inches tall, a fast grower that blooms ten to twelve weeks from seed; 'Goldmarie' is vegetatively-propagated, 16 to 20 inches tall, bright yellow, fragrant.

BRACHYCOME IBERIDIFOLIA

(bra-KIK-o-mee i-beh-ri-di-FOH-lee-uh)

Swan River daisy

9"

12"

- Blue, violet, or white daisy flowers
- Delicate mounds of feathery foliage
- Delightfully fragrant

This low-growing Australian has clouds of cool-colored daisies, with contrasting centers and fine foliage.
USES: Wonderful for edging, rock gardens, and cut flowers, and dazzling in hanging baskets. It mixes well with other edgers.

GETTING STARTED: Sow indoors six to eight weeks before last frost, barely covering the seeds. In cool-summer areas, sow outdoors every few weeks.

SITING AND CARE: After last frost, plant 6 inches apart in rich, well-drained soils, in full sun or light shade. They decline in hot weather, but peak from late spring through early summer. Bloom season can be extended with successive sowings.

SELECTED VARIETIES: The 'Splendor' series comes in blue, purple, or white with black eyes and grows 10 inches tall. 'Bravo' is a new, more varied mix, 8 to 10 inches tall. 'New Amethyst' is a vegetatively grown hybrid, 10 to 12 inches tall, with purple flowers and increased heat tolerance.

Brachycome 'Summer Skies' bears dainty, dark-eyed daisies in shades of blue, purple, and white.

BRASSICA OLERACEA

(BRA-sih-kuh oh-lur-AY-see-uh)

Ornamental cabbage and kale

12"

12"

- Marvelously colorful foliage
- Stiff, formal appearance
- Striking in fall and winter

Brassica oleracea capitata is ornamental cabbage, distinguished by smooth tight heads like the familiar culinary cabbage. Its close relative, *B. oleracea acephala,* ornamental kale, has lacy foliage arranged in a funnel-shaped cluster. Both types grow 10 to 15 inches tall, and have thick, blue-green outer leaves with centers of white, pink, red, magenta, or purple.
USES: Too tough and bitter for culinary uses, ornamental kale and cabbage shine in late season gardens, where the colors intensify as fall advances. They will remain handsome for months in mild winters. Excellent for pattern plantings, but the stiff rosettes are a challenge to combine with other plants; try ornamental grasses for a softening effect, or mass in beds with pansies, calendulas, and mums for a dazzling fall garden. Also effective in urns and other formal containers.

GETTING STARTED: Sow seed indoors six to eight weeks before planting, which is best done in early spring or fall. Harden off before setting out. Or sow directly into loose, fertile soil outdoors.

SITING AND CARE: Plant in full sun in moist, soils, spacing 12 to 18 inches apart. No special care is needed, however once hot weather arrives the plants will bolt. Fall plantings will give a longer season of beauty.

SELECTED VARIETIES: A dizzying array of hybrids offers the gardener a choice between leaf forms (smooth, ruffled, lacy, or frizzy) and striking color combinations (usually green outer leaves with contrasting centers in pink, purple, cream, or red) and patterns.

White ornamental kale and English daisies make ideal companions.

Ornamental cabbage is stunning in cool season gardens.

'Coral Queen' (left), 'Coral Prince' (center), and 'Nagoya Red' (right) are but a few of the captivating varieties of ornamental kale.

BROWALLIA SPECIOSA

(bro-WAHL-ee-uh spee-see-OH-suh)

Browallia

Browallia is a nice addition to cool, shady areas, where it adds blues and purples to the summer color mix.

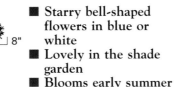

10"
8"

- Starry bell-shaped flowers in blue or white
- Lovely in the shade garden
- Blooms early summer through fall

The 8- to 18-inch tall plants have a delicate upright habit, colors from pale-to deep-blue and white, and a long season of bloom. Native to South America.

USES: Blends nicely with lobelia, impatiens, and ferns. Works well in window boxes and planters, where it cascades lightly over the rim.

GETTING STARTED: Start seeds indoors, six to eight weeks before last frost. It can also be direct sown, but blooming will be much later.

SITING AND CARE: Plant outside in spring once temperatures remain over 40° F. Space 6 to 12 inches apart in cool, shady areas. Pinch young plants to encourage bushiness. Water and feed moderately; overfeeding gives lots of foliage but few flowers.

SELECTED VARIETIES: 'Bells' hybrids, 10 to 12 inches tall, profuse white, mid- or deep-blue flowers on graceful stems; 'Troll' hybrids, white or blue, 10 inches tall and compact: 'Starlight' series, earlier flowering in dark of sky blue, or white.

CALADIUM X HORTULANUM

(kuh-LAY-dee-um hor-too-LAY-num)

Caladium

'Little Miss Muffet' (above) and mixed caladiums (left) make beautiful specimens.

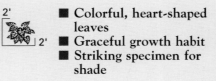

2'
2'

- Colorful, heart-shaped leaves
- Graceful growth habit
- Striking specimen for shade

On these elegant 1- to 3-foot plants, the leaves are bi- or tricolored, with contrasting borders and veining in combinations of white, green, red, and pink. Native to South America.

USES: A valuable addition in shady gardens and containers. Great with hostas, or with elephant's ear (*Colocasia*) and tall grasses.

GETTING STARTED: Usually started from tubers. Plant tubers 2 inches deep in well-drained soil and provide warmth. For outdoor planting, wait until temperatures remain above 60° F.

SITING AND CARE: Plant in late spring, 8 to 12 inches apart. Rich, well-drained organic soils are best, in light to deep shade. Water and feed regularly. Will naturalize in warm climates, otherwise dig in fall and overwinter in cool, dry conditions.

SELECTED VARIETIES: 'Freida Hemple' 18 inches tall, leaves of rich red edged in green; 'Little Miss Muffet', 8 to 12 inches tall, lime-green leaves overspeckled with crimson; 'White Christmas' 21 inches tall, large white leaves with intricate green veining.

CALENDULA OFFICINALIS

(kuh-LEN-doo-luh oh-fiss-ih-NAH-liss)

Pot marigold

Pot marigold has a long tradition as a healing and culinary herb, and is equally useful as an ornamental.

20"
12"

- Cheerful cream, yellow, and orange flowers
- Thrives in cool conditions
- Blooms early summer through fall

Myriad varieties offer heights from 6 to 24 inches, and single or double daisy flowers in sunny colors. Native to Mediterranean region.

USES: Good for bedding, mixing in borders, containers, naturalizing, and cutting. Shorter types work well in pots. Nice in fall gardens.

GETTING STARTED: Start six to eight weeks before last frost, or direct sow outdoors in early spring. Sowing in late summer will provide fall and winter bloom in mild climates.

SITING AND CARE: After last frost, plant in ordinary soil in full sun, 6 to 12 inches apart. Feed occasionally, water, and deadhead often. Best in cool summers, or used as a fall bedder in mild climates. Tolerates lean soils; will self-sow.

SELECTED VARIETIES: Select for dwarfness ('Calypso', 8 inches, 'Fiesta', 12 inches); height for cutting ('Prince Mix', 24 inches, 'Kablouna', 20 inches); or unusual colors ('Touch of Red', 14 inches, red-tipped petals, 'Pacific Apricot', 24 inches, pale orange).

CALIBRACHOA HYBRID

(kah-lih-brih-KOH-uh)

Calibrachoa

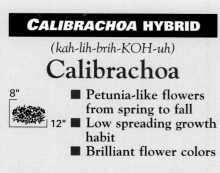

8"

12"

- Petunia-like flowers from spring to fall
- Low spreading growth habit
- Brilliant flower colors

Although it looks like a miniature petunia, *Calibrachoa* is an entirely new commercial species. A fast-growing plant, it covers itself with hundreds of flowers at a time.
USES: Good for baskets and other containers, alone or combined with verbena, petunias, and dianthus.

It also makes a beautiful annual ground cover.
GETTING STARTED: This recent introduction must be acquired as cuttings or prestarted plants.
SITING AND CARE: Plant in average, well-drained soil, in full sun to light shade, 12 inches apart. Plants are self-cleaning, and will tolerate summer heat and fall temperatures down to the mid-teens.
SELECTED VARIETIES: All varieties fall under the trade name Million Bells: 'Cherry Pink', 7 to 10 inches tall, vibrant hot-pink with yellow center; 'Trailing Blue', 5 to 8 inches tall, purple-blue with yellow center; 'Trailing Pink', 5 to

8 inches, soft, lavender-pink with yellow center; 'Trailing White', 7 to 10 inches, white with yellow center.

Sold in garden centers under the name Million Bells™, Calibrachoa is a new annual ideal for baskets.

CALLISTEPHUS CHINENSIS

(ka-LISS-teh-fuss chih-NEN-sis)

China aster

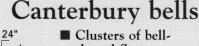
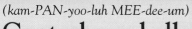

18"

12"

- Mum-like flowers in rich, vivid colors
- Popular for cutting
- Single- or double-flowered varieties

Breeding efforts have resulted in improved disease resistance, as well as a huge choice of heights and flower types. Colors include white, pink, red, blue, and purple, with yellow centers. Native to Japan.
USES: Primarily for bedding and cutting, and it is also good in

borders and containers, with airy plants such as baby's breath (*Gypsophila*) or sea lavender (*Limonium*).
GETTING STARTED: Direct seed outdoors after the last frost, or start indoors six to eight weeks earlier. Use good cultural practices to prevent damping-off.
SITING AND CARE: Plant outside after last frost into rich, well-drained neutral soil, spacing 12 inches apart, in full sun or light shade. Feed occasionally, water regularly, and stake tall varieties. Blooming can be extended by successive plantings.

SELECTED VARIETIES: 'All Change', 15 to 18 inches tall, has blue or red flowers with white edges. 'Pinocchio' is a 6-inch dwarf in mixed colors. 'Matsumoto' is 24 inches tall, with 2-inch flowers in myriad color blends.

China aster is a bit of a prima donna, but worth growing for its jewel-like colors in gardens and for cutting.

CAMPANULA MEDIUM

(kam-PAN-yoo-luh MEE-dee-um)

Canterbury bells

24"

12"

- Clusters of bell-shaped flowers
- White, pink, or violet-blue flowers
- Blooms late spring to early summer

Old-fashioned flowers on 2- to 3-foot stems add columns of blue, pink, or white to the garden. Native to southern Europe.
USES: Perfect in cottage gardens with hollyhocks (*Alcea*) and larkspur (*Consolida*). Use them in

meadow plantings, borders, or try the smaller types in the rock garden.
GETTING STARTED: For flowers the first year, sow seeds indoors six to eight weeks before planting out. May be sown outdoors in late summer to overwinter as young plants, and blooms the following spring.
SITING AND CARE: Plant in early spring, 10 to 15 inches apart, into well-drained, average soil. Fine in full sun or partial shade. Keep the soil moist, and feed lightly. Tall plants may need staking.
SELECTED VARIETIES: 'Calycanthema' (Cup and Saucer) has a flattened calyx resembling a

saucer and the petals fused into a cup form. Comes in pink, blue, or white. 'Canterbury Bells Mixed', 3 to 4 feet tall, pink, blue, or white. 'Russian Pink', 15 inches tall, blooms 16 weeks after sowing.

Canterbury bells lend a fairy tale quality to early summer gardens, and blend well in perennial borders.

CANNA X GENERALIS

(KAN-nuh jen-ur-AH-lis)

Canna

Classic cannas 'King Midas' (front) and 'Assault' (back) combine for a striking display summer to fall.

- Dramatic foliage and flowers
- Adds height to plantings
- Use for formal or exotic effects

Modern varieties offer flowers in pastel or hot colors, and foliage colors from green to blue-green, burgundy, purple, and stripes. Heights vary from 1 to 5 feet.
USES: Use in containers, as a background, or in the center of formal beds. Combine with ginger lily (*Hedychium*) and elephant's ear (*Colocasia*) for a moody, tropical effect.

GETTING STARTED: Usually grown from rhizomes, planted 3 to 4 inches deep, started in pots indoors or planted outside in late spring to early summer.
SITING AND CARE: Space 1 to 3 feet apart in full sun, in rich, fertile soils. Some shade and poorer soils will be tolerated. Water in dry spells and feed regularly. In cold winter regions, lift and store rhizomes.
SELECTED VARIETIES: 'Tropical Red' and 'Tropical Rose', 24 to 30 inches tall, are easily grown from seed; 'Pretoria' (Bengal tiger canna), 6 feet tall, features yellow-striped foliage, and orange flowers.

CAPSICUM ANNUUM

(KAP-sih-kum AN-yoo-um)

Ornamental Pepper

'Fiesta' is one of the many varieties of ornamental pepper, all of which offer bright fruits and a neat habit.

- Attractive multi-colored fruit
- Compact habit for edging and bedding
- Brilliant color late summer through fall

Ornamental peppers plants range in height from 10 to 20 inches, and the 1 to 3-inch fruit may be round, conical, or candle-shaped. Native to the Americas.
USES: Works well in containers, alone or mixed with other hot-colored sun-lovers. Mass in patterns with dusty miller (*Senecio*), or wax begonia. Also good in borders.
GETTING STARTED: Start seeds indoors 8 to 10 weeks before last

frost, provide steady warmth. Pinch seedlings to encourage bushiness.
SITING AND CARE: Plant outside in late spring, once the soil has warmed. Space 6 to 12 inches apart in moist, organic soil, in full sun. Will tolerate some shade, especially in very hot conditions. Water regularly and feed lightly.
SELECTED VARIETIES: 'Black Prince', 10 inches, black leaves, fruits turn from black to red; 'Candlelight', ripens to orange and red; 'Jigsaw', white- and purple-splotched leaves; 'Treasures Red', 8 inches tall, conical fruits that mature from white to red.

CATHARANTHUS ROSEUS

(kath-uh-RAN-thus ROH-zee-us)

Vinca

'Tropicana Mix' shows vinca's lovely foliage and long-blooming flowers.

- Long-lasting, white, pink, or red flowers
- Undaunted by heat
- Lush, glossy green foliage

Also known as Madagascar periwinkle, comes in heights from 4 to 18 inches, and several colors. Native to Madagascar and India.
USES: Bedding, borders, ground cover, and baskets. Try with red snapdragons or begonias.
GETTING STARTED: Sow seeds

indoors 12 to 16 weeks before planting out. In warm climates, seed may be direct-sown outdoors in late winter.

SITING AND CARE: Plant once weather is warm, 12 inches apart in well-drained soil, in full sun or partial shade. Tolerates heat and drought, although responds well to light feeding and regular watering. Never needs deadheading. Frost-tender. Wilt can be a problem in humid, cool climates.
SELECTED VARIETIES: 'Cooler' series, 14 inches tall, colors from pale pink to deep rosy-purple, some with contrasting eyes; 'Pretty In' series, 12 inches, shades of pink and rose; 'Pacifica' series, 14 inches, offers bright red, soft apricot, and other new colors. Look for varieties with good wilt resistance that will soon be offered.

CELOSIA

(seh-LOH-zee-uh)

Celosia

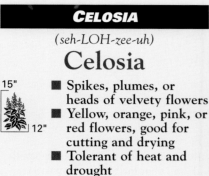

15" 12"

- Spikes, plumes, or heads of velvety flowers
- Yellow, orange, pink, or red flowers, good for cutting and drying
- Tolerant of heat and drought

There are 3 species of celosia popular with gardeners. *C. argentea var. cristata*, commonly called cockscomb, has tight, convoluted flowers resembling a rooster's comb. Plume celosia (*C. plumosa*) displays vertical, feathery flowers that look like flames. There are many varieties of both types, in varying heights and flower and foliage colors. Wheat celosia (*C. spicata*) also has erect, feathery flowers, but these are smaller and spirelike. Native to tropical Africa.

USES: Celosia is suitable for containers, edging, borders, bedding, cut or dried flowers, and specimens. Works well massed for color effects. Try the variety 'Apricot Brandy' backed by blue salvia 'Victoria'.

GETTING STARTED: May be sown indoors six to eight weeks before last frost, in peat pots. Better to sow directly into the garden as soon as soils warm in the spring.

SITING AND CARE: Does best in rich, well-drained, organic soil, but also tolerates poor dry soil. Space 6 to 12 inches apart in full sun. Keep soil moist and fertilize lightly.

SELECTED VARIETIES: 'Apricot Brandy', a 12-inch plume type with apricot-orange flowers. 'Castle Mix' is 12 inches tall and wide, a plume type in yellow, pink, or red. 'Treasure Chest' is a dwarf cockscomb, 8 inches tall with large, velvety combs in shades of yellow, pink, and red. 'Pink Candle' is a wheat type, with rose-pink plumes on 30-inch stalks.

The brilliant spikes of plume celosia are wonderful for enlivening sunny beds and borders. With regular deadheading, it will bloom summer through fall.

Celosia 'Red Fox' looks like a flame suspended in a moment of time.

'Flamingo Feather' wheat celosia provides a strong vertical design element, and is excellent for drying.

Velvety 'Toreador' cockscomb

'Coral Garden Mix' cockscomb displays crests in several colors.

CENTAUREA CYANUS

(sen-TOR-ee-uh sye-AN-us)

Bachelor's button

A mass of 'Choice Mix' bachelor's button blends classic cornflower blue with pink, purple, and white.

18"
10"
- ■ Good for cutting
- ■ Blossoms of blue, white, pink, or purple
- ■ Self-sowing

Also known as cornflowers, these cheerful cottage-garden favorites are best known for their blue flowers, but they also bloom in shades of pink, purple, and white. Bloom early to midsummer, and off and on till frost. Native to Europe.
USES: In beds, borders, and cottage gardens (often included in wildflower mixes). Use shorter varieties in mixed containers. Pair with orange pot marigolds (*Calendula*), or larkspur (*Consolida*). Good as a cut flower.

GETTING STARTED: Start indoors six to eight weeks before planting out. Easy to grow by direct-seeding outdoors just before last frost. Plants often reseed.
SITING AND CARE: Plant from midspring on, 8 to 12 inches apart in ordinary, well-drained soil, in full sun or light shade. Feed once in spring, water regularly, deadhead to prolong bloom. Short-lived; reseed repeatedly for bloom.
SELECTED VARIETIES: 'Blue Diadem' has 2-inch, intense blue flowers on 30-inch plants. 'Blue Midget' has sky blue flowers on 10-inch mounds. 'Florence' mix has pink, white, red, and blue flowers.

CERINTHE MAJOR PURPURASCENS

(ser-IN-thee MAY-jur pur-pur-ESS-enz)

Honeywort

Honeywort's muted coloration and relaxed habit combine well with many other plants.

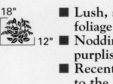
18"
12"
- ■ Lush, silvery blue foliage
- ■ Nodding clusters of purplish flowers
- ■ Recently introduced to the U.S.

This unusual newcomer to American gardens grows 18 to 24 inches tall, producing multiple stems lined with frosty blue-green leaves and tubular bluish purple flowers. Native to the Mediterranean region.
USES: An interesting addition to beds and containers. Use with gold-colored plants such as golden grass (*Hakonechloa*) or purple basil (*Ocimum*), or with other silvery

plants like lamb's-ears (*Stachys*).
GETTING STARTED: Start seeds indoors 6 weeks before last frost, or sow directly into the garden after danger of frost is past.
SITING AND CARE: Plant outside after last frost, spacing 9 to 12 inches apart in ordinary, well-drained soil, in full sun or light shade. Honeywort prefers cool conditions and may die out in hot areas. Reseeding can provide plants for fall into winter.
RELATED SPECIES: *Cerinthe major* is the straight species, similar to *C. major purpurascens* except for the flower color, which is reddish purple with yellow stripes.

CHEIRANTHUS CHEIRI

(kih-RAN-thus KIH-rye)

Wallflower

Wallflower adds warm tones to a cool-season garden, providing a perfect foil for blue forget-me-nots.

15"
12"
- ■ Fragrant flowers in bright colors
- ■ Beautiful in cool season gardens
- ■ Good for massing with spring bulbs

Cool climates are perfect for wallflower. Bright green mounds of leaves are crowned with 1- to 2-foot spikes of four-petalled flowers in shades of yellow, orange, red, mahogany, and purple. Native to Europe.
USES: A spring bloomer, it is useful in rock gardens and with spring bulbs. Magnificent massed with tulips, forget-me-nots (*Myosotis*), and pansies (*Viola*). Also good in containers.

GETTING STARTED: Perennial in mild climates, it is an annual in most of the United States. May be started indoors in late winter, but direct sowing in early spring is better.
SITING AND CARE: Plant in average, well-drained soil in full sun or light shade, 12 inches apart. Cut back after flowering. Discard plants once summer heat causes decline.
RELATED GENERA: Siberian wallflower (*Erysimum asperum*) is a U.S. native, with fragrant flowers in yellow and orange. It often reseeds. Alpine wallflower (*E. linifolium*) is a 12-inch cousin that adds purple to the family colors. 'Glastnost Mixed' offers wallflower in all its hues.

CHRYSANTHEMUM MULTICAULE

(krih-SAN-thuh-mum mul-tih-KAWL)

Annual chrysanthemum

9" 12" ■ **Wonderful, low-growing plant**
■ **Bright daisy flowers all summer**
■ **Perfect for edging and containers**

Chrysanthemum multicaule tends to be underused in gardens. It grows only 9 inches tall but spreads 12

inches wide; it flowers all summer. **USES:** The low, spreading habit goes nicely in hanging baskets and other containers, makes a fine ground cover or edger, and is suitable for rock gardens.
GETTING STARTED: Sow seeds indoors six to eight weeks before last frost. In mild climates, direct seeding in fall provides winter to spring bloom.
SITING AND CARE: Plant after last frost, 10 to 12 inches apart in ordinary, well-drained, neutral soil, in full sun. Will tolerate some frost.
SELECTED VARIETIES: 'Gold Plate' has 1-inch bright yellow double or semidouble flowers on

6-inch plants. 'Moonlight' has single lemon yellow flowers and is 9 inches tall with a compact, uniform habit good for edging and bedding.

*Chrysanthemum multicaule **bears a wealth of cheerful yellow flowers. A close-up of 'Moonlight' (inset)***

CLARKIA

(KLAR-kee-uh)

Godetia, Clarkia

18" 9" ■ **Satiny flowers in white, pink, and mauve**
■ **Cool-season bloom**
■ **Good for cut flowers**

There are two species of Clarkia for gardens: *C. amoena*, called godetia, bears blossoms with contrasting margins and centers; *C. unguiculata*, called farewell-to-spring or just clarkia, has ruffled, single or double flowers. Both grow 2 to 3 feet tall, with shorter hybrids available. Native to the U.S. west coast.

USES: Mass in beds and borders or containers, where they bloom spring to summer in cool-summer areas, or spring to early summer in summer heat. Lovely with annual poppies (*Papaver*) and larkspur (*Consolida*).
GETTING STARTED: *Clarkia* does 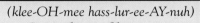 best sown directly in the garden in early spring. Barely cover the seeds.
SITING AND CARE: Plant in well-drained, poor to average soil, in full sun or light shade, 8 to 10 inches apart. Feed lightly in spring and water only when dry. Tall plants may need staking. Pull out plants as they decline in hot areas.
SELECTED VARIETIES: 'Grace

Hybrid' is a 30 inches tall, heavy-flowering godetia in mixed colors, good for cutting. 'Royal Bouquet Mixed' has double, carnation-like flowers in a wide range of colors.

*Hybrid godetia **is a vision of loveliness in cool season plantings, and wonderful as cut flowers.***

CLEOME HASSLERIANA

(klee-OH-mee hass-lur-ee-AY-nuh)

Spider flower

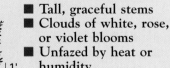

4' 1' ■ **Tall, graceful stems**
■ **Clouds of white, rose, or violet blooms**
■ **Unfazed by heat or humidity**
■ **Never needs staking**

The 3- to 6-feet-tall, airy, long-blooming stems of cleome are invaluable for elegance and ease of culture. Flowering lasts all summer to frost. Native to South America.
USES: Suitable for the back of the border, and as a screen or temporary

shrub. Use as the center of island beds, mix in perennial borders, cottage gardens, or shrub groupings. Combines beautifully with verbena (*V. bonariensis*). Good for cutting. Attracts hummingbirds.
GETTING STARTED: Sow after last frost, or start indoors four to six weeks prior to planting out.
SITING AND CARE: Plant 2 to 3 weeks after last frost, in full sun or light shade, in any soil. Space 1 to 3 feet apart. Withstands heat and drought, but likes abundant moisture. It self-seeds prolifically.
SELECTED VARIETIES: 'Helen Campbell', 3 to 4 feet tall,

glistening white flowers; the 'Queen' series, 3 to 4 feet tall, in pink, purple, or rose. Shorter varieties are available.

*Cleome **'Mauve Queen' and 'Pink Queen' bloom in cool pastel shades on tall, durable stems.***

COLEUS X HYBRIDUS

(KOH-lee-uss HYE-brih-duss)

Coleus

The glowing reds of 'Wizard Mix' are just a taste of the many foliar effects in the wonderful world of coleus.

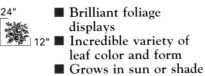
24"
12"

- Brilliant foliage displays
- Incredible variety of leaf color and form
- Grows in sun or shade

Available in a huge variety of leaf colors, patterns, shapes, and sizes, coleus is grown for foliar effects rather than its lavender flower spikes, which some people remove. Native to the Old World tropics.
USES: Useful for bedding, borders, or containers. It's a natural with silver plants like dusty miller *(Senecio)* or mugwort *(Artemisia)*.
GETTING STARTED: Seed-grown varieties can be sown indoors six to eight weeks before setting out.

Coleus can also be grown from cuttings, which root easily. Pinch young plants to encourage bushiness.
SITING AND CARE: Plant after last frost, 6 to 18 inches apart in moist, rich, well-drained soil. Coleus thrives in shade, and many kinds tolerate sun. Provide adequate moisture and feed regularly with high nitrogen fertilizer. Overwinter by taking cuttings before frost.
SELECTED VARIETIES: Too many to mention. Seed-grown types are quite variable from seed, and usually sold as mixes. Beautiful new named selections sold as cutting-grown plants are just hitting the market.

COLOCASIA ESCULENTA

(kohl-oh-KAY-see-uh ess-kyoo-LEN-tuh)

Elephant's ear

Few plants can equal the drama and exotic allure of elephant's ear.

5'
6'

- Huge, tropical leaves
- Hardy in southern and coastal regions
- Tolerates wet soils

The 5- to 7-foot height and enormous heart-shaped leaves give elephant's ear a starring role wherever it appears. Native to tropical Asia.
USES: Use it as a specimen in a tub, or in a tropical grouping with ginger lily *(Hedychium)* and hibiscus. It can be grown in bog or water gardens, and is ideal for poolside.
GETTING STARTED: Plant tubers outside in late spring, after night temperatures reach 60° F, 2 to 3

inches deep, and 6 feet apart. For an earlier start, pot up tubers indoors, four to six weeks before planting outdoors.
SITING AND CARE: Best in rich, organic soils, in sun or shade. Tolerates wet soils and standing water. Keep it well-watered and feed regularly with complete fertilizer. Evergreen in frost-free areas; elsewhere it must be lifted and stored over winter in dry conditions.
SELECTED VARIETIES: 'Black Magic', 3 feet tall, maroon to black; 'Illustris' (black elephant ear) light green leaves marked with bluish-black; 'Fontanesii' (Violet-stemmed Taro) dark green leaves with violet flushing and veining.

CONSOLIDA AMBIGUA

(kon-SOL-ih-duh am-BIH-gyoo-uh)

Larkspur

Larkspur grow 1 to 2 feet tall, with spikes of casually elegant flowers in both soft and intense colors.

30"
8"

- Spurred summer flowers in pinks, blues, purples, and white
- Good for cutting and drying
- Reseeds itself

This annual delphinium blooms through fall in cool summer areas, but declines by midsummer in hot areas. Native to southern Europe.
USES: In the middle to back of borders, in cottage, meadow, and cutting gardens, or with perennials and early summer annuals.
GETTING STARTED: Can be started indoors, sowing in peat pots six to eight weeks before planting out, but it's preferable to sow

directly, in late autumn or early spring. Thin seedlings to stand 8 to 12 inches apart.
SITING AND CARE: Best in rich, fertile soil, but will tolerate less ideal conditions. Full sun to light shade. Feed occasionally, and keep soil moist. Stake tall varieties, and deadhead to prevent self-seeding.
SELECTED VARIETIES: Many available, including dwarf ('Dwarf Hyacinth Mix'), tall ('Sublime Mix', 3 to 4 feet, 'Giant Imperials', 4 to 5 feet), early('Early Bird Hybrids', 20 inches), large-flowered ('Giant Double Hyacinth'), and unusual colors ('Frosted Skies', 12 to 18 inches, white with blue edges).

CONVOLVULUS TRICOLOR

(kon-VOL-vyoo-lus TRY-kuh-ler)

Dwarf morning glory

15"

8"

- A nonclimbing morning glory
- Abundant showy trumpet-shaped flowers
- Blooms spring into summer

This relative of morning glory grows 12 inches tall and wide, and bears multicolored, 2-inch flowers in bright blue, pink, and purple. Native to southern Europe.

USES: Good in rock gardens, rock walls, and as a neat, colorful edging. It performs well in containers.

GETTING STARTED: Start seed indoors five to six weeks before last frost in peat pots. Nick or soak seeds in warm water for 24 hours before planting. Direct seed after hard frosts in spring, or in the fall in mild winter climates.

SITING AND CARE: Sandy, poor, well-drained soils are best, but will tolerate other conditions, except for poor drainage. If using seedlings, plant after last frost, 12 inches apart, in full sun. Water moderately; fertilizing discourages flowering.

SELECTED VARIETIES: 'Ensign' varieties, rose, royal blue, light blue, and white flowers, all with starburst centers of yellow and white. 'Dwarf Rainbow Flash', 6 inches tall and 15 inches wide, comes in both pastel tints and deep shades of blue, pink, and purple.

'Blue Ensign' has flowers of an unusually intense blue beautifully set off by white throats.

COSMOS BIPINNATUS

(KOZ-mohs bye-pih-NAY-tus)

Cosmos

36"

24"

- Tall plants with saucer-shaped flowers
- Pink, white, lavender, or magenta flowers summer to fall
- Ferny foliage

Cosmos is an old-fashioned favorite, 3 to 4 feet tall. New varieties offer shorter habits. Native to Central and South America.

USES: Appropriate for back of the border, scattering among perennials, and cut flowers. Use shorter types for mixed containers, and with 'Blue Horizon' ageratum and tall verbena (*V. bonariensis*).

GETTING STARTED: Sow directly  in place after last frost, or indoors five to seven weeks before.

SITING AND CARE: Best in dry, lean soil with good drainage, but will grow in most soils. Space 1 to 3 feet apart. Avoid overwatering, and don't feed. Lanky plants may be cut back. May need staking.

SELECTED VARIETIES: The classic 'Sensation' is 3 to 4 feet tall, in single colors and picotees. 'Seashells Mix' is 3 feet tall, with tubular petals. 'Sonata' varieties are 2 feet tall in various colors, of which the standout is white.

Cosmos is beloved in both gardens and vases for its lacy foliage and clear pastel flowers.

COSMOS SULPHUREUS

(KOZ-mohs sul-FUR-ee-uss)

Yellow cosmos

20"

15"

- Flowers of yellow, orange, and scarlet
- Finely textured
- Blooms heavily all summer

Clouds of hot-colored, semidouble blossoms on wiry stems 18 to 36 inches tall. Native to Central and South America.

USES: Use in informal and cutting gardens. Short varieties in mixed container plantings, tall types at the back of the border. Plant an orange variety with larkspur (*Consolida*) for a smashing effect.

GETTING STARTED: Sow directly in place after last frost, or indoors five to seven weeks before.

SITING AND CARE: Flowers best in dry, lean soil with good drainage, but will grow in most soils. Space 1 to 3 feet apart, depending on variety. Avoid overwatering, and don't feed. May need staking.

SELECTED VARIETIES: 'Bright Lights', 3 feet tall, mixed colors; 'Diablo', 18 to 30 inches tall, burnt-orange flowers; 'Ladybird' series, 10 to 14 inches tall; 'Sunny Red', 12 to 14 inches tall, scarlet flowers.

The hot colors of Cosmos sulphureus illuminate summer borders. Here it mingles with datura and tuberoses.

CUCURBITA PEPO VAR. OVIFERA

(kew-KUR-bi-tuh PEP-oh oh-VIH-fur-uh)

Ornamental gourds

The meandering vines of ornamental gourds are a strong and playful presence in the garden.

6" 12'

- Trailing or climbing vines
- Bright multicolored fruits
- Easy to grow plants

Whether you let them sprawl or climb, the lush vines of ornamental gourds are an interesting addition to the garden. The decorative fruits can be dried and used indoors. The plants grow best in warm weather.

USES: Can be used to climb structures and create living screens, walls, and tunnels. Plant with scarlet runner bean (*Phaseolus*), morning glory (*Ipomoea*) or other annual vines. The fruits are edible, as well as decorative.

GETTING STARTED: Sow directly where they will be grown, two weeks after last frost, or start indoors three to four weeks before planting.

SITING AND CARE: Plant 1 to 2 feet apart, in rich, well-drained soil, in full sun. Feed at planting time, and water regularly. Allow plenty of room for growth. Support vines, and keep fruit off the ground. Harvest fruits when thoroughly ripe.

SELECTED VARIETIES: Often sold as mixes such as 'Choose Your Weapon', to give variety. Individual types are usually varieties of *Cucurbita*, but the genera *Lagenaria* and *Luffa* are also included.

CYNOGLOSSUM AMABILE

(sin-oh-GLOS-um am-uh-BIL-ee)

Chinese forget-me-not

'Blue Showers' provides a rich note of blue in early summer, and will naturalize where it's happy.

18" 10"

- Sprays of clear blue flowers
- Showier than other forget-me-nots
- Blooms late spring into summer

Most beloved for their wonderful shade of blue, these 2-foot-tall plants also come in bright white or pink. Native to eastern Asia.

USES: Situate in the middle of beds and border, or the rock garden. Plant near the complementary orange of California poppy (*Eschscholzia*) or pot marigold (*Calendula*).

GETTING STARTED: For earliest bloom, start indoors six to eight

weeks ahead of planting. Direct seeding outdoors provides bloom midsummer and later.

SITING AND CARE: Space 8 to 12 inches apart in full sun, in ordinary, well-drained soil. Tolerates both wet and dry conditions. Water and feed moderately. Cut back after flowering. Reseeds itself.

SELECTED VARIETIES: 'Blue Showers', 24 to 30 inches tall, lapis-blue flowers; 'Avalanche', pure white, 18 to 24 inches tall; 'Firmament', 15 inches tall, sky blue flowers; 'Mystery Rose', 30 inches tall, muted pink flowers.

DAHLIA HYBRIDS

(DOLL-yuh)

Bedding dahlia

Bedding dahlias bear large, long-blooming flowers on compact plants.

15" 12"

- Large single or double pompom flowers
- All colors except blue
- Blooms midsummer till frost
- Spectacular cut flowers

Less well-known than their tall siblings, dwarf dahlias bloom prolifically and have a compact bushy habit, 12 to 24 inches tall. Native to Mexico and Guatemala.

USES: Good in borders, bedding, containers, and for cutting. Try in combinations with snapdragons (*Antirrhinum*), nicotiana, or edgers such as dusty miller (*Senecio*).

GETTING STARTED: Sow indoors four to six weeks before last frost. May also be sown directly in the garden 1 to 2 weeks before last frost, or started from tubers.

SITING AND CARE: Plant outside four weeks after last frost, spacing 12 to 15 inches apart in moist, well-drained organic soil, in full sun or light shade. Keep well-watered and feed regularly. After tops are killed by frost, dig tubers and store.

SELECTING VARIETIES: 'Figaro Mix', 10 inches tall, single and double blooms, wide color range. 'Redskin', 12 to 15 inches tall, bronze foliage, double-flowered mix.

DAHLIA HYBRIDS

(DOLL-yuh)

Exhibition dahlia

- Large single or double pompom flowers
- All colors except blue
- Blooms midsummer till frost
- Spectacular cut flowers

Extravagantly showy garden plants range in height from 1 to 7 feet, and bear button-sized to dinner-plate-sized flowers in a huge assortment of forms and colors.

USES: Use in borders, beds, rose gardens, or cutting gardens. Plant with Bengal tiger cannas or Joseph's coat (*Amaranthus*) to bedazzle, or with cleome and red fountain grass (*Pennisetum*) for a full, misty effect.
GETTING STARTED: Plant tubers in the spring, set horizontally, 3 inches deep. Place stakes at planting time to avoid injuring roots later.
SITING AND CARE: Space 12 to 18 inches apart in well-drained organic soil, in full sun. Water and feed with low-nitrogen fertilizer regularly. Pinch shoot tips for fullness. Dig and store tubers in fall.
SELECTED VARIETIES: There is a wealth of varieties, classified by flower size and form.

Dinnerplate dahlia 'Blithe Spirit'

Giant dahlia 'Karenglen' is a glowing red.

The flushed beauty of 'Audacity'

DATURA METELOIDES

(dah-TOOR-uh meh-tuh-LOY-deez)

Datura

- Trumpet-shaped, fragrant flowers
- Large, tropical-looking plants
- Grows in sun or shade

This exotic-looking beauty grows 3 to 5 feet tall and wide, and produces large, upright, flared trumpets. Blooms midsummer to frost. All plant parts are poisonous.
USES: Use it in the border, next to patio or pool, or in containers. Try

it with red-leaved types of canna or spider flower (*Cleome*).
GETTING STARTED: Start seeds indoors two to three months before last frost. Direct seeding gives later bloom. Perennial in mild climates, it self-sows in cold-winter areas.
SITING AND CARE: Plant two to three weeks after last frost, ideally in rich, moist, soil, but will tolerate poor soil. Grow in full sun or light shade. Pick off seed pods to prevent reseeding, or after they ripen to collect seeds.
SELECTED VARIETIES: 'Double Blackcurrant Swirl', 5 feet tall, violet flowers; 'Evening Fragrance', 3 to 4 feet tall, 8 inches long, lilac-white flowers.

RELATED GENUS: *Brugmansia*, the angel's trumpets, grow as a soft-wooded shrubs with large, hanging, trumpet flowers in shades of yellow, pink, and peach.

Although it looks exotic, datura is easy to grow, and its large, fragrant flowers are good for cutting.

DIANTHUS CHINENSIS

(dye-AN-thus chye-NEN-sis)

China pink

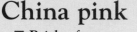

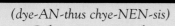

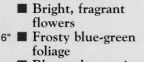

- Bright, fragrant flowers
- Frosty blue-green foliage
- Blooms late spring to early summer

China pink forms 6- to 12-inch mounds of foliage, and bears flowers with fringed petals, single or double, in shades of pink, red, and white. Native to eastern Asia.
USES: For edging and bedding, growing in containers or rock

gardens, and cut flowers. Try it with Swan River daisy (*Brachycome*) and white lobelia.
GETTING STARTED: Sow outdoors in place after final frost, or start indoors six to eight weeks ahead.
SITING AND CARE: Best in well-drained alkaline soils, in sun or light shade. Declines in summer, but some hybrids are heat resistant.
SELECTED VARIETIES: 'Ideal Hybrids', 12 inches tall, heat and cold tolerant, in a dozen shades; 'Magic Charms', 6 inches tall, in pink, crimson, white, and scarlet; 'Telstar Hybrids', 4 to 6 inches tall, early-blooming.

RELATED SPECIES: *D. barbatus* (sweet William) 6 to 10 inches tall, spicily fragrant, and reseeds itself.

Sweet William bears clusters of spice-scented flowers (left). A drift of 'Color Magic' China pinks (right).

DIMORPHOTHECA SINUATA

(dye-mor-foh-THEE-kuh sin-yoo-AY-tuh)

Cape marigold

Sparkling masses of cape marigold bloom for many months in cool climates.

1'
1'

- Pastel or white daisy flowers
- Contrasting centers of yellow, blue, or orange
- Winter bloom in mild climates

These large-flowered daisies grow 6 to 15 inches tall, and bloom late spring through summer. Native to South Africa.

USES: In large masses, good for beds, borders, and containers. Use with petunias, coleus, or verbena for a nice contrast. An evergreen perennial in mild climates with cool summers (such as coastal California), where it is popular as a blooming ground cover.

GETTING STARTED: Start indoors six to eight weeks before planting out, barely covering seeds. In mild climates direct sow in early fall for winter blooms, in winter for spring bloom.
SITING AND CARE: Plant outdoors in late spring, when soil is warm. Space 6 to 12 inches apart, in rich, well-drained soil, in full sun. Stands drought well, but prefers cool summers. Water and feed sparingly. Cut stems to the ground after flowering.
SELECTED VARIETIES: 'Salmon Queen', 12 inches, shades of salmon and apricot; 'Aurantica Hybrids', 12 inches, orange, buff, and yellow.

DOLICHOS LABLAB

(DOH-lih-kohs LAB-lab)

Hyacinth bean

Hyacinth bean—lovely in every stage of its life, from seed to plant to flower to pod—is endlessly useful.

15'

1'

- Annual climber with purplish green leaves
- Fragrant purple or white flowers
- Dark purple stems and pods

This quick-growing vine is a great accent plant. Blooms midsummer to frost. Native to the Tropics.
USES: Use to screen undesirable views, decorate fences and trellises, and create contrasting foliage effects. Mix with other climbers, such as scarlet runner bean, or decorate the vegetable garden by training it up corn stalks. The pods can be used in flower arrangements. Also good in containers.

GETTING STARTED: Sow outdoors after soils have warmed up, or indoors six to eight weeks before last frost, sowing in peat pots. Soak in warm water for 24 hours before planting.
SITING AND CARE: Plant seedlings in late spring, when night temperatures remain above 50° F. Space 1 to 3 feet apart, in a sunny location, in ordinary well-drained soil. Harvest seed from dried pods.
SELECTED VARIETIES: 'Alba' is a white form. 'Ruby Moon' has bicolored pink flowers and dark purple to brown pods.

ESCHSCHOLZIA CALFORNICA

(eh-SHOL-zee-uh kal-i-FOR-ni-kuh)

California poppy

Mixed colors of California poppy glow in late spring (right); 'Ballerina Rose' is a stunning hybrid (inset).

12"

6"

- Brilliant orange, yellow, red, pink, and white blooms
- Drought tolerant
- Naturalizes well

A West Coast native, California poppy is tough and free-flowering. The species produces 12-inch mounds of gray-green foliage with bright orange blossoms. Varieties are available in many colors.
USES: Good in beds, borders, and rock gardens. Often included in wildflower mixes with bachelor's button (*Centaurea*).
GETTING STARTED: Direct seed into the garden after the last frost, or start indoors, two to three weeks

before last frost, sowing in peat pots. In mild climates, sow outdoors in fall or winter.
SITING AND CARE: Prefers sandy, alkaline soil with excellent drainage. Best in full sun, but tolerates shade. Avoid overwatering, and don't feed. Self-seeds, and perennializes in mild climates.
SELECTED VARIETIES: 'Dalli', 12 inches, orange-red with yellow centers; 'Mission Bells', 15 inches tall, is a mix with double flowers in creams, oranges, and pinks; 'Thai Silk' series, 10 inches tall, bears ruffled, semidouble flowers in mixed pinks, reds, oranges, and golds.

EUPHORBIA MARGINATA

(yoo-FOR-bee-uh mar-jih-NAH-tuh)

Snow-on-the-Mountain

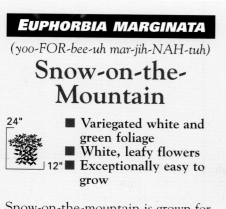

24"
12"

- Variegated white and green foliage
- White, leafy flowers
- Exceptionally easy to grow

Snow-on-the-mountain is grown for its silvery green and white variegated foliage and showy white flower bracts. Native to the central United States.

USES: These 2-foot, bushy plants will tolerate nearly any conditions in full sun. Useful in beds, borders, and for massing in difficult, dry areas. Try contrasting it with colorful shrubs such as red barberry, or to cool down hot colored summer annuals, like celosia.

GETTING STARTED: Sow outdoors in place after last frost, or indoors 6 to 8 weeks before.

SITING AND CARE: Plant outdoors after last frost, spacing 8 to 12 inches apart in full sun or light shade, in any kind of soil. Tolerates heat, drought, and neglect.

SELECTED VARIETIES: 'Summer Icicle' is an 18 inches dwarf type.

'White Top' is an erect, uniform 3- feet-tall variety.

Snow-on-the-mountain is sometimes called ghost weed due to its erect silvery-white growth.

GAILLARDIA PULCHELLA

(gay-LAR-dee-uh pul-KEL-uh)

Blanket flower

14"
12"

- Cheerful daisy-like flowers
- Hot colors with contrasting tips
- Tolerant of heat and drought

The bright colors and banded patterns of these 18- to 24-inch plants shine from June to frost, unfazed by heat or drought. Native to central and western United States.

USES: At home in informal beds and borders, with zinnia, marigolds, and orange cosmos. Mixes well with perennials or shrubs, and can be used in containers or for cut flowers.

GETTING STARTED: Sow indoors at surface depth four to six weeks before planting out. Direct seeding can be done after the last frost, or in the fall where winters are mild.

SITING AND CARE: Plant after last frost, 1 foot apart in ordinary soil, in full sun. Tolerant of dry, infertile soil, but not heavy clay. Deadhead to prolong blooming.

SELECTED VARIETIES: The species is usually single. Breeders have developed heavily-double varieties: 'Double Mixed', 24 inches, cream, gold, crimson, and bicolors; 'Red Plume', 12 inches tall, brick red flowers on bushy plants; and 'Yellow Sun', 18 to 20 inches, golden yellow.

'Red Plume' blanket flower grows compatibly with marigolds in sunny spots and is good for cutting.

GAZANIA RIGENS

(guh-ZAY-nee-uh RYE-jenz)

Gazania

10"
9"

- Daisy-like flowers with vibrant petals
- Silvery green foliage
- Tolerates heat, drought, and wind

Gazania bears bright daisy-type flowers on 6- to 12-inch plants. The yellow, orange, red, or muted pink flowers are often dazzlingly striped and banded, and close at night. They bloom summer to frost, and prefer hot summers. Native to South Africa.

USES: Use in borders, beds, and containers, as edgers and ground covers. Try combining with signet marigolds *(Tagetes tenuifolia)* and verbena 'Imagination' for a drought-proof planting.

GETTING STARTED: Start seeds indoors four to six weeks before the last frost. May be sown outdoors in place after final frost.

SITING AND CARE: Plant two weeks after last frost, 8 to 12 inches apart. Best in light, sandy, well-drained soil in full sun. Once established, water only in dry spells, and feed lightly. Deadhead regularly.

SELECTED VARIETIES: 'Daybreak Hybrids', early-blooming, 8 inches tall, in several colors, some with stripes. 'Chansonette Mix', 8-inch plants, with 4-inch flowers. 'Talent Mixed', silvery white foliage, 8-inch plants, wide color range.

Gazania bears brilliant daisy flowers with interesting bands and stripes, and attractive divided leaves.

GOMPHRENA GLOBOSA

(gom-FREE-nuh gloh-BOH-suh)

Globe amaranth

'Buddy Purple' fills the midborder with long-lasting bloom (left); a rich tapestry of mixed colors (right).

18"
12"

- Everlasting, clover-like flowers
- Dense, bushy plants
- Blooms summer into fall

Famous for their longevity in the vase, globe amaranth's colors include white, pink, purple, orange, and red. Native to the tropics of the Eastern hemisphere.

USES: Erect plants for borders, beds, containers, and cutting gardens. Shorter varieties are good edgers. Layer 'Strawberry Fields' with blue salvia and white cleome.

 GETTING STARTED: For earliest bloom, sow indoors six to eight weeks before last frost, barely covering the seeds. Direct seeding outdoors can be done after last frost.

SITING AND CARE: Plant in spring, when temperatures remain above 50° F. Space 12 inches apart in light, well-drained soil, in full sun. Water and feed lightly. For drying, pick flowers before they open fully, hang upside-down to dry.

SELECTED VARIETIES: 'Bicolor Rose', 2 feet tall, soft lilac-rose with a white center. 'Gnome' series, 6-inch dwarf in pink, white, and 'Buddy Purple'. 'Full Series', 18 to 24 inches tall, with large flowers in wide color range. 'Strawberry Fields', 2 feet tall, bright red flowers.

GYPSOPHILA ELEGANS

(jip-SOF-ih-luh EL-uh-ganz)

Annual Baby's breath

Annual Baby's breath forms tight, rounded mounds of lacy flowers useful for edging and bedding.

18"
18"

- Early summer sprays of white flowers
- Valuable for flower arranging
- Good for drying

Annual baby's breath produces tight mounds of airy blooms on plants from 8 to 24 inches tall, and pink forms are available. Native to eastern Europe and northern Asia.

USES: Good in borders and containers, or grown in the cutting garden. A natural for the rock garden, or growing out of wall niches, along with trailing lobelia.

GETTING STARTED: Seed directly in the garden in early spring while soil is still cool, or start indoors, six

 to eight weeks before last frost. For continuous bloom, sow every few weeks throughout spring.

SITING AND CARE: Space seedlings 8 to 12 inches apart, in well-drained, non-acid soil, in full sun. Water and feed sparingly.

RECOMMENDED VARIETIES: 'Carminea' and 'Rosea' mixture, 18 inches, shades of pink. 'Covent Garden', 18 inches, classic single white. 'Garden Bride', 10 to 12 inches tall, single pink flowers. 'Gypsy', 12 inches tall, semidouble light pink flowers.

HEDYCHIUM

(heh-DIK-ee-um)

Ginger lily

Grow the tropical beauties white ginger (left) and 'Kahili' ginger (right) for striking elegance and fragrance.

5'
3'

- Showy, orchid-like blooms
- Sublime fragrance
- Lush, bold foliage
- Tall, dramatic form

Heights of 6 to 8 feet, lush green leaves, and heavily scented flowers of various colors and forms make these plants invaluable additions to the garden. Bloom lasts summer to frost. Native to India and Malaysia.

USES: Use as a specimen, or mix it with canna, elephant's ear *(Colocasia)* and caladium. Good for moist woodland edge or waterside.

GETTING STARTED: Start by rhizome or root division, planted after soil has warmed in the spring.

Or start from seed indoors, sowing six to eight weeks before last frost, barely covering seeds, or outdoors, direct seeding in early spring.

SITING AND CARE: Plant 2 to 3 feet apart in moist, rich well-drained soil, in sun or part shade. Water and feed regularly. Cut back faded flower stalks. Hardy in warm areas; in the North, lift rhizomes and store over winter, like canna.

SELECTED VARIETIES: *Hedychium coronarium* (white ginger) 7 feet tall, large moth-shaped white flowers. 'Kahili' 6 to 7 feet tall, yellow flowers with intense orange stamens. 'Orange Crush', 5 to 6 feet tall, large spikes of orange flowers attractive to butterflies.

HELIANTHUS

(hee-lee-AN-thus)

Sunflower

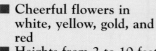

- ■ Cheerful flowers in white, yellow, gold, and red
- ■ Heights from 2 to 10 feet
- ■ Beloved by children and birds

The familiar, tall, golden-headed sunflower has been hybridized into a multitude of new forms among which gardeners can choose. Native to North America.

USES: Tall varieties can be used at the back of borders, to create living screens, fences, and playhouses for children, lined along buildings and fences. They can also play host to twining annual vines such as hyacinth bean (*Dolichos*). Shorter types are more easily integrated into beds, containers, and other mixed plantings. They associate well with perennial, tall grasses, shrubs, and other bold annuals. Pair with red fountain grass (*Pennisetum*) for a glorious effect. Dwarf types can be bedded in masses. All types are good for cutting, and edible seeds.

The deep-toned gem 'Velvet Queen'

GETTING STARTED: May be started in peat pots indoors four to eight weeks before last frost; but probably best sown directly where it is to be grown, after last frost.

SITING AND CARE: Grow in any soil, but best conditions are light, well-drained soil, in full sun or light shade. Spacing depends on variety. Tall types will need staking or other support, especially in windy areas.

SELECTED VARIETIES: There is a wide range of varieties, some selected for dwarfness (such as 'Music Box' and 'Teddy Bear'), tallness ('Moonwalker'), new flower colors ('Chianti', 'Inca Jewels', and 'Italian White'), lack of pollen ('Sunrich Lemon and Orange'), and classic appearance ('Sunbeam'). Another good feature is multiple branching, which results in more flowers (although smaller) and an extended season of bloom.

The bicolored flowers of 'Floristan' sunflowers are wonderful in the garden or for cutting.

Use dwarf 'Teddy Bear' for bedding.

'Moonbright' is a lovely cool yellow.

'Autumn Beauty' is 6 to 9 feet tall.

'Sunbeam' is a classic.

'Sonja' is good for cutting.

Award-winning 'Valentine'

HELICHRYSUM BRACTEATUM

(heh-lih-KRY-sum brak-tee-AY-tum)

Strawflower

The vivid colors of 'Bright Bikini' strawflower will last all summer in the garden, and indefinitely indoors.

24"
9"

- Everlasting flowers
- Brilliant colors
- Good for cutting and drying

Strawflower is probably the most popular of the everlastings. Heights range from 18 to 36 inches tall, and colors include white, yellow, orange, red, pink, and purple. Native to Australia.

USES: Good for beds and borders, with annuals, perennials, or shrubs. Use tall types for cottage gardens and for cutting and drying.

GETTING STARTED: Start seed indoors, six to eight weeks before planting out. In long summer areas, outdoor seeding may be done after last frost.

SITING AND CARE: Plant after last frost, 6 to 24 inches apart, in well-drained soil in full sun. Water in dry spells. Best in hot, dry summers.

SELECTED VARIETIES: 'Bright Bikini', 15 inches tall, 8 bright colors; 'Dragon Hill Monarch', 2 feet, golden yellow; 'Monstrosum Mix', 3 feet tall, large doubles. 'Silver Bush', 16 to 18 inches, white flowers, silver-green foliage.

RELATED SPECIES: Licorice plant (*Helichrysum petiolare*) is grown for its wooly, vinelike foliage, in a range of subtle colors, including silver, chartreuse, yellow, and variegated.

HELIOTROPIUM ARBORESCENS

(hee-lee-oh-TROH-pee-um ar-boh-RES-enz)

Heliotrope

Heliotrope, sometimes called cherry pie plant for its scent, is an old-fashioned favorite.

20"
12"

- Flower clusters in blue, violet and white
- Strong, fruity fragrance
- Long period of bloom

Heliotrope grows as 1- to 2-feet-tall, bushy plants which bloom indefinitely. Beloved for its fruity, vanilla fragrance. Native to Peru.

USES: Used most commonly in containers, either alone or with trailers such as alyssum (*Lobularia*) and ivy geraniums (*Pelargonium*). It's good for edging or for mixed plantings. Can be trained as a standard. Place where the fragrance can be enjoyed.

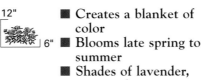

GETTING STARTED: Sow indoors ten to twelve weeks before planting. May be grown from cuttings.

SITING AND CARE: Plant two to three weeks after last frost, into rich, well-drained, organic soil, 1 to 2 feet apart, in full sun or light shade. Keep soil evenly moist, feed regularly, and deadhead to prolong bloom. Very frost tender.

SELECTED VARIETIES: Most varieties are bred for compactness, such as 'Blue Wonder' (12 inches, deep blue flowers) and 'Mini Marine' (10 inches, deep purple flowers). Other varieties, such as 'Fragrant Delight' focus on fragrance.

IBERIS UMBELLATA

(eye-BEER-iss um-bel-LAY-tuh)

Globe candytuft

Annual candytuft forms a mass of sparkling color in late spring and early summer.

12"
6"

- Creates a blanket of color
- Blooms late spring to summer
- Shades of lavender, rose, and mauve

These 16-inch plants have a mounded growth habit and bear neat flower clusters. Native to southern Europe.

USES: Well suited to massing in beds, for edging, border plantings, rock gardens, and in wall and rock crevices. Good with spring bulbs, or used as a cut flower.

GETTING STARTED: Start seeds six to eight weeks before last frost, in peat pots. Sow directly after last frost. For extended bloom, sow successively through midsummer.

SITING AND CARE: Plant after last frost, 6 to 12 inches apart in ordinary well-drained soil, in full sun. Once established, water sparingly. Deadhead after blooming, and shear back to maintain tidiness. Tolerant of heat and drought. May self-seed.

SELECTED VARIETIES: 'Brilliant Mix' grows 10 inches tall, with purple, pink, white, and red flowers. 'Dwarf Fairy Mixed' is 9 inches tall, in colors ranging from white to carmine. *Iberis crenata* is a related species with bright white, umbrella-shaped flowers on 12-inch plants.

IMPATIENS

(im-PAY-shens)

Impatiens

12"
10"

- Lush, mounded plants
- Continuous bloom summer to frost
- Flowers in many colors and bicolors
- Indispensable for shady areas

Impatiens has become the most popular annual of our time because of its mounds of glossy foliage, constant bloom, luminous flower colors, and ability to flourish in shade. Plant breeders have developed a wide range of heights and flower types, and the colorful New Guinea Hybrids.

USES: Impatiens are useful throughout the garden, in beds, borders, and containers, for edging and massing, and as ground cover under trees. They mix beautifully with hostas and ferns in shade gardens.

GETTING STARTED: Start indoors ten to twelve weeks before last frost, sowing on the surface. Highly susceptible to damping-off; sow into vermiculite, and water from bottom only. Some New Guinea types must be started from cuttings.

SITING AND CARE: Plant outdoors after last frost, spacing 1 to 2 feet apart in well-drained organic soil, in partial to full shade. Tolerates sun in cool areas. Keep soil moist and feed lightly. Pinch young plants to promote dense growth.

SELECTED VARIETIES: A tremendous range of varieties exists, from heights of 6 to 24 inches, single to rosebud-shaped flowers, a rainbow of flower colors and, especially within the New Guinea hybrids, foliage colors and variegations. Shorter types include the 'Accent' and 'Super Elfin' series. 'Blitz' is taller. 'Frost', 'Swirl', and 'Mosaic' offer new flower patterns, 'Confection' and 'Victorian Rose' offer doubles. Within the New Guineas, 'Tango' is an award-winning seed-grown type.

Impatiens blanket shade with color.

New Guinea types have jazzy foliage.

Blooms of double varieties such as 'Fiesta Pink Ruffles' resemble roses.

Delicately-hued 'Super Elfin Twilight'

IPOMOEA BATATAS

(ih-poh-MEE-uh buh-TAY-tus)

Sweet potato vine

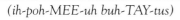

6"
7'

- Dense, trailing vine
- Wonderful foliage colors
- A rapid grower

The ornamental varieties of sweet potato vine are relative newcomers to American gardens, but gaining popularity quickly. The long vining stems of beautifully colored and shaped foliage add drama to any mixed planting. The vines grow to 7 feet long, and foliage colors include white, pink, red, dark purple, gold, green, and variegations.

USES: Excellent for hanging baskets, window boxes, and containers. Valuable as an annual ground cover, as it will quickly fill areas in sun or shade.

GETTING STARTED: From tubers, cuttings, or pre-started plants.

SITING AND CARE: Plant after last frost, 1 to 2 inches apart in light, well-drained soil, in full sun to partial shade. Pinching back and pruning will keep vines shorter, if desired.

SELECTED VARIETIES: 'Blackie' has deeply-lobed leaves that are a dark purplish green that almost looks black; 'Margarita' has large, chartreuse, heart-shaped leaves.

'Terrace Lime' is another chartreuse variety.

Ornamental sweet potato vine comes in fabulous colors and is useful for containers and gardens.

IPOMOEA ALBA

(ih-poh-MEE-uh AL-buh)

Moonflower vine

Moonflower vine's large white flowers unfurl at night, releasing a rich fragrance.

15'
2'

- Lush twining vine
- Large white fragrant flowers
- Flowers open at night

Moonflower vine is a rapid grower with 6-inch, scented white flowers, and large, heart-shaped leaves. Flowers take about 5 minutes to open in early evening, a dramatic show. Native to tropical America.

USES: Train moonflower vine onto a trellis, fence, or arbor. Plant with morning glory, or other flowering vines. Or train it onto sunflowers (*Helianthus*). Its nighttime flowers and fragrance are especially useful around patios, porches and outdoor dining areas.

GETTING STARTED: Seed directly where plants are to grow, or start indoors three to four weeks before last frost. Soak seeds in warm water for 24 hours, or nick the seed coat before planting.

SITING AND CARE: Plant three to four weeks after last frost, when temperatures remain above 45° F, 12 to 18 inches apart. Best in full sun. Prefers well-drained soil of low fertility, but tolerates a range of conditions. Do not fertilize, and water only lightly. Provide support for twining growth. Drought tolerant. Perennial in mild climates. All plant parts are poisonous.

IPOMOEA TRICOLOR

(ih-poh-MEE-uh TRY-ku-ler)

Morning glory

Brighten the day with 'Scarlett O'Hara' (left), 'Star of Yalta' (right), or 'Early Call Blue' (inset).

10'
3'

- Twining annual vine
- Graceful climbing form
- Heavy bloom midsummer to frost

Morning glory vines grow vigorously to 10 feet or more, and bloom in purple, blue, red, pink, and white. Native to the Tropics.

USES: Train onto fences, trellises, roses, other vines, or any other structure. Can also ramble sideways or down, to cascade over a wall, or from a hanging basket. Suitable for containers, where restricted roots stimulate more flower production.

GETTING STARTED: Sow directly where plants are to grow or start

indoors three to four weeks before last frost. Soak seeds in warm water for 24 hours or nick the seed coat before planting.

SITING AND CARE: See *Ipomoea alba*.

SELECTED VARIETIES: The best known is 'Heavenly Blue', sky blue with white throat. Some other classics are 'Flying Saucers', white with sky blue streaks; 'Pearly Gates', white; 'Scarlett O'Hara', crimson; and 'Early Call Mix'. Some newer varieties are *I. × imperialis*: 'Mt. Fuji Mix', mixed colors with pinwheel patterning, and 'Tie Dye', deep purple with lavender streaking.

IPOMOEA QUAMOCLIT

(ih-poh-MEE-uh KWAM-o-klit)

Cypress vine

Cypress vine (left) and cardinal climber (right) are fine textured vines to grace the late summer landscape.

25'
1'

- Twining vine
- Scarlet, parasol-shaped flowers
- Feathery, bright green foliage

A vigorous plant, growing up to 25 feet in warm climates, it bears clusters of 1-inch, bright red, funnel-shaped flowers midsummer to fall. Native to the Tropics.

USES: Use as other *Ipomoea*, to festoon fences, latticework, and trellises, to train up stems of tall plants, lampposts or other vertical elements, or to ramble over the landscape. The delicate foliage and brilliant flowers are magnificent entwined with tall shrub roses.

GETTING STARTED: See *Ipomoea tricolor*.

SITING AND CARE: As for *Ipomoea tricolor*, but a bit more fussy about soil, requiring excellent drainage and high organic matter.

SELECTED VARIETIES: A white-flowered form is sometimes found.

RELATED SPECIES: *I. × multifida*, known as cardinal climber, is similar, with palm-like leaves, purple stems, and slightly larger flowers, scarlet with a white throat. *I. coccinea* (scarlet starglory) has heart-shaped foliage, and 1-inch scarlet flowers with a yellow throat. All types are sometimes categorized as Quamoclit.

IONOPSIDIUM ACAULE

(eye-on-op-SID-ee-um uh-KAWL)

Diamond flower

2"
4"
- Tiny tufted plant
- Dainty lilac or white flowers
- Covers itself with bloom
- Blooms summer to fall

Diamond flower, also called violet cress, is a very pretty but little known annual. It grows only 2 to 3 inches tall, creeps horizontally, and bears a profusion of four-petalled, white, or lilac tinged with violet flowers. Native to Portugal.

USES: A creeping rock plant in its native habitat, diamond flower is suited to growing in rock gardens and crevices, between paving stones, on stone walls, and as an edger. Combine it with tiny sedums, sweet alyssum (*Lobularia*), and moss rose (*Portulaca*). It's also lovely grown in small pots.

GETTING STARTED: Sow directly where it is to grow in early spring for summer bloom, in summer for fall bloom, or in autumn for bloom the following spring. It is easily grown.

SITING AND CARE: Best grown in cool, light, moist soil, in full sun or partial shade. In containers, add gravel to give perfect drainage. Water in dry spells. Tolerant of drought, but not heat, and will languish in hot weather. Reseeds pleasantly.

Use diamond flower to add a dainty touch to sunny slopes, rock gardens, and pathways.

LAGURUS OVATUS

(lah-GUR-uss oh-VAY-tuss)

Hare's tail grass

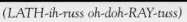

18"
6"
- Erect, slender grass
- Flowers resemble rabbits' tails
- Long-lasting, good for drying
- Best grown in masses

A darling grass in both the garden and dried arrangements. It's stiff, 10- to 20-inch stems are tipped with 2-inch, furry, ivory flower heads. Native to the Mediterranean region.

USES: Grow this slender grass in clumps, as a border plant, in meadow and wildflower plantings, cutting gardens, or mixed with other grasses or shrubs. It's buff color goes well with red or purple foliage, such as that of perilla. Cut for fresh or dried arrangements. The dried heads accept dye readily

GETTING STARTED: Start seed indoors six to eight weeks before last frost. May also be direct sown outdoors, either three weeks before last frost, or in fall.

SITING AND CARE: Plant seedlings outdoors after last frost, spacing 4 inches apart in light, well-drained soil, in full sun. Tolerant of dry conditions, but will perform best with regular watering. Self-seeds.

SELECTED VARIETIES: Only available as the species, but it may be sold either individually, or in ornamental grass seed mixes.

Hare's tail grass, sometimes called rabbit-tail grass, is great for casual gardens and dried arrangements.

LATHYRUS ODORATUS

(LATH-ih-russ oh-doh-RAY-tuss)

Annual sweet pea

6'
2'
- Vine that climbs with tendrils
- Clusters of fragrant ruffled blossoms
- A rainbow of colors

Breeding efforts have produced a wide range of varieties in every color except yellow, larger sizes, various heights, and improved heat tolerance. Native to Italy.

USES: Sweet pea can be trained onto teepees of stakes or brushwood, up netting, trellises, bamboo canes, or strings, or allowed to ramble at will. Wonderful as a cut flower.

GETTING STARTED: Soak seed for 48 hours, then sow outdoors in early spring, or start indoors four to six weeks earlier. Sow outdoors in late fall for winter bloom in mild climates.

SITING AND CARE: Plant seedlings outdoors after last frost, spacing 6 to 12 inches apart in fertile, alkaline soil, in full sun. Water and feed abundantly, provide support, mulch, and deadhead faithfully. Best growth occurs in long, cool growing seasons, and they fail under hot conditions.

SELECTING VARIETIES: Besides flower color and size, watch for height and growth habit (there are bush forms), heat tolerance, and fragrance.

Annual sweet pea is beloved for its beautifully colored and scented flowers.

LAURENTIA AXILLARIS

(loh-REN-tee-uh ax-ih-LAR-iss)

Laurentia

Laurentia is little-known but well worth growing in gardens, baskets, and containers.

8" | 12"

- Low mounded plants, a refined bedding plant
- Shades of blue, white and lavender
- Flowers early summer to frost

Laurentia grows as 6- to 12-inch spreading cushions of fine-textured foliage, and bears masses of starry, softly fragrant, five-petalled flowers in shades of blue, purple, and white. Also known as *Isotoma* and *Solenopsis*.

USES: Well-suited to bedding, edging, rock gardens and walls, and growing in hanging baskets and other containers. Combines well with diamond flower (*Ionopsidium*).

GETTING STARTED: Start seeds indoors, in late winter for midsummer bloom, or in fall for spring bloom. Sow without covering into well-drained potting soil. Can be direct sown in fall in mild winter areas.

SITING AND CARE: Plant after last frost, 4 to 6 inches apart in light, well-drained acidic soil, in full sun. Will reseed and naturalize in warm climates.

SELECTED VARIETIES: 'Blue Stars', sky blue, 1-inch flowers. 'Shooting Stars', white flowers, finer foliage; 'Starlight Pink', lavender-pink flowers; 'Stargazer' is a blend of all three colors.

LAVATERA TRIMESTRIS

(lav-uh-TEE-ruh try-MESS-tris)

Tree mallow

Tree mallow creates a summer symphony of color and form in sunny borders.

30" | 18"

- Tall, bushy plants
- Hollyhock-like flowers in white and pink
- Blooms midsummer

Tree mallow is valuable for its 2- to 4-foot, sturdy, shrub-like habit and large flowers in glowing pinks and white. Native to the Mediterranean region.

USES: Use in the middle to back of the border, in beds, or as a low screen or temporary shrub. Use it to add fullness to rose gardens, or with 'Sensation Mix' cosmos and baby's breath (*Gypsophila*) for a misty effect. It's also good for cutting.

GETTING STARTED: Sow outdoors in early spring, or indoors in peat pots six to eight weeks before planting. May be sown outdoors in the fall in mild areas.

SITING AND CARE: Set out plants after last frost, 12 to 18 inches apart in well-drained, ordinary garden soil, in full sun. Water regularly and feed monthly with low-nitrogen fertilizer.

SELECTED VARIETIES: 'Loveliness' is 3 to 4 feet tall, deep pink. Midheight varieties, all 2 feet, include 'Mont Blanc' (white), 'Mont Rose' (pink), and 'Ruby Regis' (cerise). 'Dwarf White Cherub' grows only 14 inches tall.

LIMONIUM SINUATUM

(lih-MOH-nee-um sin-yoo-AY-tum)

Statice

Statice is well-known as a dried everlasting, but deserves more attention as a plant for the garden.

20" | 12"

- A favorite for cutting and drying
- Attractive undulating leaves
- Tolerates heat, drought, and salt spray

These long-lasting flowers are widely used for drying and arranging. Stems 12 to 24 inches tall rise above rosettes of dark green leaves, with flowers in white, blue, lavender, yellow, and pink. Native to the Mediterranean region.

USES: In mixed beds and borders, as well as the cutting garden. Blooming starts midsummer. Combine with snapdragons, China asters (*Callistephus*), and salvia.

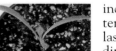

GETTING STARTED: Start seed indoors eight to ten weeks before last frost, or direct sow after final frost.

SITING AND CARE: Plant seedlings after last frost, 1 to 2 feet apart in light, sandy soil, in full sun. Will tolerate hot, dry conditions, but not wet feet. Water only during dry spells. Stake tall plants if needed. To harvest for drying, cut flowers when they are fully open, and hang upside down in a cool, dark place.

SELECTED VARIETIES: There is a wide choice, offering various colors and heights.

LINARIA MAROCCANA

(lih-NAH-ree-uh mar-oh-KAN-uh)

Toadflax

12"
6"

- Flowers like miniature snapdragons
- Delicate, mounded plants
- Good for naturalizing

These 8- to 12-inch tall plants bloom for an amazingly long period, from April to frost. Native to Morocco.

USES: Use in rock gardens and walls, cottage gardens, window boxes, for bedding and edging. It will reseed and naturalize.

GETTING STARTED: Seeds should be sown outdoors in place in early spring as soon as the ground thaws. Reseed every few weeks to lengthen the bloom season. Can be sown the previous fall in mild-winter areas.

SITING AND CARE: Plant in loose, sandy soil with perfect drainage, spaced 6 inches apart, in full sun. Best in areas with cool summer nights, or as a spring flower in hot climates. Water and feed lightly.

SELECTED VARIETIES: Color mixes include 'Fairy Lights Mixed' (12 inches, white-throated flowers), and 'Northern Lights' (24 inches,

bright colors). 'Fantasy' series (8 to 10 inches) comes in separate colors of white, blue, yellow, rose, or white speckled with pink. 'Gemstones' (6 inches tall) blooms in shades of red.

The bright colors of Linaria 'Fairy Bouquet' will bring a festive atmosphere to any garden.

LINUM GRANDIFLORUM

(LYE-num gran-dih-FLOH-rum)

Flowering flax

18"
12"

- Erect delicate plants
- Satiny flowers open daily
- Beautiful in masses

The slender wiry stems of flax grow 15 to 24 inches tall, and are tipped by clusters of 1-inch round flowers. The blooms are white, red, pink, or purple, and renew themselves each morning. Native to North Africa.

USES: Use it as a filler in borders, cottage and meadow gardens, associating well with other casual

beauties like annual poppies *(Papaver)* and bachelor's button *(Centaurea)*. It's most effective planted in masses.

GETTING STARTED: Sow seeds directly outdoors, where they are to be grown, when soil is still cool. As bloom period is short, repeated sowings every few weeks will keep it going. Fall sowing can be done in mild-winter areas.

SITING AND CARE: Plant in ordinary well-drained soil, in full sun, spacing 6 to 12 inches apart. Water lightly. Does best under cool conditions.

SELECTED VARIETIES: Limited available varieties, among them:

'Album', 24 inches tall, white; 'Bright Eyes', 18 inches tall, white with dark center; 'Rubrum', 18 inches, scarlet.

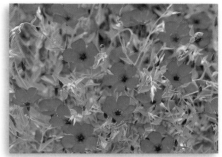

'Rubrum' flowering flax has translucent blossoms in a rare shade of rosy-red.

LISIANTHUS (EUSTOMA)

(lih-zee-AN-thus)

Lisianthus

18"
6"

- Cup-shaped flowers of ivory, pink, and purple
- Long stems, perfect for cutting
- North American native

Lisianthus has won many fans for its gray-green leaves and lustrous 2- to 3-inch blossoms, beautiful in bud and flower.

USES: A long-lasting cut flower, it can be grown in borders, and containers. It harmonizes with roses, snapdragons, and delphinium.

GETTING STARTED: Start seed indoors ten to twelve weeks before planting out. Where growing seasons are very long, outdoor seeding may be done in early spring, or the previous fall.

SITING AND CARE: Plant in spring, once temperatures remain above 40 ° F, 12 inches apart, into moist, well-drained soil, in full sun. Pinch young plants to increase flowering. Water lightly. Established plants tolerate heat and drought.

SELECTED VARIETIES: Shorter types include 'Mermaid Extra Dwarf' and 'Lisa Blue', 6 inches tall; doubles include 'Echo Hybrids' and 'Mariachi'; 'Heidi' hybrids offer

improved branching; 'Red Glass', 12 inches tall, adds red to the choices.

The exquisite flowers of the 'Echo' hybrids (left) and 'Heidi Deep Blue' (right) are wonderful for cutting.

LOBELIA ERINUS

(loh-BEE-lee-uh er-RYE-nus)

Edging lobelia

'Palace Royal' lobelia is smothered with delicate indigo-blue flowers over a long season.

4"
6"

- Low, trailing plants
- Flowers in fabulous shades of blue
- Blooms spring into summer

Low, trailing plants which bloom in vivid shades of blue, lavender, pink, and white. Native to South Africa.
USES: For hanging baskets, edging, bedding, as a ground cover, rock gardens, and rock walls. Contrast it with dwarf marigolds (*Tagetes*) or forget-me-not (*Myosotis*).
GETTING STARTED: Sow indoors ten to twelve weeks before final frost, at surface depth.

SITING AND CARE: Plant two to three weeks after last frost, 4 to 6 inches apart in fertile, well-drained, humus-rich soil. Grows well in shade, or sun in cool summer areas. Keep soil moist. Cut back lightly after first bloom. Flowering stalls in heat, but resumes in cool weather.
SELECTED VARIETIES: 'Crystal Palace', dark blue flowers with bronze foliage, and 'Cambridge Blue', sky blue. Splashed and picoteed colors ('Riviera Series'), contrasting eyes ('Sapphire' and 'Mrs. Clibran'), increased earliness ('Moon' and 'Regatta' series), and cascading habit ('Fountain' and 'Cascade' series). 'Compact Royal Jewels', rich blue with white eye.

LOBELIA X SPECIOSA 'FAN'

(loh-BEE-lee-uh spee-see-OH-suh fan)

Fan hybrid lobelia

'Fan Scarlet' is one of the new hybrids which are improved forms of tall lobelia.

2'
1'

- Erect, slender flower spikes
- Mid-green or bronze foliage
- Blooms midsummer through fall

The plants are uniform and compact, 20 to 24 inches tall, bloom for months on end, and come in red, rose, orchid, and scarlet, some with bronze foliage.
USES: Splendid addition to flower beds and borders, as well as large containers. The vertical spikes can be used as an accent in any mixed planting, or dazzle in sweeps of color, perhaps with *Rudbeckia* 'Goldsturm' and ornamental grasses.

GETTING STARTED: Start from  seed indoors in late winter; sowing in January will give blooms in July.
SITING AND CARE: Plant after last frost, 12 to 18 inches apart in moist, rich soil, in full sun or partial shade. Water regularly; cut back faded flower spikes.
SELECTED VARIETIES: 'Cinnabar Rose' has rich pink flowers, and green foliage. 'Fan Scarlet' grows 24 inches tall, with scarlet flowers and bronze foliage. 'Fan Series Mixed' offers a four-color mix, blending rose and scarlet with red and orchid.

LOBULARIA MARITIMA

(lob-yoo-LAR-ee-uh muh-RIT-i-muh)

Sweet alyssum

Sweet alyssum is a long-time favorite for its low habit, pastel colors, and easy-going nature.

4"
10"

- Low, mounded plants
- Masses of lavender, pink, or white flowers
- Blooms spring to frost

Sweet alyssum is a low (4- to 6-inch), trailing annual with fine foliage covered with small thimbles of scented flowers. Native to the Mediterranean region.
USES: A favorite for edging, also lovely mixed in baskets and containers, in beds and rock gardens, tucked into walls or between paving stones. Try it with dwarf snapdragons (*Antirrhinum*), and China pinks (*Dianthus*). Very easy to grow.

GETTING STARTED: Easy to sow outdoors in early spring, or indoors four to six weeks before the last frost.
SITING AND CARE: Plant after last frost, 6 inches apart, in ordinary well-drained soil, in full sun or light shade. Tolerant of poor soil and dry conditions. Water regularly, and cut back for tidiness and rebloom.
SELECTED VARIETIES: Classics are 'Carpet of Snow' and 'Rosie O'Day'. Newer varieties, such as 'Apricot Shades', 'Snow Crystals', and 'Wonderland Red' offer wider spread; trailing form ('Trailing Rosy Red'); or fragrance ('Sweet White').

LUPINUS HARTWEGII

(loo-PYE-nuss hart-WEH-jee-eye)

Hartweg lupine

3'
2'

- ■ **Tall plants with multiple flower stems**
- ■ **Strong, sweet citrus fragrance**
- ■ **Good for cutting**

This 3-foot-tall annual lupine blooms late summer into fall, in tiers of white, rose, red, or bicolored flowers. More tolerant of heat than other lupines. Native to Mexico. **USES:** In the mixed borders it combines well with daylilies, tall ageratums, and nicotiana.

GETTING STARTED: Sow seeds outdoors after last frost, directly where plants are to grow. Chipping seeds or soaking in warm water will speed germination. Seeding every few weeks will extend bloom season. **SITING AND CARE:** Plant at 1-foot intervals in moist, well-drained soil, in full sun or light shade. Water and deadhead regularly, feed with high phosphorus fertilizer, and cut back after blooming. **SELECTED VARIETIES:** Only a few varieties are available: 'Pink Javelin', 3 to 4 feet, mixed white, pink, and gold; 'Sunrise', 3 to 4 feet,

mixed white, gold, bronze, and azure blue; and 'Sunset White', a 40-inch white form.

Hartweg lupine is a recent introduction that is more tolerant of heat than other lupines. Shown here is 'Sunrise'.

MATTHIOLA INCANA

(mah-THEE-oh-luh in-KAY-nuh)

Stock

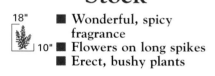

18"
10"

- ■ **Wonderful, spicy fragrance**
- ■ **Flowers on long spikes**
- ■ **Erect, bushy plants**

Stock bears spiked clusters of single or double flowers in white, pink, yellow, crimson, and purple. Native to the Mediterranean coast. **USES:** Flower beds and borders, in containers, and for cutting. Perfect in cottage gardens, or mixed with late tulips. Plant where its scent can be savored.

GETTING STARTED: For earliest bloom, start seed indoors, six to eight weeks before last frost. Outdoor sowing after last frost gives summer bloom. In mild climates, outdoor sowing in late fall provides late-winter and early-spring bloom. **SITING AND CARE:** Plant after last frost in the North, in fall in the South. Space 1 foot apart in moist, fertile, well-drained soil, in full sun or partial shade. Water regularly and feed monthly. Best in cool weather. **SELECTED VARIETIES:** 'Ten Weeks Mixed' (available as 12-inch dwarf or 18-inch plants), 'Trysomic Seven Week' (earliest, 12 to 15

inches), 'Legacy' (12 to 15 inches, very fragrant), 'Cinderella' (8 to 10 inches, early, multiple branching), 'Excelsior Mammoth' (30 inches).

'Color Magic' stocks wave their spicily scented flowers among other cool-season bloomers.

MELAMPODIUM PALUDOSUM

(mel-am-POH-dee-um pal-uh-DOH-sum)

Melampodium

10"
12"

- ■ **Golden yellow star-shaped flowers**
- ■ **Blooms summer to frost**
- ■ **Heat and drought tolerant**

Melampodium, a fairly recent introduction to American gardens, is a long-blooming, 8- to 12-inch mounded plant, with golden daisy flowers all season long, and is virtually self-maintaining. It is superb in hot, humid climates.

USES: In beds, borders, as edging, and as a tolerant container plant. The bushy habit fills open spaces nicely, and looks good alone or mixed with perennials or annuals. **GETTING STARTED:** Start from seed indoors six to eight weeks before last frost. Later bloom will result from outdoor seeding in late spring. **SITING AND CARE:** Plant after last frost, 8 to 12 inches apart, in ordinary, well-drained soil, in full sun. Water moderately, and avoid high nitrogen fertilizer, which results in lots of leaves and few flowers. Tolerates heat and humidity well.

SELECTED VARIETIES: 'Derby', 8 to 10 inches, 1-inch flowers; 'Million Gold', 8 to 10 inches, early blooms; 'Showstar', 8 to 12 inches.

Melampodium, sometimes called black-foot daisy, blooms prolifically till frost. 'Showstar' is shown here.

MESEMBRYANTHEMUM

(meh-zem-bree-ANTH-eh-mum)

Ice plant

Livingstone daisy, M. bellidiformus, blooms in shimmering hues that are hard to resist.

6" | 6"
- Low, creeping plant
- Bright daisy flowers
- Very drought tolerant

This 6-inch creeping succulent bears mats of daisylike flowers in neon shades of white or rose. Perennial relatives are widely used as ground covers in coastal California.

USES: This low plant works well for edging, as bedding, in rock gardens and walls, in window boxes and other containers. Compatible growing with other succulents, such as sedum and moss rose (*Portulaca*), with alpine plants, and between paving stones.

GETTING STARTED: Start indoors ten to twelve weeks before last frost, or sow outdoors after last frost; reseed every few weeks to extend bloom.

SITING AND CARE: Plant after last frost, 6 inches apart in poor, dry, sandy or gravelly, well-drained soil, in full sun. Though best suited to sandy soils in dry Western climates, they will give several weeks of bloom in other areas if planted in lean, well-drained soil.

SELECTED VARIETIES: The Mesembryanthemum family is large and confusing. (*M. crystallinum*) or Livingstone daisy (*Dorotheantus bellidiformis*) are most available.

MIMULUS X HYBRIDUS

(MIM-yoo-lus)

Monkey flower

Monkey flower brings its cheerful personality to cool, moist settings or water's edge.

6" | 6"
- Brightly colored and patterned flowers
- Grow well in shade
- Tolerant of wet areas

Monkey flower is an attractive plant for cool, moist, shady conditions. The 6- to 8-inch-tall plants bear speckled flowers in combinations of yellow, cream, orange, red, and maroon. Native to Chile.

USES: Monkey flower is useful for bedding, borders, stream or poolside gardens, rock gardens and walls, and in containers. Plant alongside forget-me-not (*Myosotis*), ferns, impatiens, and other moisture-loving, shade-tolerant plants. May naturalize near water.

GETTING STARTED: Sow indoors ten to twelve weeks before last frost. It may also be sown outdoors in late winter.

SITING AND CARE: Plant after last frost, 6 inches apart in moist, well-drained, rich soil, in shade. Best in a cool, damp location near water, as it is found in nature.

SELECTED VARIETIES: It may take some searching, but numerous varieties can be found, among them: 'Calypso', a hybrid speckled mix, 5 to 8 inches tall, with large flowers; 'Magic Mix', compact plants, several colors; 'Shade Loving Mixed', 6 to 9 inches tall, scarlet, orange, or yellow, some with speckles.

MINA LOBATA

(MY-nah loh-BAH-tuh)

Firecracker vine

The unusual flowers of Mina lobata have inspired various nicknames, such as Spanish flag and exotic love.

10' | 2'
- Showy, twining vine
- Sprays of colorful flowers
- Blooms late summer to fall

Graceful sprays of boat-shaped blossoms change from scarlet to yellow to creamy white, giving a multihued effect. The vine also has attractive three-lobed leaves, and grows 10 to 20 feet long. Native to Mexico.

USES: Grow this self-twining vine on trellises, fences, arbors, or anywhere adequate supports can be created. It's lovely tumbling out of baskets and other containers, or woven among other climbers.

GETTING STARTED: Start seeds indoors six to eight weeks before planting out. Seeds may be direct sown outdoors two weeks after last frost. Nick seeds or soak in warm water overnight.

SITING AND CARE: Plant seedlings outdoors when spring temperatures remain above 50° F. Space 2 feet apart in light, sandy soil, in full sun or light shade. Provide support. Water moderately and don't feed.

SELECTED VARIETIES: Besides the species, there is also *Mina lobata* 'Citronella', with lemon yellow flowers that turn white.

MIRABILIS JALAPA

(mih-RAH-bih-lis jah-LAH-puh)

Four-o'clock

2'
2'

■ Large, bushy plant
■ Fragrant blooms open late afternoon into evening
■ Abundant, colorful flowers

Also known as marvel of Peru, this 2- to 3-foot plant blooms summer through fall, opening every evening just in time for dinner on the patio. The small umbrella-shaped flowers come in white, yellow, red, pink, and bicolored, often with different colors on the same plant. Native to American tropics.

USES: Used as low, temporary shrubs or hedges, or in flower beds and borders. Useful to fill gaps, to mass around patios and pools, or to line pathways.

GETTING STARTED: Can be easily sown outdoors after last frost, or indoors four to six weeks ahead, sowing into peat pots.

SITING AND CARE: Plant after last frost, 1 to 3 feet apart in average, well-drained soil, in full sun to partial shade. Tolerates heat, drought, humidity, and neglect, but blooms best if watered regularly and fed monthly. Cut to the ground after frost. Self-sows freely and is perennial in mild climates.

SELECTED VARIETIES: Usually available in mixed colors; varieties include 'Jingles' and the 'Teatime' series (24 inches, flowers remain open longer than the species).

A close-up view of 'Jingles' (left), shows different colored flowers on the same plant; a happy mix (right).

MUSA

(MYOO-suh)

Banana

8'
4'

■ Large treelike plants
■ Huge, lush leaves
■ Grow in sun or shade

Ornamental banana offers a tropical element in the landscape. Started ahead from seed and given enough heat, it can easily reach 5 feet or more in height by midsummer, even in northern gardens. Foliage colors include greens, reds, and yellows, sometimes with contrasting patterns. Native to the Tropics.

USES: In containers or gardens. Use singly, or group with ferns, caladiums, hostas.

GETTING STARTED:  Easy to start indoors from seed, sowing ten to twelve weeks before planting out. Or purchase as divisions or started plants.

SITING AND CARE: Plant after all danger of frost, in moist, organically rich soil, in full sun or partial shade. Likes warm, humid conditions. Water and feed regularly, using a high potassium fertilizer. Protect from wind. Will overwinter in mild climates; in cold areas, pot up and bring inside as a houseplant.

SELECTED VARIETIES: Many types are available, including seed mixes. Two red-leaved forms are bloodleaf banana (*M. zebrina*) 6 to 8 feet tall, green leaves with splashes of burgundy, and 'Dwarf Jamaican Red', 8 feet tall, reddish leaves.

Handsome and impressive foliage make red-leaved banana a striking accent plant.

MYOSOTIS SYLVATICA

(my-oh-SOH-tis sil-VAH-tih-kuh)

Forget-me-not

6"
8"

■ Sky-blue flowers
■ Bloom throughout spring
■ Grow in sun or shade

The cool blue of forget-me-not is like the breath of spring. Bloom peaks in spring, and continues intermittently in summer and fall. The species can be open to 15 inches tall; varieties have been selected for neat, low, mound forms and blue, white, or pink flowers. Native to Europe and Asia.

USES: Massed as a ground cover or under spring bulbs, in borders, water and bog gardens, for edging or in woodlands. Also with primrose (*Primula*), viola, and wildflowers.

GETTING STARTED: Easily started by direct seeding outdoors, in late summer for spring bloom, in early summer for fall bloom. Or sow indoors four to six weeks before planting out.

SITING AND CARE: Plant in early spring in fertile, moist, well-drained soil, spaced 8 to 12 inches apart, in sun or shade. Performs well in wet soil; best in cool conditions. Water and feed generously. Self-sows.

SELECTED VARIETIES: 'Carmine King', 8-inches rosy-carmine; 'Blue Ball', 6-inches, bright blue; 'Royal Blue Improved', 12 inches, deep indigo-blue; 'Rosylva', 6 inches, clear pink; 'Victoria Mix', 8-inch mounds in white, blue, and pink.

'Royal Blue' forget-me-not is a vision of loveliness whether massed alone, or with other spring bloomers.

NEMESIA STRUMOSA
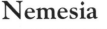

(neh-MEE-see-uh stroo-MOH-suh)

Nemesia

Like a carnival in bloom, nemesia flowers come in nearly every color of the rainbow.

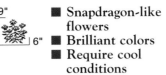

- **Snapdragon-like flowers**
- **Brilliant colors**
- **Require cool conditions**

Nemesia grows 1 to 2 feet tall, bearing two-lipped flowers of white, yellow, red, pink, orange, or mauve. Native to South Africa.

USES: For bedding, edging, borders, rock gardens and walls, containers, and cut flowers. Goes well with linaria and lobelia.

GETTING STARTED: Start seed indoors eight to ten weeks before last frost in hot-summer areas; in cool-summer areas, start four to six weeks before last frost. Can also be sown outside after frost, but only in cool climates.

SITING AND CARE: Plant after last frost, 6 inches apart, in fertile, moist, well-drained organic soil, in full sun or partial shade. Won't tolerate much heat and humidity. Pinch young plants to encourage branching. Water and feed liberally.

SELECTED VARIETIES: 'Blue Gem', 8 to 10 inches, rich blue; 'Carnival Mixed', 9 to 12 inches, mixed colors; 'KLM', 10 inches, top petals blue and lower lip white; 'Mello Red and White', 8 inches, red and white contrasting blossoms; and 'Tapestry', 10 inches, mixed glowing colors.

NEMOPHILA MENZIESII

(neh-MAH-fih-lah men-ZEE-see-eye)

Baby blue-eyes

Few flowers are more charming than baby blue-eyes (left) or the variety 'Pennie Black' (right).

- **Blue flowers with white centers**
- **Good companion for spring bulbs**
- **Naturalizes well**

This California native forms 6- to 12-inch mounds of attractive foliage covered in fragrant, cup-shaped flowers of clear blue and white. It can only be grown in cool conditions, where it blooms from June to frost.

USES: For edging and naturalizing among wildflowers, for flower beds, rock gardens, and containers. Useful at the front of the border, or tucked among paving stones.

GETTING STARTED: Can be sown indoors in peat pots six to eight weeks before planting out, or seeded directly outdoors in early spring.

SITING AND CARE: Plant after last frost, 6 to 12 inches apart in light, sandy, perfectly drained soil, in full sun or partial shade. Water and feed moderately. May be killed by high heat and humidity.

SELECTED VARIETIES: 'Pennie Black', 3-inch height and 12-inch spread, deep blackish purple with white edge; 'Snowstorm', white speckled with black. A related species is *N. maculata;* '5-Spot' has white petals with deep blue spots.

NICOTIANA

(nih-koh-shee-AY-nuh)

Flowering tobacco

Nicotiana sylvestris (left) is tall and richly fragrant. Hybrids such as 'Metro Hybrids' (right) offer compact color.

- **Tall, graceful plant**
- **Tubed flowers with starry tips**
- **Blooms in sun or shade**

Nicotiana, a long-blooming beauty, comes in a wide range of heights and colors, some with a rich evening fragrance. Native to Brazil.

USES: In borders, beds, and containers, spotted, or massed. Place fragrant *N. alata* near doorways and sitting areas. Try 'Nikki Red' with 'Star White' zinnia for a happy pair.

GETTING STARTED: Easy to sow outdoors in place after final frost, or start seed indoors six to eight weeks ahead, sowing without covering.

SITING AND CARE: Plant after last frost, 1 to 2 feet apart in well-drained soil, in sun or partial shade. Water and feed moderately, deadhead.

SELECTED VARIETIES: Hybrids include: 'Domino', 14 inches, bright colors, good branching; 'Heaven Scent', 2 to 3 feet, fragrant; 'Havana Appleblossom', 14 inches, pink reverse on white blossoms; 'Havana Lime Green', 14 inches, green with pink reverse. Species types include: *N. grandiflora* 'Fragrant Cloud', 3 feet, white, and very fragrant; *N. langsdorffii*, 3 to 5 feet, greenish yellow tubular flowers; *N. sylvestris*, 3 to 4 feet, candelabra of fragrant white flowers and bold-textured, large leaves.

NIGELLA DAMASCENA

(nye-JEL-uh dam-uh-SEE-nuh)

Love-in-a-mist

15"
8"
- Pink, white, or blue flowers
- Feathery bracts surround blossom
- Popular for drying

Nigella creates a misty quality unlike any other plant. Flowers are followed by handsome seed pods. Native to the Mediterranean region.
USES: Best in informal borders and cottage gardens, or used as an airy foil to dense plants, such as vinca (*Catharanthus*). Harmonizes with

forget-me-not (*Myosotis*). Also use it for cutting and drying. Often self-sows profusely.
GETTING STARTED: Difficult to transplant, best sown outdoors in early spring as soon as soil can be worked. Can be sown in fall in mild climates. Repeated sowings will give extended bloom.
SITING AND CARE: Plant in ordinary well-drained, or dry, gravelly soil, in full sun, spaced 1 foot apart. Water only when soil is dry, and feed monthly.
SELECTED VARIETIES: 'Dwarf Moody Blue', 6 to 8 inches, semi-double sky-blue; 'Miss Jekyll' series, 18 inches, bright blue, white, or

rose; 'Oxford Blue', 30 inches, large double blue; 'Persian Jewel', 15 inches, classic color mix; 'Transformer', 15 to 20 inches, yellow flowers followed by seed pods that can be turned inside out.

Mixed colors of 'Persian Jewel' display the unusual flower form that has earned love-in-a-mist its fame.

NOLANA PARADOXA

(noh-LAY-nuh par-uh-DOX-uh)

Nolana

10"
18"
- Low, trailing plant
- Likes dry, sunny areas
- Good for edging

A perennial grown as an annual, nolana reaches 4 to 12 inches tall, and bears handsome 2-inch-wide flowers, dark blue with white or yellow throats. Native to South America.
USES: Superb for bedding, nolana is well-adapted to rock gardens and walls, hanging baskets and other

containers, and edging. Group it with other low plants such as signet marigolds (*Tagetes*), verbena, or sweet alyssum (*Lobularia*). Useful in seaside plantings.
GETTING STARTED: Start indoors four to six weeks before last frost, barely covering in peat pots. It can also be sown in the garden after last frost.
SITING AND CARE: Plant seedlings outdoors after last frost, spacing 6 inches apart in poor, dry, sandy soil, in full sun.
SELECTED VARIETIES: 'Blue Bird', 6 inches, dark blue with white throat; 'Sky Blue', 10 inches, sky blue with white throat; 'Snowbird',

6 inches, pure white. A related species, *N. humifusa*, grows 10 inches high, trails 18 to 24 inches wide, and has silvery blue flowers with dark throats.

The throated flowers of Nolana *'Blue Bird' look rather like ruffled-edged morning glories.*

OCIMUM BASILICUM

(AW-sih-mum buh-SIH-lih-cum)

Basil

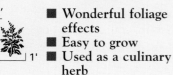

2'
1'
- Wonderful foliage effects
- Easy to grow
- Used as a culinary herb

This heat-loving plant comes in a range of colors, heights, and forms. Native to Old World tropics.
USES: Useful for color bedding, for accents in informal gardens, container plantings, and flower arrangements. Contrast purple basil with silver dusty miller (*Senecio*), or

green forms with red-leaved celosia. And cook with it, too!
GETTING STARTED: Easily started from seed. Start indoors four to six weeks before planting out. May also be sown outdoors after soil warms in late spring.
SITING AND CARE: Plant when temperatures remain above 65° F, 6 to 10 inches apart, in rich, well-drained soil in full sun. Pinch back to promote bushiness. Water regularly, feed occasionally, and shear for tidiness.
SELECTED VARIETIES: Select for dwarf tidy habit ('Spicy Globe', 'Dwarf Bush', 'Minette'), foliage color ('Dark Opal', purplish bronze;

'Osmin', dark purple), ruffled leaves ('Purple Ruffles'), or fragrance (cinnamon, lemon, licorice, and other scents).

Beauty of foliage and form make basils such as 'Purple Ruffles' useful in both flower and herb gardens.

PAPAVER

(puh-PAY-ver)

Annual poppy

20"

8"

- Translucent, cup-shaped flowers
- Shades of white, yellow, pink, and red
- Blooms spring to early summer

Mixed 'Oregon Rainbows' Iceland poppies

Shirley poppies come in single or double forms.

Annual poppies are of several sorts, all with delicate nodding stems and glowing, brilliantly-colored blossoms of a pronounced beauty that is fleeting, but well worth planting.

USES: Poppies are best used in mixed beds and borders, rock gardens, cottage gardens, or naturalized in meadow plantings. Scatter them among late spring bloomers, such as iris, foxglove (*Digitalis*), and stocks (*Matthiola*). Also used for cutting.

GETTING STARTED: Annual poppies are best seeded directly in the garden, in fall in mild-winter areas, in early spring elsewhere. Repeated sowings will extend bloom period.

SITING AND CARE: Plant into moist, well-drained soil in full sun, spaced 8 inches apart. Performs best under cool conditions. Remove plants as they decline. Self-sows.

SELECTED VARIETIES: *Papaver rhoeas*, known as Shirley, corn, or field poppy, is 2 to 3 feet tall, single or double flowered, in mixed pastel

shades; available varieties include 'Angel Choir' (double mix) and 'Mother of Pearl' (single mix). *P. commutatum*, the Flanders poppy, is 20 inches tall, with crimson single flowers with a black blotch. *P. somniferum*, the opium or breadbox poppy, is 3 to 4 feet tall, red, white, pink, or purple, in single, and very double forms called "peony-flowered." *P. nudicaule*, Iceland poppy, is 1 to 2 feet tall, with wide flowers in bright yellow, orange, white, greenish, and pink; varieties include 'Oregon Rainbows', 'Red Sails', and 'Wonderland Mixed'.

A heavily double breadbox poppy vividly demonstrates the reason it's called "peony-flowered."

PELARGONIUM X HORTORUM

(pel-ar-GOH-nee-um hor-TOR-um)

Geranium

18"

15"

- Abundant bright flowers
- Long period of bloom
- Handsome foliage

A red zonal geranium offers dazzling color.

There are many varieties of ivy geraniums, which are stars in hanging baskets and window boxes.

Easy and vigorous, geranium is one of the most highly bred and readily available of all annuals. Flowers are intensely colored and produced freely from spring through fall. Of hybrid origin, parents are native to South Africa.

USES: Traditionally grown in pots, geraniums are also useful for bedding, borders, hanging baskets and other containers, and as houseplants.

GETTING STARTED: All types can be rooted from stem cuttings. Reliable seed-grown strains are also available; start them indoors eight to ten weeks before last frost. Pinch seedlings for compactness.

SITING AND CARE: Plant one week after last frost, 12 to 18 inches apart, ideally in rich, moist soil, in full sun. Tolerant of less-than-ideal soil and some shade. Water and feed regularly; deadhead for neatness. Bring plants indoors to overwinter.

SELECTED VARIETIES: *P. × hortorum* is the common garden or zonal geranium, available in shades of red, pink, white, salmon, and purple, in many varieties; some good seed-grown lines are 'Elite', 'Maverick', 'Orbit', and 'Ringo'. Other types include:

Ivy geraniums (*P. peltatum*) have small starry flowers and cascading stems; they are particularly suited to baskets and window boxes. Some good varieties are: 'Breakaway Red', 'Summer Showers', 'Swiss Balkans', and 'Tornado Series'. Scented geraniums (various species) are a large group, among them apple, coconut, lemon, peppermint, rose, and many other fragrances.

A variegated ivy geranium and catmint cascade gracefully from a planter.

PENNISETUM SETACEUM

(pen-ih-SEE-tum seh-TAY-see-um)

Annual fountain grass

3'

2'

- Tall, graceful grass
- Various foliage colors
- Lovely midsummer through fall

This grass adds elegant form and foliage to plantings. It grows 2 to 4 feet tall, with a vase-shaped habit, fuzzy pink flower spikes, and colorful foliage. Native to Mexico.
USES: Use in containers or borders, as a background for lower plants, as a specimen plant, and for fresh arrangements. A single plant can be a focal centerpiece, a mass provides bold contrast. Try it with tall *Nicotiana sylvestris* and cleome.

GETTING STARTED: May be started from seed indoors, or in prepared soil outdoors, six to eight weeks before last frost.
SITING AND CARE: Plant in moist, fertile, well-drained soil, spacing 18 to 30 inches apart, in full sun or partial shade. Water regularly. It is perennial in warm climates, and can become invasive.
SELECTED VARIETIES: The runaway favorite of this group is the variety 'Rubrum', commonly called purple-leaved fountain grass, 2 to 3 feet tall, with burgundy foliage and reddish purple plumes. 'Atrosanguineum', 4 feet tall, has reddish purple leaves.

Purple fountain grass offers fabulous color, form, and durability from midsummer through frost.

PENSTEMON

(PEN-steh-mon)

Beard-tongue

18"

12"

- Spikes of tubular flowers
- Many bright colors
- Blooms late spring to midsummer

The penstemons are a large group of perennial plants often treated as annuals. Erect plants of varying heights, they bear long spikes of tubular, lipped flowers. Native to North America.
USES: In mixed borders, wildflower, meadow, and cottage gardens, containers, and for cut flowers. Blend them with larkspur (*Consolida*) or Canterbury bells (*Campanula*).
GETTING STARTED: From seed indoors eight to ten weeks before last frost, or sow outdoors in spring or fall.

SITING AND CARE: Plant after last frost, 12 to 20 inches apart in fertile, well-drained soil, in full sun or light shade. Water and deadhead regularly. Cut plants back and mulch before winter. May self-sow.
SELECTED VARIETIES: A few are: *P. barbatus*, 3 to 4 feet, pendulous scarlet flowers; *P. digitalis* 'Albus', 4 feet, white flowers with purple stamens; 'Early Bird Mix', 18 inches, large flowers, mixed colors; *P. hartwegii* 'Finest Mixed', 30 inches, mix of rose, lavender, and white.

The lovely 'Colgrave's New Hybrids' is just one of the many desirable varieties of beard-tongue.

PERILLA FRUTESCENS

(per-ILL-uh froo-TEH-senz)

Perilla

3'

2'

- Purplish-green foliage
- Tall and substantial
- Good for accent or contrast

Perilla is cultivated as a culinary herb in Asia, but American gardeners grow it for handsome foliage. The 2- to 3-foot-tall plants have purple-bronze foliage with a metallic sheen, and can be used like a coleus for full sun. Native to India and Japan.
USES: Perilla is sometimes called "purple hedge," suggesting one good use for the plant. Its color can be spotted, lined out, or massed in borders, beds, containers, along driveways or other landscape edges, or among shrubs. Use it to back up delicate plants such as flax (*Linum*) or baby's breath (*Gypsophila*). It looks wonderful with silver plants, and striking paired with deep pinks such as 'Rosy Wave' petunia.
GETTING STARTED: Start seeds indoors in peat pots, ten to twelve weeks before last frost. Or sow directly in the garden after last frost.
SITING AND CARE: Plant outdoors after last frost, spacing 12 inches apart in ordinary well-drained soil, in full sun or partial shade. It needs no special care, but deadheading will help counter its tendency to self-sow. Unwanted plants are easily yanked out.

Perilla's metallic purple leaves look great juxtaposed with lighter foliage, such as here with feverfew.

PETUNIA X HYBRIDA

(pe-TOO-ni-uh HY-bri-duh)

Petunia

1'

■ **Cheerful round-faced flower**
■ **Mounded or trailing plants**
■ **Blooms all season long**

Dependability, versatility, and variety are the hallmarks of the petunia. Flowers can be single or double, smooth or ruffled, clear, edged, striped, or veined, in every color except orange, mounded or cascading, but always abundant, fragrant, and tolerant. Native to Argentina.

USES: Petunia combines with any other plant, and can be used for bedding, borders, hanging baskets, window boxes, and other containers. Some types, especially the 'Wave' hybrids, make good ground covers.

GETTING STARTED: Sow the seed indoors ten to twelve weeks before last frost.

SITING AND CARE: Plant after the last frost, ideally into moist, well-drained, organic soil, in full sun or partial shade. It tolerates a wide range of soil types. Water regularly and feed occasionally. Deadhead and prune for tidiness, vigor, and extended bloom. Tolerates light frost.

SELECTED VARIETIES: Petunias break down into several types:

Grandifloras have the largest flowers, single or double, and are best used in containers, since rain tends to push the heavy blossoms face-first into the garden.

Multifloras have smaller flowers, single or double, borne in greater quantity, with better tolerance to weather and disease; fine in gardens or containers.

Floribunda hybrids offer many small flowers and good weather tolerance.

Milliflora hybrids are more compact, and yet more floriferous with loads of very small flowers.

The 'Wave' series is a recent form that grows 6 inches tall and up to 4 feet wide, suitable for ground cover or containers. Other new types include the 'Supertunia' and 'Surfinia' forms, developed for trailing habit, intense color (some with veining), prolific flowering, and ease of culture.

Petunia integrifolia **is a species type with a multitude of tiny flowers.**

Deep-toned centers add to the appeal of Surfinia petunia 'Pink Vein'.

'Fantasy Crystal Red' is a milliflora type.

'Prism Sunshine' is an award-winning yellow.

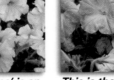

This is the floribunda 'Celebrity Pink Morn'.

'Heavenly Lavender' is a double grandiflora.

The blue form of the popular 'Daddy' series

PHACELIA CAMPANULARIA

(fuh-SEE-lee-uh kam-pan-yoo-LAR-ee-uh)

California bluebell

9"   6"

■ **Upturned bell-shaped flowers**
■ **Intense blue color**
■ **Low, bushy plant**
■ **Native to California**

California bluebell, a bushy annual that grows 10 inches tall, has small fleshy leaves that are hidden by clusters of intense, gentian blue flowers when in bloom. Performs best under cool conditions.

USES: Can be used as an annual ground cover, in rock gardens or borders, or in containers. It is most effective planted in masses or naturalized with wildflowers. Try it with forget-me-not (*Myosotis*) or white lobelia.

The flowers of California bluebell provide one of the most intense blues available to gardeners.

GETTING STARTED: Sow indoors in midspring, or outdoors in early spring. In mild winter areas, sow outdoors in late summer or early fall.

SITING AND CARE: Plant seedlings outdoors after last frost, spacing 8 inches apart in light, well-drained soil, in full sun. Pinch to promote bushiness. Tolerant of dry conditions, but not of heat.

SELECTED VARIETIES: Related species and varieties include: 'Lavender Lass', 12 inches, lavender with pale center; *P. parryi* 'Royal Admiral', 10 inches, purple-blue; 'Tropical Surf', 9 to 12 inches, midblue, spreading habit.

PHASEOLUS COCCINEUS

(fay-zee-OH-liss kok-SIN-ee-uss)

Scarlet runner bean

15'

1'

- Fast-growing twining vine
- Bright bean flowers
- Edible pods

Scarlet runner bean vines climb to 15 feet, with dark green leaves and scarlet flowers followed by long pods. Native to tropical America.

USES: Train it onto bamboo teepees, create a living screen with wire or twine, decorate fences, trellises, light poles, or any vertical structure. Use it with climbing roses, or as a vibrant follow-up to spring-blooming clematis.

GETTING STARTED: It can be started indoors in peat pots four to six weeks before planting out, but it's easier to sow directly outdoors two weeks after last frost.

SITING AND CARE: Plant into moist, well-drained soil in full sun, spacing 6 to 8 inches apart. Provide support for the vines, and water regularly. Pick pods for eating while still tender, at about 4 inches long.

SELECTED VARIETIES: 'Scarlet Bees', a 2 feet bush form with abundant scarlet flowers and improved heat tolerance; 'Painted Lady', an heirloom form with bicolored coral and cream blossoms.

Scarlet runner bean is an easily grown annual vine that blooms brilliantly throughout the summer.

PHLOX DRUMMONDII

(floks druh-MON-dee-eye)

Annual phlox

8"

6"

- Low, spreading mounds of foliage
- Rounded flowers in clusters
- Bloom summer to frost

Low mounded plants bear tight flower clusters in shades of pink, red, salmon, purple, mauve, white, and bicolors. Good cut flower.

USES: Use for bedding, edging, containers, rock and cottage gardens. Mix with small-flowered petunias and vinca *(Catharanthus)*.

GETTING STARTED: Can be sown indoors six to eight weeks before planting out, into peat pots, but does better direct sowing outdoors in early spring as soon as soil can be worked.

SITING AND CARE: Plant into well-drained soil, moist, sandy, and high in organic matter, in full sun. Allow moderate crowding, and mass for best effect. Water and feed liberally, and deadhead. Excessive heat may cause decline; shear back to promote new growth.

SELECTED VARIETIES: 'Dolly', 6 inches, early, mixed colors and bicolors; 'Phlox of Sheep', 10 to 12 inches, pastels, some bicolor; 'Twinkle Mixed', 6 inches, bright colors, star-shaped.

Sometimes called "Texas pride" for its native state, annual phlox forms attractive mounds in lovely hues.

PLECTRANTHUS

(plek-TRAN-thus)

Plectranthus

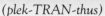

4"

12"

- Graceful branching habit
- Interesting foliage
- Subtle colors and variegations

These members of the mint family include Swedish ivy and some less familiar plants that are becoming popular for foliage accents. Native to Old World tropics.

USES: In beds, borders, hanging baskets, or other containers, to add brightness and soften edges. Use with Ipomoea 'Blackie' and flowering annuals for a rich mix.

GETTING STARTED: Start from cuttings, rooting in water or a well-drained soil mix, or purchase started plants. Pinch young plants for more branching.

SITING AND CARE: Plant outdoors after last frost, in average, well-drained soil or potting mix, spaced 1 foot apart, in full sun or light shade. Water and feed lightly.

SELECTED VARIETIES: Various species and types are available, among them: *P. coleoides* 'Albo-marginatus', 2 feet long, white-edged leaves; 'Aureo-marginatus', scalloped, gold-variegated leaves; 'Variegata', scalloped, white-variegated; Cuban oregano, crinkly, scented green foliage, trailing habit.

Plectranthus is an exciting new bedding plant for shade. Shown here is P. madagascariensis *'Variegata'.*

PORTULACA GRANDIFLORA

(por-too-LAH-kuh gran-dih-FLOR-uh)

Moss rose

A mass of 'Cloudbeater Mix' moss roses turns this rocky slope into a celebration of color.

6"
12"

■ Low, trailing plant
■ Brilliant flowers close on cloudy days
■ Tolerates heat and drought

Portulaca will thrive in extreme heat, drought, and poor soil, where it forms mats of tiny fleshy leaves and 1-inch single or double flowers in neon colors. Blooms last early summer to frost. Native to Brazil.
USES: In hot, dry areas such as sunny slopes, edges by concrete, walls, and cracks between paving stones. Also good in massed beds, rock gardens, and containers. Grows well with gazania, small marigolds, and statice *(Limonium)*.

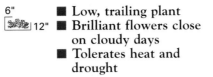

GETTING STARTED: Easy to start by seeding directly outdoors after last frost, or indoors four to six weeks ahead.
SITING AND CARE: Plant in hot, dry, perfectly drained soil, in full sun. It requires no care. Flowers close late in the day; some new varieties stay open longer.
SELECTED VARIETIES: All grow 4 to 6 inches, mostly in mixed colors: 'Afternoon Delight', double flowers, stays open later; 'Cloudbeater Mix', double flowers, stays open all day; 'Sundial', individual colors or mix, vigorous and uniform; 'Swan Lake', large white double.

RICINUS COMMUNIS

(RYE-sih-nuss kom-MYOO-nis)

Castor bean

Castor bean grows rapidly from a seed to a massive shrublike plant. 'Carmencita' is shown here.

5'
3'

■ Bold plant, 5 to 15 feet tall
■ Large, palmate leaves
■ Poisonous seeds

Castor bean's leaves grow to 3 feet wide in various colors, depending on variety, for an immense tropical effect in the garden. All parts of the plant, but especially the seeds, are poisonous. Native to the tropics.
USES: A temporary shrub used for screening, living fences, or as a specimen. Combine it with other tall plants such as cannas, grasses, Mexican sunflower *(Tithonia)*, or cleome. Attractive in waterside settings. Plantings repel moles.
GETTING STARTED: Start indoors

in peat pots six to eight weeks before planting out, or direct seed outdoors after last frost. Presoak in warm water for 24 hours. Keep seeds away from children, and handle with care, especially after soaking.
SITING AND CARE: Plant after last frost, in almost any soil in full sun, 3 to 4 feet apart. Grows best with regular watering and feeding. Stake if needed. Remove spent flowerheads to prevent seeding.
SELECTED VARIETIES: 'Carmencita', 5 to 6 feet, reddish brown leaves and rosy-red flowers; 'Sanguineus', 8 feet, red leaves; 'Zanzibariensis', 15 feet, green.

RUDBECKIA HIRTA VAR. PULCHERRIMA

(rud-BEK-ee-uh pul-KUR-ri-muh)

Gloriosa daisy

The warm beauty of 'Goldilocks' (left) and 'Indian Summer' (right) last from the peak of summer into fall.

2'
1'

■ Daisylike flowers with dark centers
■ Blooms midsummer to fall
■ Great for cutting

Also known as brown-eyed Susan, these are short-lived perennials that bloom the first year from seed, in solid or bicolored yellow, gold, orange, and bronze, single or double, all with chocolate brown centers. Native to United States.
USES: Good for borders, bedding, and cut flowers. Combine with red zinnias, lobelia 'Fan Scarlet', and purple fountain grass *(Pennisetum)*.

GETTING STARTED: Start seed indoors six to eight weeks before last frost. In long-summer areas, sow outdoors in spring.
SITING AND CARE: Plant after last frost, 1 to 2 feet apart, ideally in rich, well-drained soil, but tolerant of many kinds. Full sun to light shade. Water regularly. Some may need staking. Use fungicide to prevent mildew. Reseeds freely.
SELECTED VARIETIES: 'Becky Mix', 8 inches, single; 'Goldilocks', 8 to 10 inches, gold semidouble; 'Indian Summer', 3 feet, gold, single and semidouble; 'Irish Eyes', 28 inches, single gold with green center; 'Marmalade', 24 inches, single, gold.

SALPIGLOSSIS SINUATA

(sal-pih-GLOSS-iss sin-yoo-AY-tuh)

Painted tongue

24"

8"

- Tall, graceful plants
- Velvety funnel-shaped flowers
- Summer bloom

A relative of petunia and nicotiana, but somewhat difficult to grow. The 2- to 3-foot erect plants bloom in clear white and yellow as well as veined purples, reds, bronzes, blues, and pinks, often with contrasting throats. Native to Chile.

USES: Near the back of the border, planted close to sturdier plants to help support the somewhat lax stems. Try them with daylilies (*Hemerocallis*) and delphiniums, and annuals such as Chinese forget-me-not (*Cynoglossum*) and snapdragons (*Antirrhinum*). Definitely use as a cut flower.

GETTING STARTED: Best started indoors in peat pots eight to ten weeks before planting out. Darkness is needed for germination. Pinch young plants to induce branching.

SITING AND CARE: Plant just before last frost, 8 to 12 inches apart in rich, moist, perfectly drained soil, in full sun. Best in cool-summer areas. Water and feed lightly. May need staking.

SELECTED VARIETIES: 'Bolero', 18 to 24 inches, mixed rich colors; 'Casino', 15 to 20 inches, more basal branching; 'Royale', 15 to 20 inches, basal branching, 3-inch flowers, mixed colors and bicolors.

A close look at 'Bolero Mix' show the lavish colors and markings that make painted tongue a choice cut flower.

SALVIA

(SAL-vee-uh)

Salvia

18"

10"

- Erect bushy plants
- Tall spikes of tubular flowers
- Blooms summer through fall

The genus Salvia, also known as the sages, is full of many exquisite species. Those raised as annuals include scarlet sage (*S. splendens*), blue salvia (*S. farinacea*), Texas sage (*S. coccinea*), and clary sage (*S. viridis*). All four are native to the Americas.

USES: These salvias are all suitable for bedding and borders, for use in containers, and cut flowers. Blue salvia and clary sage are good for drying. Most types attract hummingbirds. Blue and scarlet salvia both provide season-long color, and are extremely useful for ribbons of constant color, combining wonderfully with other flowering plants.

GETTING STARTED: Start seeds indoors, sowing blue salvia twelve weeks before planting out, six to eight weeks for other types.

SITING AND CARE: Plant after last frost, 1 to 2 feet apart in rich, moist, well-drained soil in full sun or light shade. Deadhead, water during dry spells, and feed lightly.

SELECTED VARIETIES: Scarlet sage (*S. splendens*) has many varieties, selected for height, uniformity, and color groups. Some dwarf types are: 'Blaze of Fire', 16 inches, red; 'Salsa' series, 16 inches, shades of rose, salmon, purple, and red. Medium and tall types include: 'Bonfire', 24 inches, red; 'Flare', 18 inches, scarlet.

Blue salvia (*S. farinacea*) varieties include: 'Victoria', 18 inches, violet-blue; 'Silver White', 18 inches, white; 'Strata', 14 to 18 inches, blue and white bicolor.

Texas sage (*S. coccinea*) has a few standout varieties: 'Cherry Blossom' ('Coral Nymph'), 24 inches, salmon and cream bicolor; 'Lady in Red', 15 to 24 inches, scarlet flowers in loose spikes; and 'Snow Nymph', 24 inches, white.

Clary sage (*S. viridis*) has a different look, grown for its colorful, papery bracts of pink, white, or blue, rather than its flowers.

'Sizzler Mix' demonstrates the range of colors now available among scarlet sages.

'Victoria' blue salvia

The bicolor 'Strata' is an award-winner.

Scarlet sage blazes away.

S. horminium 'Art Shades'

'Coral Nymph'

SANVITALIA PROCUMBENS

(san-vih-TAL-ee-uh proh-KUM-benz)

Creeping zinnia

Creeping zinnia is a free-flowering, low-maintenance trailing plant for warm, sunny areas.

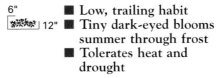
6" | 12"

- Low, trailing habit
- Tiny dark-eyed blooms summer through frost
- Tolerates heat and drought

Cheerful golden-yellow or orange flowers bloom from June through frost. It's a pretty and reliable plant. Native to Mexico.

USES: A tough, uniform edging or ground cover, and is also useful in beds and borders, rock gardens and walls, hanging baskets and other containers. Use with 'White Star' zinnia for a perfect pairing, or with low blue ageratum for contrast.

GETTING STARTED: It can be started indoors in peat pots, six to eight weeks before planting out, but best when direct sown after last frost. In mild climates, it can also be fall-sown for early spring bloom.

SITING AND CARE: Best in light, well-drained soil in full sun, but will tolerate other soils and some shade. Space 6 inches apart. Requires minimal watering and no feeding.

SELECTED VARIETIES: 'Mandarin Orange', 8 inches tall by 12 inches wide, orange with dark center; 'Golden Carpet', 4 to 6 inches, single orange with black center; 'Yellow Carpet', 4 to 6 inches, single lemon yellow with black center.

SCAEVOLA

(skuh-VOH-luh)

Fan flower

Scaevola 'Blue Wonder' has quickly become popular for its lovely flowers and habit and ease of culture.

10" | 12"

- Full, trailing habit
- Blue flowers late spring to frost
- Great for baskets

Fan flower has a tidy, well-branched growth habit and nonstop bloom of pretty fan-shaped flowers in shades of blue.

USES: Most frequently used for hanging baskets and mixed container plantings, but also works well in flower beds, cascading over walls, or as an annual ground cover. Mixes well with creeping verbena, petunias, ivy geraniums, and bidens.

GETTING STARTED: This is a vegetatively propagated plant, started by rooting cuttings or buying prestarted plants. Pinch young plants to promote bushiness.

SITING AND CARE: Move outside after frost, once soil has warmed up, planting into well-drained, fertile soil or planting mix. Space 15 inches apart in full sun. Water and feed regularly. Before fall frosts, dig and pot a plant from which to take cuttings for next season.

SELECTED VARIETIES: 'Blue Fans', 12 inches, sky blue with white eye; 'Blue Shamrock', 10 to 14 inches, intense blue; ' Blue Wonder', 12 inches, sky-blue with white eye; 'New Wonder', 10 to 14 inches, blue-violet; 'Petite Wonder', 4 to 6 inches, lavender; 'Sun Fan', 10 to 12 inches, light blue.

SCHIZANTHUS X WISETONENSIS

(sky-ZAN-thus wye-zeh-toh-NEN-sis)

Butterfly flower

The blooms of Schizanthus truly look like tiny butterflies, hovering in great masses over delicate, lacy foliage.

12" | 12"

- Mounded pyramidal habit
- Flowers resemble small butterflies
- Requires cool conditions

Butterfly flower blooms from late summer till frost, and can be potted and brought inside for winter bloom. Also known as poor man's orchid. Native to Chile.

USES: Where it can be grown, use it for bedding, edging, borders, containers, and cut flowers. Likely plant partners include tuberous begonias, coleus, and lobelia.

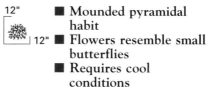

GETTING STARTED: Sow indoors eight to ten weeks before last frost, or, in zones 9 to 10, outdoors in early spring or fall.

SITING AND CARE: Plant seedlings outdoors a few weeks after last frost, spacing 12 inches apart in rich, moist, perfectly drained soil, in full sun to light shade. Water moderately.

SELECTED VARIETIES: 'Disco', 6 to 9 inches, mixed intricate colors, good for gardens; 'Hit Parade', 12 inches, wide color range, bushy; 'Star Parade', 6 to 9 inches, compact, bright colors; 'Sweet Lips', 12 to 15 inches, deep colors with striping, veining, and picotee edges.

SENECIO CINERARIA

(sen-EE-see-oh sin-uh-RAH-ree-uh)

Dusty miller

10"

6"

- Compact bushy plants
- Silver foliage
- Reliable, season-long color

Dusty miller is grown for its wonderful lacy silver foliage and compact, tidy form. Heights can range from 8 to 16 inches, and there are several different leaf forms. Native to the Mediterranean region. **USES:** In beds and borders and mixed containers, for edging and carpet bedding. It's particularly

handsome along brick walkways, and contrasted with deep shades of purple like heliotrope, or the blue of *Convolvulus* 'Blue Ensign'. It glows in white flower groupings, and cools down hot oranges and yellows.
GETTING STARTED: Start seed indoors eight to ten weeks before last frost; avoid overwatering.
SITING AND CARE: Plant after last frost; fall planting can be done in mild regions. Space 8 to 10 inches apart in light, well-drained organic or sandy soil, in full sun or light shade. Drought tolerant. Water lightly; shear for tidiness or flower removal.
SELECTED VARIETIES: 'Cirrus',

8 inches, large, rounded leaves, whitest of all types; 'Silverdust', 12 inches, finely divided silvery leaves; 'Silver Lace', 10 inches, wiry-thin steel gray leaves; and 'Silver Queen', 8 inches, lacy silvery white.

Dusty miller is endlessly useful, and comes in several varieties, such as 'Cirrus' (left) and 'Silver Lace' (right).

SILENE

(sye-LEE-nee)

Catchfly

9"

12"

- Erect airy plants
- Red, pink, or white blossoms with cleft petals
- Long-blooming

Catchflies are not common in American gardens, but there are several lovely types that are easy to grow, bloom over a long period, and add a delicate note of color.
USES: Tall types for planting in beds, borders, cottage gardens, or naturalizing in meadow or

wildflower plantings. They go well with bachelor's buttons (*Centaurea*), nicotiana, flax (*Linum*), and other informal annuals and perennials. Use the short types in border edges, rock gardens, and in containers.
GETTING STARTED: Start seeds indoors eight to ten weeks before planting out, or sow outdoors in early spring. It may also be sown outside in the fall for earliest bloom.
SITING AND CARE: Plant in early spring, 12 inches apart in well-drained soil high in organic matter, in full sun or light shade. Water regularly and feed occasionally.
SELECTED VARIETIES 'Angel Series', 9 to 12 inches, mixed colors;

'Cherry Blossom', 24 inches, pink with white center; 'Hot Pink', 6 inches, pink, profuse bloom; 'Peach Blossom', 4 to 6 inches tall, 12 inches wide, double, shades of pink; *S. uniflora*, 10 inches, white flowers.

'Peach Blossom' catchfly has clusters of double flowers in the most delicate shades of pink.

STIPA TENUISSIMA

(STEE-puh ten-yoo-ISS-ih-muh)

Ponytail grass

30"

20"

- Delicate narrow foliage
- Tan flower plumes
- Forms dense clumps
- Attractive spring through winter

Ponytail grass is a southwestern native that performs splendidly in gardens. Also known as "Mexican feather grass" because of its fine foliage which forms an airy clump with 2-foot, tan, silky flower plumes that emerge in early summer. The

color and form remain attractive for months on end, even into winter.
USES: Can be used in beds and borders, spotted among shrubs, massed as a ground cover, or grouped with other grasses. The tan color is a great neutralizer; try it to tone down hot-colored annuals or create a muted mix with deep reds, purples, or blues.
GETTING STARTED: Start seed indoors six to eight weeks before planting out, or sow outdoors in spring.
SITING AND CARE: Plant seedlings outdoors after last frost, spacing 1 to 2 feet apart in fertile, well-drained soil, in full sun to light shade. Water well while getting

established. Overwinters in mild climates.

Graceful form and interesting texture make ponytail grass an intriguing design element.

TAGETES

(tuh-JEE-teez)

Marigold

12"

12"

- Tough, long-blooming plants
- Round, cheerful flowers
- Brilliant, easy color
- Wide range of colors and sizes

This justifiably popular annual has been extensively hybridized, resulting in a huge array of types and forms. All bear either single or double flowers in yellows, golds, oranges, some bicolored with red or brown stripes. Native to Mexico.

USES: Marigolds can be used for bedding and edging, in borders and containers, in cutting, herb, vegetable, and kitchen gardens. Cool their warm tones by planting with blue- or white-flowered companions, or celebrate their gaiety with other hot-colored plants. The tallest types can be used as an annual hedge.

GETTING STARTED: Start from  seed indoors, sowing six to eight weeks before last frost, barely covering. Smaller types are easily started outdoors in late spring, but tall African types need longer to come into bloom.

SITING AND CARE: Plant outside after last frost, ideally into moist, well-drained soil, but many types will be tolerated. Water in dry spells, and deadhead.

SELECTED VARIETIES: Marigolds break down into four major types. The African marigold (*T. erecta*) is the tallest, from 1 to 3 feet, with large flowers that resemble carnations. The French marigold (*T. patula*), is 6 to 18 inches tall, bushy with smaller single or double flowers. Triploid types look like French marigolds, but never set seed, so they bloom indefinitely. Signet marigolds (*T. tenuifolia*) are 6 to 8 inches tall, with lacy foliage and tiny edible flowers.

A glowing mix of French marigolds

French marigold 'Disco Flame'

French marigold 'Queen Sophia'

French single 'Cinnabar'

African 'French Vanilla'

African 'Antigua Primrose'

African 'Primrose Lady'

THUNBERGIA ALATA

(thun-BER-jee-uh uh-LAY-tuh)

Black-eyed Susan vine

6'
1'

- Twining vine
- Orange, yellow, or white flowers
- Bloom summer through fall

Thunbergia is an easily grown vine with perky funnel-shaped flowers that often have dark throats, thus the black eyes of its common name. It grows quickly, but only to about 6 feet, which makes it usable in small spaces and containers. Native to South Africa.

USES: For climbing up trellises, netting, fences, or other supports. Try it with cypress vine (*Ipomoea*) or hyacinth bean (*Dolichos*) for variety. Also used as a ground cover, or in hanging baskets.

GETTING STARTED: Sow indoors  in peat pots six to eight weeks before, or outdoors after final frost. In warm climates, it can be sown outdoors in late fall or early spring.

SITING AND CARE: Plant in late spring, after it's thoroughly warm, 12 inches apart in moist, fertile soil or planting mix, in full sun or light shade. Potted plants may be brought indoors for the winter and replanted the following spring.

SELECTED VARIETIES: 'Susie' series comes in orange with black eye, or a mix of orange, yellow, and white. A related species, *T. fragrans* 'Angel Wings' is a climber with fragrant white flowers.

The 'Susie' series of Thunbergia may have flowers of orange (right), pale yellow, or white (inset).

THYMOPHYLLA TENUILOBA

(*tye-moh-FYE-luh ten-yoo-ih-LOH-buh*)

Dahlberg daisy

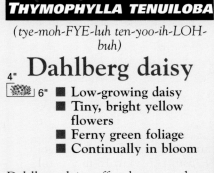

4"
6"

- Low-growing daisy
- Tiny, bright yellow flowers
- Ferny green foliage
- Continually in bloom

Dahlberg daisy offers low growth only 4 to 8 inches tall, fine texture, nonstop bloom of petite golden yellow daisies, and a fresh look even during the hottest summer. Native to southwest Texas and Mexico.
USES: It is ideal for edging, bedding, desert, and rock gardens, walls and spaces between pavers, and suitable for hanging baskets and other containers. Try it with moss rose (*Portulaca*), and low-growing forms of sedum. Under less severe conditions, it's a good companion for ageratum, sweet alyssum (*Lobularia*), and trailing verbena.
GETTING STARTED: Sow in place in fall, or start indoors six to eight weeks before last frost.

SITING AND CARE: Plant after last frost, 4 to 6 inches apart in any soil with good drainage, in full sun. Water and feed sparingly. It will reseed, especially into edges and cracks.

SELECTED VARIETIES: 'Golden Fleece', 8 inches, yellow daisy-like flowers, with crested centers.

The dainty-looking flowers of Dahlberg daisy are actually tough, long-lasting, and unfazed by heat.

TITHONIA ROTUNDIFOLIA

(*tih-THOH-nee-uh roh-tun-dih-FOH-lee-uh*)

Mexican Sunflower

5'
2'

- 4- to 6-foot plants
- Red-orange daisies with yellow centers
- Tolerates heat and drought

One of the largest plants grown as an annual, it bears brilliant fiery 3-inch daisy flowers from midsummer through fall. Native to Mexico and Central America.

USES: Use in the back of the border, for a temporary screen or hedge, or as a specimen. Plant it with sunflowers (*Helianthus*), cannas, perilla, or other bold structural plants. Good for cutting, but the ends of the hollow stems must be seared. Attractive to hummingbirds and butterflies.

GETTING STARTED: Sow indoors six to eight weeks before last frost, or, in mild winter areas, outdoors after last frost.
SITING AND CARE: Plant after last frost, 2 feet apart in any well-drained soil. Water only during dry spells. Stake plants if needed.
SELECTED VARIETIES: 'Aztec Sun', 4 feet tall, golden yellow flowers; 'Goldfinger', 30 to 42 inches tall, neon scarlet-orange; 'Sundance', 3 feet, scarlet-orange; 'Torch', 4 to 6 feet, fiery orange.

Tithonia 'Torch' (left) and 'Goldfinger' (right) bloom in saturated color on statuesque plants.

TORENIA FOURNIERI

(*toh-REE-nee-uh for-nee-AIR-ee*)

Wishbone flower

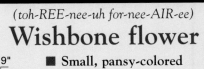

9"
6"

- Small, pansy-colored flowers
- Abundant bloom, summer to frost
- Shade-loving

Wishbone flower is a favorite of the discerning shade gardener. Growing 8 to 12 inches tall, its flowers are rather like a snapdragon, but colored like a pansy, in rich purple or pink bi-tones with light throats and markings. Native to South Vietnam.

USES: For bedding, edging or hanging baskets. It harmonizes with hostas, ferns, and impatiens.
GETTING STARTED: Sow seeds indoors eight to ten weeks before final frost, or outdoors one week after final frost.

SITING AND CARE: Plant two weeks after final frost, in fertile, moist soil high in organic matter. Space 8 inches apart, in partial to deep shade. Keep well watered.
SELECTED VARIETIES: 'Clown Mix', 8 to 10 inches, larger flowers, mix of seven tri-colors (violet, rose, plum, burgundy, blush, blue, blue/white), all with cream and yellow throats; 'Panda', 4 inches, compact, blue or pink tri-colors. A related plant, *T. flava* 'Suzie Wong', has trailing foliage and yellow flowers with deep purple throats; good for beds or baskets in shade.

Wishbone flower offers gardeners another option for shade; 'Clown Mix' is shown here.

TROPAEOLUM MAJUS

(troh-PEE-oh-lum MAY-jus)

Nasturtium

Nasturtiums are used for mounding, cascading, or even eating; a classic trailer (left), 'Empress of India' (right).

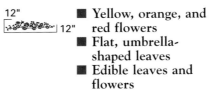

- Yellow, orange, and red flowers
- Flat, umbrella-shaped leaves
- Edible leaves and flowers

Among the most beloved of annuals, with flowing growth, round leaves, and bright 5-petalled flowers. Colors range from hot colors into shades of cream, salmon, and apricot. Native to the Andes.

USES: As a trailing edger, in window boxes, or over walls, trained onto trellises as a vertical screen, or in beds and borders. A relative of watercress, both the leaves and flowers are edible.

GETTING STARTED: Best sown outdoors after final frost.

SITING AND CARE: Ideally grown in sandy, infertile soil, it will tolerate any average soil that is well-drained. Space 8 to 12 inches apart, in full sun. Water regularly, but do not feed, or you'll get leaves but few flowers. Best in cool, dry conditions.

SELECTED VARIETIES: 'Alaska', variegated foliage, 12 to 15 inches, mixed colors; 'Empress of India', blue-green leaves, red flowers, 2 feet; 'Soft Fruit' series, 12- to 15- inch plants, in many colors; 'Whirlybird' series, 12-inch mounds, mixed or single colors.

TROPAEOLUM PEREGRINUM

(troh-PEE-oh-lum per-uh-GRY-num)

Canary creeper

The graceful texture and habit of canary creeper merits wider use among today's gardeners.

- Dainty vine with lobed foliage
- Fringed canary yellow flowers
- Bloom early summer until frost

This little-known annual offers delicate flowers and foliage, and a vining habit, to 6 to 10 feet. It grows rapidly and blooms continually until killed by frost. Native to Peru.

USES: Canary creeper can be trained onto trellises, fences, wires, lattice, or other structures, or onto other vines, tall roses, or shrubbery. It looks especially pretty twining itself into evergreens. Very suitable

for baskets and containers, mixing its yellow flowers with blue lobelia, for instance. Try growing it onto a teepee of stakes in a pot.

GETTING STARTED: It may be sown into peat pots indoors, starting two to four weeks before last frost, or sown directly where it will grow, one week after last frost.

SITING AND CARE: See *Tropaeolum majus*.

RELATED SPECIES: Scotch flame flower, *T. speciosum*, is a perennial vine grown as an annual, with tiny scarlet flowers and finely lobed leaves. It is particular about growing conditions, requiring a cool, moist location and rich soil.

VERBENA X HYBRIDA

(ver-BEE-nuh HY-bri-duh)

Garden verbena

'Peaches and Cream' (left) and 'Homestead Purple' (right) are some wonderful new verbena hybrids.

- Trailing or upright plants
- Masses of rounded flower clusters
- Blooms all summer

Verbena is one of the easiest ways to brighten sunny spots. Only 6 to 8 inches tall but up to 4 feet wide, it has deep green or grayish aromatic foliage. Flowers may be neon blue, red, white, pink, or purple. Of hybrid origin; parents are native to South America.

USES: As a ground cover in beds, borders, containers, in rock gardens, or over walls. It mixes well with bidens, multiflora petunias and calibrachoa. Also as a cut flower.

GETTING STARTED: Sow seed indoors twelve to fourteen weeks before last frost.

SITING AND CARE: Plant after last frost 12 to 18 inches apart in light, fertile, well-drained soil, in full sun. Moderately tolerant of heat and drought. Water moderately and feed regularly. Prone to mildew in heavy soil and damp locations.

SELECTED VARIETIES: 'Amour Light Pink', 10 by 10 inches, warm pastel pink; 'Blaze', 9 inches, compact, vivid red; 'Tapien' hybrids, 6 inches, several colors, ferny foliage, mildew resistant; 'Temari', 6 inches, violet, pink, red, and burgundy.

VIOLA X WITTROCKIANA

(vye-OH-luh wit-rok-ee-AY-nuh)

Pansy

6"
 6"

- Low mounded habit
- Large bright flowers
- Charming colors and faces
- Cool season bloom

Pansies are perennials that are usually treated as annuals, and short-season ones at that, because they are destroyed by heat. Enjoy their jubilant faces and colors in cool seasons, but expect to replace them with later-bloomers by early summer. Of hybrid origin; parents native to Europe and possibly Asia Minor.

USES: Useful for bedding and edging, in rock gardens and containers, and as cut flowers. They are superb in mass bedding schemes with spring bulbs, and in fall displays with calendulas or mums.

GETTING STARTED: Sow indoors eight to ten weeks before planting out; in mild climates they can be sown outdoors in late summer or winter.

SITING AND CARE: Plant in early spring as soon as soil can be worked. In mild areas they can be grown outdoors all winter. Space 4 to 6 inches apart in rich, moist, well-drained soil, in sun or light shade. Best performance is in cool-summer areas. Water and feed regularly. Deadhead to prolong bloom. Choose heat-resistant varieties.

SELECTED VARIETIES: There is a huge range of pansy types, divided by flower size (large, medium, or small), some with faces, some without, in bright shades, pastels, with varying degrees of uniformity, heat resistance, and cold tolerance.

RELATED SPECIES AND HYBRIDS: *V. tricolor* (Johnny-jump-up) is like a miniature pansy, growing 4 to 8 inches tall, usually with tricolored flowers. *V. cornuta* is similar, and these two species are often collectively called violas. Their starting and culture is as for pansies, although they are somewhat more heat resistant and likely to reseed themselves. There are many adorable and garden-worthy hybrids, among them: 'Bluebird', 6 inches, fresh blue; 'Bowles' Black', 4 inches, deepest purple-black; 'Chantreyland', 6 to 8 inches, apricot; 'Sorbet' hybrids, 6 by 12 inches, good heat and cold tolerance, several lovely colors; 'Yesterday, Today, and Tomorrow', 5 inches, color changes from white to light blue to deep blue.

'Yesterday, Today, and Tomorrow'

Mixed colors of 'Paramount' pansies

Viola 'Blackberry Sorbet'

Pansy 'Faces Apricot Shades'

Viola 'Columbine'

Pansy 'Jolly Joker'

Pansy 'Antique Shades'

WAHLENBERGIA

(wall-en-BER-jee-uh)

Rock bell

12"
 14"

- Open, spreading habit
- Flowers in shades of blue
- Superb container plant

Wahlenbergia is a relatively unknown annual that definitely merits attention. The plant grows 12 inches tall and spreads to 14 inches, and produces 1- to 2-inch bell-shaped flowers that change from slate blue to lilac to pale blue, creating a multihued effect. Native to South Africa.

USES: Suitable for bedding and edging, rock gardens, and especially hanging baskets and all kinds of containers. Its open, spreading habit cascades gracefully over rims, and the beautiful flowers never fail to delight. Combines nicely with linaria, China pinks (*Dianthus*), and fibrous begonias.

GETTING STARTED: Sow indoors in late winter for late spring bloom. Earlier bloom can be had by sowing in fall.

SITING AND CARE: Plant after final frost into rich well-drained soil, 10 to 12 inches apart in sun or shade. Water and feed moderately, and deadhead regularly to extend bloom.

SELECTED VARIETIES: *W. undulata* 'Melton Bluebird' is a blue variety; a white form is also available.

The lavishly borne bellflowers of Wahlenbergia make stunning subjects for hanging baskets.

ZANTEDESCHIA AETHIOPICA

(zan-tee-DESS-kee-uh ee-thee-OH-pih-kuh)

Calla lily

- Elegant, fragrant flowers
- Popular for flower arrangements
- Tolerates shade and waterlogged soils

In addition to the classic white form, there are yellow callas (right) and hot colors such as 'Pacific Pink' (left).

Many people are familiar with the calla lily, but few realize how easy it is to grow. Its large, waxy flowers, usually a creamy white, are also available in shades of yellow, pink, red, purple, and apricot. Some varieties have dappled leaves. Native to South Africa.
USES: In containers, in beds and borders, and as a cut flower. Combine it with caladiums or coleus for a lush contrast.

GETTING STARTED: Grown from tender rhizomes planted 4 inches deep and 1 to 2 feet apart in the garden, or 3 inches deep in pots.
SITING AND CARE: Plant in spring, once temperatures reach 50° F, into rich, moist, organic soil. Tolerant of boggy conditions. Best in part shade, tolerates sun. Feed occasionally with liquid fertilizer and water frequently. In cold-winter areas, may be lifted and stored.
SELECTED VARIETIES: 'Green Goddess', flowers green flushed with white; 'Sunrise Mix', 1 to 2 feet, in red, cream, yellow, pink, and apricot.

ZINNIA ANGUSTIFOLIA

(ZIH-nee-uh an-gus-tih-FOH-lee-uh)

Narrowleaf zinnia

Whether you choose a white form (inset) or gold (right), narrowleaf zinnia is a winner for sunny spots.

- Loose, bushy mounds
- Small single white, gold, or orange blossoms
- Blooms all summer till frost

A truly marvelous plant, with wiry, tumbling stems, linear leaves, and a wealth of 1-inch daisy flowers all through the growing season. Its appearance is delicate, but its nature is tough—tolerant of heat, drought, and humidity. Native to Mexico.
USES: Ideal for ground cover and edging purposes, and also good in borders, rock gardens and walls, hanging baskets, window boxes, and other containers. Mix it with verbena, scaevola, sweet potato

'Blackie', or ivy geranium (*Pelargonium*). Also useful as a cut flower.
GETTING STARTED: Sow indoors five to seven weeks before final frost, or directly in the garden after final frost.

SITING AND CARE: Plant after last frost, 8 to 12 inches apart in average garden soil in full sun. Water and feed lightly.
SELECTED VARIETIES: 'Crystal White', 8 to 10 inches tall and wide, white with orange centers; 'Star' series, 9 to 12 inches, comes in orange, gold, and white, individually or as the mix 'Starbright'.

ZINNIA ELEGANS

(ZIH-nee-uh EL-eh-ganz)

Zinnia

'Dreamland Mix' (right) is ideal for midborders; grow long-stemmed types for cut flowers (inset).

- Erect bushy plants
- Large round double flowers
- Rugged, long-bloomers

Many heights (from 6 to 40 inches) and forms means there is a zinnia for nearly every garden. It comes in an enormous range of bright, festive colors. Native to Mexico.
USES: In borders, beds, for edging, cut flowers, and in containers.

GETTING STARTED: May be sown indoors four to six weeks before final frost, or seeded directly after final frost.

SITING AND CARE: Plant in ordinary well-drained soil, spacing 6 to 12 inches apart, in full sun. Does well in hot, dry conditions. Pinch young plants to promote bushiness. Mildew can be a problem; water carefully to avoid wetting foliage. Feed lightly, and remove spent flower heads.
SELECTED VARIETIES: Huge range, including dwarf bedding types ('Dasher', 'Dreamland', and 'Small World' hybrids), tall cutting types ('Blue Point', 'Big Red', 'Ruffles Hybrid'), unusual colors ('Envy', chartreuse; 'Peppermint Stick', streaked and blotched). The 'Pinwheel' series is mildew resistant, and compact, 12 inches tall.

FIRST AND LAST FROST DATES

These maps indicate the average dates for the first and last frosts across North America. Many factors influence the accuracy of these dates. For example, at the bottom of a north-facing hill, spring comes later and fall earlier than on the top of the hill. It wouldn't hurt to contact your local cooperative extension service to find a more precise date for your location.

Light frosts occur when the temperature falls below 33° F. Light frost rarely poses a threat to cool-season annuals, such as pansies and ornamental cabbage, which grow quite well in cold weather in spring and fall.

Warm-season annuals are more variable. Some quickly succumb to light frost, while others, such as petunias, survive until a hard frost (around 28° F) knocks them down. However, it's best to wait until after the last frost in spring to set out warm-season annuals in the garden, and to rely on cool-season annuals to provide fall bloom.

**Average Dates of
Last Spring Frost**
May 30 or After
April 30 to May 30
March 30 to April 30
February 28 to March 30
January 30 to February 28
January 30 or before

**Average Dates of
First Autumn Frost**
June 30 to July 30
July 30 to August 30
August 30 to September 30
September 30 to October 30
October 30 to November 30
November 30 to December 30

INDEX

Pages numbers followed by t indicate material in tables, numbers in italics denote photographs. Boldface numbers refer to lead entries in the "Selection and Growing Guide."

METRIC CONVERSIONS

U.S. Units to Metric Equivalents			Metric Units to U.S. Equivalents		
To Convert From	Multiply By	To Get	To Convert From	Multiply By	To Get
Inches	25.4	Millimeters	Millimeters	0.0394	Inches
Inches	2.54	Centimeters	Centimeters	0.3937	Inches
Feet	30.48	Centimeters	Centimeters	0.0328	Feet
Feet	0.3048	Meters	Meters	3.2808	Feet
Yards	0.9144	Meters	Meters	1.0936	Yards
Square inches	6.4516	Square centimeters	Square centimeters	0.1550	Square inches
Square feet	0.0929	Square meters	Square meters	10.764	Square feet
Square yards	0.8361	Square meters	Square meters	1.1960	Square yards
Acres	0.4047	Hectares	Hectares	2.4711	Acres
Cubic inches	16.387	Cubic centimeters	Cubic centimeters	0.0610	Cubic inches
Cubic feet	0.0283	Cubic meters	Cubic meters	35.315	Cubic feet
Cubic feet	28.316	Liters	Liters	0.0353	Cubic feet
Cubic yards	0.7646	Cubic meters	Cubic meters	1.308	Cubic yards
Cubic yards	764.55	Liters	Liters	0.0013	Cubic yards

To convert from degrees Fahrenheit (F) to degrees Celsius (C), first subtract 32, then multiply by 5⁄9.

To convert from degrees Celsius to degrees Fahrenheit, multiply by 9⁄5, then add 32.